The
Prodigal Project

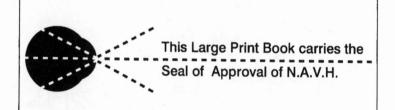
This Large Print Book carries the
Seal of Approval of N.A.V.H.

The Prodigal Project

Book I
Genesis

Ken Abraham
and
Daniel Hart

Thorndike Press • Waterville, Maine

Published in 2003 by arrangement with Plume, a member of Penguin Group (USA) Inc.

Thorndike Press® Large Print Christian Fiction.

The tree indicium is a trademark of Thorndike Press.

The text of this Large Print edition is unabridged. Other aspects of the book may vary from the original edition.

Set in 16 pt. Plantin by Myrna S. Raven.

Printed in the United States on permanent paper.

Library of Congress Cataloging-in-Publication Data

Abraham, Ken.
    Genesis / Ken Abraham and Daniel Hart.
       p. cm. — (The Prodigal Project ; bk. 1)
      ISBN 0-7862-5758-X (lg. print : hc : alk. paper)
      1. Rapture (Christian eschatology) — Fiction. 2. Large type books. I. Hart, Daniel. II. Title.
PS3601.B68G4 2003b
  813'.54—dc21
                                         2003054752

For John Chase Bennett IV,
September 4, 1982–February 12, 2002

— D.H.

ACKNOWLEDGMENTS

Special thanks to Dr. J, the "Great Facilitator," and to Daniel Hart for sharing such an intriguing story with me.

— K.A.

I would like to thank my agent, Jane Gelfman, my editor, Gary Brozek, and my family for their guidance, support, and unwavering faith.

— D.H.

Heartfelt thanks to Joel Fotinos, Gary Brozek, and the great team at Plume for believing in this book and making it happen.

"For the Lord Himself will descend from heaven with a shout, with the voice of the archangel, and with the trumpet of God; and the dead in Christ shall rise first. Then we who are alive and remain shall be caught up together with them in the clouds to meet the Lord in the air, and thus we shall always be with the Lord. Therefore comfort one another with these words."

— 1 THESSALONIANS 4:16–18

Chapter One

An odd moment of quiet, a stillness, made him raise his head as the putter contacted the ball. The ambient noise of nature stopped. No birds called, no insects hummed or whirred, no fair breeze whispered. The silence captured his attention. These small sounds were part of what he had always enjoyed about being out on the course. On this pretty Sunday he walked in a beautiful setting, and he saw it as a chance to feel close to nature and Mother Earth — even on a manufactured plot of land. He couldn't escape the fact that he stood on a golf course, not some far and exotic wilderness trail; but the place was fragrant and alive nonetheless. Beyond the green fairways, blighted fields of corn and what should have been soybeans shriveled in the heat and drought. He put from his mind thoughts of the abandoned irrigation wheels that sat like discarded Tinkertoys.

He liked it when they had an early tee time so he could watch the colors change with the warming sun, from almost silver to the deeper greens and gold. But now there was this odd pause, a sudden cessation, as if the earth itself were holding its breath.

"He who peeketh . . . putteth again, John," chided Conner Eagan with a grin. "You got to keep your head down all the way through the putt —"

John Jameson held up his hand to stop Eagan. His head was still up, cocked to the side like an alert retriever's as he listened to the stillness. "Something's not . . . ," he said. Then he felt it.

The tremor came in a wave, throbbing and rumbling across the groomed golf course. Jameson felt the vibration in his feet, was struck by the impression that a great heavy beast was scratching its back against the underside of the earth's crust. It was a pulsing, drumming vibration, not violent, and it made his feet feel funny. Not here, he thought, this can't be right. He heard one of Conner's friends cry out, and saw the man reach out for Conner, who stood staring at the ground with a fixed grin. The disturbance lasted only a few seconds, but during that time Jameson saw his golf ball dancing and skittering on the tips of the shorn grass, and a few yards away a small water hazard was ribbed with barely discernible concentric ripples.

He understood his golf game, now more than ever, to be an escape. He recognized it as a chance to turn away from the parched and hard-edged reality the world had become, a chance to be surrounded by green and gold, fertile field, rolling glade, moisture, sweet air, and hope.

It was artificial, of course, man-made, created by diesel earthmovers and irrigation. The designers had literally formed an oasis in the middle of a dry and brittle world. For years now the global warming trend had become very real. It was insidious, encroaching on the earth without drama or drumbeat until it was simply *there*. Forests were sparse and dusty, fields were barren and without promise, playgrounds were paved to keep the blowing dust down, and gardening had become an excruciating exercise in futility. He also understood it was money that formed this golf course, this place he sometimes called his cathedral, his place of solace and reflection on Sundays. But now his benign communing with nature, his quiet time in the cathedral, was stolen away by the tremors.

Then came another pause, another breath, and it was over. Jameson heard a birdcall, the distant answer, and watched as a monarch butterfly glided along the

11

edge of a sand trap. He wiggled his toes to chase the numbness in his feet, and moved his tongue around searching for spit. He found none.

"That was weird," said Conner. "Like an earthquake or somethin'."

"Earthquake? In Indiana?" said Sam, one of Conner's buddies, the fourth of the foursome, the one with the skin burnished from too much free time and sun. "What next," he grinned, "a hurricane like down in Florida? That was probably an aftershock caused by some politician dropping his wallet."

Ted, the one who had reached out for Conner during the tremor, scratched his close-cropped gray hair, spit, and mused, "Feet felt like they went to sleep. Felt it once before, long time ago . . . stood on a ridgeline maybe a mile from another ridge where a B-52 bomb strike hit. Caused that same kind of tremor . . . a soft drumming into the soles of your feet. Only time I ever felt it."

Sam jumped right in. "Oh, I see, Ted. It's not an act of God, but a simple *air strike*. Here all these years I've firmly believed being in Indiana had to be one of the safest places in the world in case of the next war. I mean, who would want to bomb anything here in Hoosierville? We may be salt of the earth Midwesterners and all that, but in the big picture we are *boring,* we are a completely zero threat . . . we are . . ." He raised his eyebrows in mock consternation. "Wait. We *do* have Chanute, that old air force base a few miles from here," he nodded toward Jameson, thinking he was telling the new guy something he didn't know, "shut down during the budget crunch a few years ago. I heard recently they may reactivate it because of all the . . . let me get this right . . . because of the 'global unrest.'"

"Okay," Ted laughed, and shook his head at his friend. "Okay, Sam, it wasn't a bomb strike."

"No," said Jameson, almost to himself, "it was a tremor, maybe far from the epicenter, or just a little one, but a tremor." He looked at the other three. He had known Conner in high school, and had recently met Sam and Ted, friends of Conner's. They were all decent guys and okay golfers, and this was the second time they had made up a foursome.

Conner was proud of his membership in the golf club, and liked to play host to the others. Jameson thought Conner tried hard to be the big deal, but he liked the others

13

and liked the course. Golf was a good thing, a chance to get out of the house, to be with "the guys," to move the old bod around a bit. Golf was good even when the ball seemed to have a mind of its own. "But you're right, Conner," he added, "it was weird."

"Does it seem to you guys that the world is a total mess nowadays?" asked Ted. He stashed his putter back in his bag, frowning. "Every time I watch the news — which I try to avoid like the plague — one of those bubbleheads is yappin' about another 'small war' or stupid 'border battle' here or there. No big ones, just enough to cause disruption, maybe kill a few people."

"It would be big enough if you were one of the few," opined Sam.

"Well, it just seems like there are more, anyway," concluded Ted as he watched Jameson grunt, bend to pluck his ball out of the cup, and slowly straighten with a soft grunt.

"Nah," said Conner. "What it is, Ted, is we have such amazing communication technology in our world now. There have always been wars and rumors of wars, tremors, storms, tidal waves, the usual burping and grunting from our fair planet. The border wars have been happening

14

since the first two guys picked up sticks. We just *hear* about each and every one now. Hey, self-confessed news junkie John Jameson here was going on yesterday about how it seems there are more military movements every day now, air force jets zipping by, army helicopters off in the distance, convoys of troops in Humvees clogging the interstate."

Conner stopped talking long enough for both Sam and Ted to putt out on the hole; after they'd all picked up their bags and begun walking toward the next tee, he charged on: "I told him, didn't I, John? Told him it's the *communications* we have now. Couple of our jet jockeys launch from Saudi Arabia or someplace against some 'threat,' and a minute later CNN is showing it in our living room in *real time*. I mean, some jerk in West-by-Camel Islamabad can't pass gas, and we hear about it fifteen minutes later."

Jameson listened, smiling like the others. His heart still beat strongly, moisture finally returned to his mouth, the sun warmed his face, he was alive. "I guess I'll take a three on that hole," he said with a grin.

"That's *right*," exclaimed Sam. "You made that putt while the world was coming to an end."

"Shoot," added Conner, "don't give him credit for that. The ball was just looking for a place to hide, and *dove* into the hole."

They set their bags down and stared down the next fairway, hoping to divine the right club for the next hole.

"Man, you ended with a ninety-three today, John," Conner Eagan said as he sat at the table with the others. "Not bad for a guy — one of our *government* men — fudging a little disability time with the oft-abused 'hurt back' ploy."

"Yes, it is a back injury, Conner. But even better, my government doctor suggested golf was *good* for what ails me." They sat, having a cold one after their round, near a large window in the Nine-teenth Hole, overlooking the practice putting green. What *does* ail me? he wondered as he answered his friend. He didn't mind Conner's style of constant ribbing, but his going out on light duty with a back injury, and coming home to the small town where he grew up, was part of a bunch of things that troubled him about himself — and his life — lately.

"What work are you in with the government, John?" asked Ted amiably.

"I'm with customs," answered John.

"Stationed in Norfolk, Virginia. I'm not a field agent anymore, though. Don't go on ship searches or cargo checks. I work in a section that coordinates intell, from our own sources and those of the other services . . . when they'll share it. My section is part of admin, so I'm just a glorified office worker, really."

"And you hurt your back jumping from a cargo net onto the deck of an Iraqi freighter?" Conner slipped in. "Or did you do it chasing some foxy secretary around your desk?"

"No, Conner," replied Jameson with a sigh, "nothing dramatic like that. I bent over to move some boxes and my stupid back went boink." The lie came easily. Who couldn't identify with a back problem? he thought.

There was no way he could tell them the real reason he was on disability, no way he could tell them what his real job was. He knew from experience how impossible it was to discuss his type of work with people who had no clue, who equated it with spy novels or action films. It was a complicated thing, his work, especially what had happened on the day he was . . . injured. Guilt shouldered into his thoughts then, as it always did — guilt, anger, a sense of What if

17

I had handled it differently? It was a matter of national security, was it not? he asked himself again. Was it not?

Sam sipped his iced tea and asked, "So you came back here to mend, John?"

"Yeah, I guess. My dad passed away a couple of months ago and the house —"

"John's mom died years ago," Conner threw in.

"And the house was sitting here and my brother works the pipeline up in Alaska and there's nobody else so I talked it over with Sylvia, my wife, and we decided I'd take some disability leave. Come back here until we figure out what to do with the house and all, and then . . ." John shrugged at the others.

"How do your kids like the change?" asked Ted.

"They hate it," admitted John. "I've ruined their lives, taken them away from their school friends and brought them here to 'a total burg,' as my fourteen-year-old girl says. Couldn't leave 'em there. You try to do the right thing, make the right decision. . . . I don't. . . ."

Truth was, he had been second-guessing himself for months now. He knew he should feel like a guy who had it made, successful in his career and still on an upward professional path, in a comfortable marriage to a good friend, two kids who didn't give him any more headaches than anybody else's kids. But there was something missing, something off-center in his life. Sylvia told him she sensed his frustration — she called it a kind of spiritual malaise. She had gone through the same thing in her own life — the questioning, the search for an answer to what a full and meaning-filled life really was. He and Sylvia had suffered through a miscarriage after the first two kids were born. They'd tried again without success, and only when Sylvia had fully committed to a life with God had she accepted what was now so clearly meant to be. Her work with teenage mothers and their various foster-care programs evidence that there was a larger plan.

Despite that, John wondered who he was, what he was, whether what he did was worth anything . . . the big picture, the meaning of life . . . the whole "Am I important in the big scheme of things?" He settled his family into his deceased father's house, lived his days of disability leave, and wondered if he would ever even go back to work.

He looked up to find the others watching

him, waiting for him to finish. "Somebody give me a sign," he said with a grin, "so I'll know what to do next."

"Join this golf club, like me," suggested Conner. "Get rid of that stupid SUV and buy yourself a hog Harley-Davidson like I got, chase fast women, tell lies, impress your buddies, cheat on your taxes, listen to your kids' music, get out there and *live life* like I do. Life is seriously way too short, John, my friend. You got to live it for the *now*."

"Now how do you chase fast women, Conner," Sam asked with a mitigating smile, "when you're a wimpy married slob like the rest of us?"

Conner shrugged, a rueful grin on his face. "I guess I keep meeting my next former wife, if you know what I mean, Sam. Got two under my belt already . . . and this one I got now went to a lawyer yesterday. Just because of that little situation I had with that honey down in order processing at the home office."

"You are a mess, Conner Eagan," said Ted.

"Guilty, my friend, I'm a mess. But I know the truth about this life, this world, buddy. And that is, carpe diem, man. Carpe diem, carpe Harley, carpe pretty girls, carpe fast cars, carpe *life*, my friend."

"Well," replied Sam easily, "with that good advice ringing in our ears, let's call it a day."

"I'll pay the bill," said Conner as they stood to leave.

John Jameson headed home, the pleasure of the golf game diluted by the questions in his heart — and the undefined feeling of unease in his mind. He turned on the car radio, already set to NPR, listened as he drove, and let the current events meld with the information he had learned from his agency's intell input. It was a time of great energy, and tumult, a time of prosperity, poverty, potential, and cessation. Social, monetary, religious, and physical borders flexed and fluctuated in seemingly random patterns. New allegiances and alliances were formed worldwide. European and Asian countries joined in promises of mutual support, protection, and gain. They made promises and pacts that would have been unthinkable even a generation before. War lived on, not the nuclear global conflict that he and an entire generation had grown up fearing, but "small wars" between peoples birthed in hate and intolerance, fed on distrust, educated by agenda-driven backward-looking fanatics, and armed by bigger powers with their own game plan. Most countries now had the draft or conscription, and many young men and women were lost to the insatiable hunger of the conflicts. Wars and rumors of war, thought Jameson as he pulled onto his street.

Sylvia's van wasn't in the driveway of the old Cape Cod house when Jameson pulled in. Even now, he still liked the house's dormers, thought they resembled a pair of watchful eyes, as though the house itself could keep them safe, provide a haven from all that messiness out there.

Sylvia had mentioned that she and the kids would be going to church this morning. He sighed as he got out of his car. That was her answer for everything now. "Just pray about it," he said as he stepped over his son's skateboard and opened the front door of the house. His eyes hung for a moment on the small wood-and-wire gong that his dad had nailed to the door over twenty years ago, and he was assailed by memories. He paused in the doorway. He had spent many years coming and going through this doorway, and he reflected that the going out was always different, while the coming back was always the same. "My door is always open for you," his father had often intoned. As if he could forget.

He shook his head. Sounded like some dumb Biblical thing Sylvia would throw at him. She even had the kids caught up in it. They missed their friends back in Virginia but seemed to be doing okay with the church youth group here. He shrugged as he closed the door behind him, hearing the many sounds in the quiet house. He admitted he had *no* problem with the kids being in the church group, especially Sonia. He found himself doing double takes at her now and then. Such a child a short time ago, and then with no warning, talking, moving, and dressing (when she could get away with it) like a young woman.

He reflected a moment about Sylvia's desire to educate him about the Bible. No, he thought, not educate, more like *share* the good message she found within its pages. He knew she looked at him with a face infused with love, nothing else, and her wanting him to understand what was in the Scripture came simply from her love for him. She felt she had discovered something incredibly rich and important — a lifesaving thing, literally — and because she loved him she was compelled to share it. He saw with his own eyes and heart how the message gave her comfort and strength, how the kids seemed to find it also. He loved her for loving him enough to share the Good Word, but she didn't try to force it. She had told him you *can't* force it anyway, you simply open your heart, and let Him in. He shook his head. He had tried, and he went through the motions with her, but for him it just didn't feel real.

He grabbed a cold drink from the fridge, clumped up the stairs to the master bedroom, and used his toes to pull off each shoe. So Sylvia had found Jesus, and the church. Hurrah, he thought. What did *he* need to find? It would have to be something of substance, something real. Maybe it was a middle-age thing, gettin' on, afraid of dying, afraid of missing out on life's treasures. I should buy myself a leather jacket, he thought with a grin. Get a leather jacket, join a gym to tighten up those long-gone abs, and perhaps have some wild fling with a twenty-year-old girl into tattoos and body piercing. "Nah," he said to the empty house. He wished he could talk with his father.

The hospital ship *Mercy Ark* steamed

ponderously along the coast of the African continent, a few miles offshore from what remained of the town of Novo Sumbe, where the country of Angola had once been: Through war, famine, disease, and the corruption of man, most of the south and central African states had been reduced to wastelands of anarchy. Those who ruled, ruled by the power of the gun, and those with the guns controlled what food was grown or shipped in from other countries still willing to share. Most starving people died where they fell, and within moments their twisted and shrunken bodies were stripped of what little they possessed. For many no medicine was available for the sick, no place for them to seek aid, and no way for any help to travel to them. Governments had completely broken down, utilities were either sporadic or nonexistent. The phrase "hell on earth" had lost almost all meaning after been used so often by journalists who still did stories about Africa.

The *Mercy Ark* was just that, a ship of mercy. Privately funded, staffed by missionary volunteers, and equipped to provide medical and health care to people who had no other access, the ship traveled to most areas of the world escorted by a naval destroyer arranged for through the United Nations. Most local governments, if there were any, allowed the ship safe harbor for a price. Once in an area, the staff would assist as many needy as possible, focusing on the children, hygiene, and life-threatening disease. Food and medicines were distributed, again with the usual warlord payoffs, and the hospital section of the ship functioned as an outpatient clinic. Most of the time it was necessary to have a contingent of armed marines from the naval vessel on the dock near the gangway to keep the desperate throngs from swarming the ship. Often the more serious cases were brought on board for care as the ship continued its cruise. On this day almost every bed was full, and the staff and crew worked tirelessly to provide comfort.

David Njorsgaard rubbed his bearded cheeks, then ran his hands through his thinning blond curls. The captain's pensive mood had infected others on the bridge. A Norwegian who had been at sea since he was thirteen years old, he'd earned his crew's respect. He was usually friendly and open, and liked to move about the ship giving encouragement where he could. The navigator and the first officer both felt their captain had changed after their last layover in Le Havre, France. He had become remote, solemn, and quiet much of the time, and ventured from his cabin less often — rare for a man who had spent his life on the bridge. Francois Druet, the navigator, had sailed with the captain for over fifteen years in various assignments, and knew that the captain had attended some special, and secret, meeting while they were in France. One of the great cathedrals, the captain had said, he was to go there, and had told the navigator hesitantly that he felt *driven* to go. The first officer and navigator suspected the meeting in the church had somehow changed Njorsgaard, and not for the good.

Francois glanced at David as he stood on the bridge now, staring off at the horizon. The first officer caught the navigator's eye, and shrugged. They both watched as the captain took something from his jacket, held it in both hands, and stared at it. The object looked like a cell phone, and the navigator, who stood closer to him, saw the captain's hands shake. Captain Njorsgaard, his troubled face a mosaic of sadness and turmoil, the corners of his ice blue eyes wet, sighed and thumbed a few numbers into the object he held.

Instantly, an explosion and fireball that erupted from her lowest deck consumed the hospital ship *Mercy Ark*. The blast blew the bottom out of her even as it turned the upper decks into a charnel house. Within seven minutes she was gone, along with all those who sailed in her.

In Eastlake, Ohio, not far from Cleveland, Shannon Carpenter watched her three-year-old son, Matt, stagger across the kitchen floor. She had just handed him his favorite "big boy" cup, not a sippy cup, and told him as he turned away, "Don't spill, Matt." Of *course* she had said, "Don't spill." She sounded like a broken record, and there was a certain inevitability to what would happen next. But this was something different, and she watched, holding her breath, as Matt staggered, recovered, staggered again, and dropped the cup, scattering the milk in fat drops and puddles everywhere. Then he sat down, turned his head to stare at her wide-eyed, and began crying.

"It's okay, Matt, it's okay," said Shannon softly. She sat beside her son and hugged him, felt his heaving chest and shoulders against her own. She thought, not for the first time, how fragile he still was — would always be — in her mind. "It's not your fault, Matt. The floor shook, and it surprised you." She looked around the kitchen, her mouth dry, and added, "It surprised Mommy, too." She held him close for a few minutes, waiting to see if there would be another tremor, but none came. Then she stood, comforted Matt until he relaxed, poured another cup of milk for him, watched him toddle away, and cleaned up the mess. She wished that she could bounce back as quickly as he did from life's little bumps.

Just what I need today, she thought, a stupid *earthquake* in Cleveland, Ohio. "Sorry," she said to the empty kitchen, "can't be bothered by earthquakes today, don't have time." Time, she thought, I need more *time*. She looked into the living room to see Matt seated before the big TV, watching *Blue's Clues*, and went back to the laundry room, where several large piles of clothing and towels awaited her. She'd discovered that Sunday morning was the only block of two or three hours she could devote to doing laundry. She and her husband never really argued, he didn't yell at her or anything, but this morning he had expressed his disapproval in a way she had come to recognize.

Sunday meant the Carpenter family would present themselves, freshly scrubbed and buttoned, to one of the center pews in the Cuyahoga Christian Church. They would listen to the sermon, sing a few hymns, visit with some of the congregation they were friendly with, and head home for a leisurely afternoon. That was the way her husband thought it should be, anyway. This morning she had helped the two older kids get dressed, and when her husband saw she was not getting ready, he asked why not.

"Laundry, honey, this week has just gotten away from me and we are flat running out of clean clothes around here," she replied. She tried to lighten it up by adding, "I've only got one bra left, and it's my most uncomfortable one."

He looked at her quietly, steadily. He didn't show anger or frustration, just looked into her eyes and waited. She watched as the frown lines around Billy's eyes, lines that had deepened from the years he spent working outside squinting against the glaring sun, softened and relaxed. For a moment she wished he was high school Billy again, rewarding her with that radiant smile of his that had her squinting. As a final effort she said, "I'll keep little Matt here with me while I catch up around the house. You go with the other two and relax. We'll make a big lunch when you get back. Okay?" But it wasn't okay, and she felt his disappointment and resignation as he picked up his Bible and left without another word.

It wasn't that she didn't like going to church as a family. The picture of them doing that actually pleased her, and the people at the church were nice for the most part. The sermons all seemed to be running together lately, though, no real clarity or impact to them. Not for her, anyway. Billy seemed to think the sermons were becoming *more* relevant, and hung on every word. He would be disappointed on the drive home when he wanted to discuss it and she couldn't seem to grasp it as he did. He'll come home all excited today, she thought as she threw a fresh fabric-softener sheet into the dryer, telling me that earthquakes had some Biblical import, it was some kind of sign or something to go along with the other crazy fighting and stuff happening all around the world.

"We should just thank God America isn't directly involved in most of these flare-ups, Shannon," Billy had told her the other day. "But we should look at all of these events as signs. . . ." She saw one of the bath mats folded on the washer, and remembered she still hadn't cleaned the upstairs bathroom. She blew out a puff of air, and said to the lint trap, "Somebody give *me* a sign."

One morning several weeks ago, Billy came home early. Thunderstorms had washed out the day, and after sending the crew home, he'd sorted through receipts in his truck before deciding to do more paperwork at home. Shannon had taken the day off to catch up at home, and she was clipping coupons when Billy walked in. She always loved the scents he carried with him when he came home — a musky, tangy mix of sweat from an honest day's labor, sawdust, and this particular morning, wet wool. While she fixed him some soup for lunch, Billy sat at the kitchen table reading his Bible.

When she set the steaming bowl in front of him, Billy looked up and smiled. Shannon pulled a chair up next to him and grinned at him before producing a second spoon. They sat side by side and ate. She held his hand, ran her fingers over the cracked ridges of his calluses, feeling the warmth of the soup and his love for her. Billy alternated eating and holding his place in the Bible with his free hand, loving the moments like this one when speaking didn't seem necessary, the acquired intimacy of years together.

"Billy," Shannon said, "Tell me what it is that you get from that." She reached across him and tapped at the pages of the Bible. "I mean, I know what's in there, but you've read it all before."

Billy shrugged and looked at her. "The only thing that I can compare it to, is that it's like when I look at you or one of the kids. Even though you're with me every day, every time I see you, I notice something else, come to some new appreciation — well, most of the time, appreciation," he squeezed her hand and wiggled his eyebrows at her, "for what a gift you all are to me."

Shannon shifted in her seat like a school girl struggling with a lesson. She shook her head. "That's not what I mean. I know that it gives you comfort, but I guess what I don't understand is how you — I don't know exactly — what you find in there to follow."

Billy pushed back his chair and stood. While he walked around the kitchen, he slapped a flat lumber pencil against his left thigh and said, "I believe that God has put his blueprint in here for me, and not just for me but for all of us. I mean, it's kind of like what I do at work most days. I follow the design that's someone else's creation. I execute it the best that I can, knowing that due to the imperfections of the materials being used, the tools, and to be honest with you, Shannon, my own imperfections as a craftsman, I may never get the work done to the exact specifications laid out in those plans."

He paused and looked at Shannon. She'd pushed her own chair away from the table and now sat with her elbows resting on her legs, her chin in her hand. She smiled at Billy and nodded. "Go on."

"Well, the way I look at it, by studying the Bible closely, I'm getting as familiar as I possibly can with the specifications and measurements. That way, the bringing it all to life becomes second nature. Almost like I don't need to think about what's wrong and what's right, I just try in what I know and what I've read and I just act on that. That's the ultimate goal, but I still have to ask myself what Jesus would do."

"That's funny, Billy, because there are times when I ask myself, 'What would Billy do?' "

His face clouded for a moment before he

spoke. "Shannon, that's flattering, but you really do need more instruction than just me. I mean, there are hundreds of people at church you could learn from, but more importantly, it's also all in here." Billy held up his Bible and held it out to her.

Shannon shook her head, let a curtain of hair fall across her face. Billy felt a sensation in the pit of his stomach, as though he was in a car going fast over the crest of a hill. Shannon's gesture, equal parts humility and uncertainty, touched him in a way that he couldn't really understand. All he knew was that it reminded him of when they were first dating. With the back of his hand Billy brushed her back. Shannon leaned into his hand, took it into her own, before gently kissing his roughened palm.

"I need time, Billy. That's all. Just a little more time." Before Billy could respond, she stood up and began clearing the table. "I'm going to have to get the kids soon. I imagine you've got things you need to get done."

Billy nodded, felt his throat constrict and marveled at God's infinite patience with his creation, and wondered if he would have enough of his own to give Shannon what she was asking for.

Shannon was married to a carpenter, but

one licensed, certified, insured, and financed up to his neck as a general contractor. He was William Carpenter, the man she had fallen in love with when they were both in middle school, the man everyone except her called Bill. For her it would always be "Billy." They had been married for twelve years now, had three children — Billy, nine; Laura, six; and little Matt, three — and lived in a house William Carpenter had built with his own hands in a nice upper-middle-class neighborhood with a small-town feel.

Billy Carpenter was a provider, a man who took seriously the fact that he was a husband and father. He worked hard, spent what time he could with his kids, and loved his wife with a simple and direct passion. Bill and Shannon Carpenter had never discussed this, but his unstated expectation had always been that she would spend most of her energy at home. They had a family, he worked to provide for them, and she would take care of the home front. Just like his father and mother.

She had gone to college after high school, though, had a degree, and wanted to *work*. Shannon had grown up in the age of empowered women and did not want to spend all of her time sitting at home, even if she *was* a soccer mom with a high-tech minivan. She and Bill had several heated discussions about it, but he finally relented with her promise that it would be part-time. She got a job as a legal assistant with a law firm that specialized in civil litigation, with a bit of criminal work, and enjoyed it. The job gave her a reason to stay sharp, to wear something besides jeans and a T-shirt, gave her a place to meet and exchange views with people — a chance to be more than just Mom. Bill Carpenter tolerated it, thought the lawyers in the firm were a bunch of weenies, and tried to hold his temper if he came home after a hard day's work to find instructions taped to the fridge regarding the heating of dinner. It hadn't taken long for part-time to become almost full-time, then almost all of the time.

Shannon Carpenter didn't like it when her husband was unhappy. She respected him, his work ethic, his morals, the way he was with their children. She wanted to be a good wife, a good partner for him. She had tried hard to stay attractive to him, and fought to keep her weight down after the kids. She was still only one size up from high school — maybe two, depending on the cut of the jeans — but knew she could hold her own in their social circles. Her mother had given her good advice about that other thing too, before she and Billy married.

Men have needs, her mom had said, and it doesn't take much to hold him a bit, hold him and give him what you can as often as he wants it. Keeps him happy, she had said, keeps him from straying. Shannon would admit it hadn't hurt *her* either. She and Billy were relaxed around each other, playful most of the time, and he was an affectionate man, always touching her hair, or telling her how good she looked and smelled, or smacking her on the rump when she was bending into the fridge looking for something.

She knew she should, or could, be happy simply being Mrs. William Carpenter, mother and wife. Keep the house, drive the kids around in the minivan like all the other soccer moms, go to church, and live the good life. Forget being a professional woman, a career woman. You can't have it all, you can't *do* it all, she had read. But she did want it all, and she was trying her best to keep the whole thing running. She bunched her right hand into a fist and pounded it lightly into the muscle of her right thigh.

Billy did not like her work, she thought ruefully, and he would for *sure* not like the one special project she did there. She glanced at her watch, and decided she could give the upstairs bathroom just a lick and a promise. She could get the neighbor's teenage daughter to sit and watch TV with Matt for a while. That would give her a little time to drive over there, even for a couple of minutes, to see if anything had . . . changed. She sighed. Lately she had the feeling, emotionally, spiritually, a bit like that tremor made her feel. Her internal gyrocompass was a few points off, or something . . . her guidance systems were out of line. She had everything going for her but was drifting somehow, drifting away from solid footing, and it worried her. She wished she could find whatever it was Billy had found in the church.

Chapter Two

The elderly priest turned his eyes away as the members of the newly formed committee filed out of the small but sumptuously appointed chambers. He was a humble and pious man, he felt, not given to pride. He admitted to feeling a little pride on this day, however, because the committee had convened in this small church in the fold of a valley in northern Italy. It had been the church of his childhood, where he had first received the blessed Word, where his heart had opened to a fullness that diminished all else he had known. That had been, truly, lifetimes ago. Now he had returned, as escort — perhaps valet — to one of the most influential and respected bishops in all of Italy.

He understood he was to remain invisible while the notables gathered, there only to carry things, or fetch a glass of water, or perhaps find a document if ordered to do so. He stopped himself before he shrugged like an old woman. To be invisible is one thing, he knew; to be stone deaf, another thing altogether. He was *not* deaf, and collected snippets, half sentences, whispers, and asides as another might collect precious stones. He bartered with what he learned, of course, and his most repeated confession concerned his delight in gossip.

He had stood out of the way, unobserved and collectively dismissed, while the committee listened to their guest. The bishops, cardinals, and senior priests on the committee were intellectuals, may the Heavenly Father bless each one, he thought. Perhaps they truly were above earthly matters, he mused, as they must surely have felt the tremor that shook the region during the meeting, even as it rattled his old bones. To his astonishment, no mention of the tremor was made. It was as if the rumblings of the earth had no import compared to the matters they discussed. These men were the best and the brightest, considered the up-and-comers in the church hierarchy. He sniffed. He was a humble man, he reminded himself, educated by the trials of life, the trials of man, certainly not an intellectual. But he knew something, he told himself, something the best and brightest apparently did not see on this day of God.

The meeting had ended with an agreement, a covenant of sorts to work with their guest on a "project." It had to do with a joyous occasion, a happening the church had longed for and prayed for since Peter, John, and Paul began writing all those letters. God alone would not make it happen, he discerned. No, the Church would help it along, and the Church would be assisted by the committee's guest. Other churches, the guest had said, other denominations, other faiths, even the confused followers of that upstart Muhammad — even various faiths in the childlike country of America — all of these would be made to embrace the plan, would eventually agree to be part of this "project."

The old priest sniffed again, and wondered how the committee's guest had managed to be gone from the church so quickly. He felt a chill, and a tumble of anger and sadness battered his heart for a moment. He wished again, prayed as he had so many times before in his worthless life, prayed for the Blessed Father to give him the strength to speak out when he saw a lie. That is what it was, he knew, this agreement, this covenant . . . a lie.

He was a simple man, a humble man, certainly not an intellectual, but he had looked directly into the eyes of the guest as he held a chair for the man. Noir was the guest's name. Yes, the man was a respected international theologian, an emerging voice of reason and cohesiveness, a unifier, supposedly. But the old priest had looked directly into those eyes, and what he saw there froze his heart.

Thomas Church did not know John Jameson, lately of Indiana. Thomas Church lived on Long Island, and spent a lot of time in nearby New York City. He didn't know Jameson, but he had something in common with him — he was a news junkie too. His interests leaned toward the financial gruntings and heavings more than people shooting at one another, but he believed money had something to do with almost any act of man anyway. If Protestants and Catholics exchanged gunfire in Northern Ireland, the Pakistanis and the Indians fretted and quarreled over Kashmir, the Israelis and Palestinians machine-gunned each other, the Chinese rattled their swords about Taiwan, North and South Koreans called each other names, the Russians were for sale, nuclear devices and all, the British Parliament demanded everyone act like gentlemen, and the French decried everything the Americans did, then money was moving around somewhere underneath, of that he was convinced. Unlike Jameson, Thomas Church gathered almost all of his information about world events from the Web. Church was a computer guy — not a computer *nerd* by any means — but a computer virtuoso. The first time his fingers caressed a keyboard, the first time he blasted from one site to another, cruising through entire worlds in seconds, he was hooked. Hooked and sure from that moment what his work would be.

He had grown up out toward the Hamptons, had lived a happy, healthy childhood in a fairly normal family, and felt pretty lucky, all things considered. He had a business degree from Brown, was a partner in a successful financial security and planning firm, and lived comfortably. True, he was now in his mid-forties and divorced, but even that had been relatively painless.

He and Iris had felt the fire during their early years, had actually known passion for a while. Then they had the children, and settled down into an American-family kind of life that often seemed almost scripted to him. They raised the children, did the PTA thing, joined a modest country club, moved once to a bigger house, and rarely fought about anything. Iris had a minivan, the kids grew into school activities and sports, and were driven here and there in the van, just as they were supposed to. Thomas had one falling-out with a partner in the early years of the Web site businesses, and the Churches spent a couple of years hanging on by the skin of their teeth, then fought back up to a healthy financial level. His daughter fell out of a tree house when she was nine and broke her arm, looked beautiful on the night of her prom, and got into trouble once with a couple of her friends by using the old "Each of us will tell our mom we're spending the night at our *friend's* house" and then driving to the shore to meet some boys. His son had done pretty well in track and field, had two minor fender benders with his first car, and was brought home by the cops once for fighting with some kids from another school. All typical Americana, he surmised as he lived those years, all as if scripted.

Then came high school graduations one year apart, and the kids were off to colleges several states away. His son had already dropped out and was working on some kind of cattle ranch in Texas, and apparently loving it. His daughter was still in college, engaged to a tall, skinny guy who ate no meat and was an expert on the Aztecs or Incas or some long-lost civilization, and they seemed happy. All scripted. Then the house had become a quiet place, and one evening he and Iris were sitting at the dining-room table, looked up from their plates, and began to speak at the same time. Divorce. No children at home, no common interests, no fire or passion. The one thing they did share was a desire for something more — or different. Scripted.

The split was so painless they almost used the same divorce lawyer, but even with the two jerks they eventually retained trying to make a fight out of it, the legal formalities went smoothly. Iris wanted very little from Thomas, and Thomas was willing to give her anything she wanted. The kids seemed heartbroken at first, but adjusted quickly, and maintained easy contact with both parents. Scripted. The only thing that didn't seem scripted was the way his wife simply disappeared after the divorce was final. He knew the kids had some way of occasionally speaking with her, but other than that she was just gone. He never let himself admit that it bothered him. All he knew was that she'd headed out west to discover herself at an ashram or some other crazy thing run by some kind of New Age guru or another.

Thomas Church became a single man, stayed fit and trim by jogging and working out in a local gym, and lived his comfortable life. He was a reasonably attractive man, thought the gray in his trimmed beard gave him a seasoned and salty look, and took precise care with his clothes and grooming. He owned the almost obligatory Harley-Davidson motorcycle and a functional but plush SUV, and was fairly successful in his pursuit of women. He was in no way looking for a new long-term relationship, but he didn't feel he was a user, either. He had had one brief affair during his years with Iris, and now he had the intense desire to experience other women. He was a taciturn man, quiet and undemonstrative, by no means a braggart. But he would allow, if asked, that he "did all right" with women, and saw himself as a gentleman.

He saw his world, his life, as scripted, but he saw *the* world as one messed-up place, and rapidly getting worse. Maybe it was his age, he sometimes mused, that made him so cynical. Whatever it was, he did not see the current state of the world as a happy one. He was a student of history, knew that old pontificators centuries ago had been bemoaning the state of the world *then*. Morals, music, the arts, politics, young people . . . it had all been doomed lifetimes ago, he had read. But here we were, the world still stumbling along, so maybe it was all old men and sour-grapes bluster. Or maybe the world was falling apart.

After Iris had moved out, he'd remodeled the house. Turned what had been the sitting-room/sewing-room portion of the master bedroom suite into another multimedia room. The flat-panel high-definition television screen, the requisite state-of-the-art multichannel home theater sound system. Along another wall stood a bank of smaller televisions, like monitors in a studio, tuned to CNN, CNBC, CNN Financial.

From New Zealand he'd imported a Perreaux stereo system, and he'd mail-ordered stacks of jazz, classical, and world music CDs that still sat unopened, a shrink-wrapped Tower of Babel. The walls were lined with a fabric whose acoustical properties dampened any noise that might interfere.

But his pride and joy was his pair of computers — a desktop and a laptop. Arrayed before him were various input and storage devices. His favorite was the wireless mouse — with it he felt free to roam around the room, though he most often sat rooted to his chair. He had Internet access via cable and a DSL line. Originally he had doubled up, thinking that he should keep his phone line free in case the kids, or Iris, or one of the women he was seeing needed to speak to him. But increasingly he'd stopped picking up the phone, preferring instead to let the machine get it. Nothing urgent taking place on the home front, but out there — that was another story.

Thomas Church saw the reflection of his own face in the flat-screen LCD monitor. The face vibrated and bounced up and down and side to side, palsied and unsettled. "What was that?" he said as he put his hands on the keyboard in front of him, steadying it. The room shook, and he heard a door slam somewhere in the house. No way, he thought, then watched as a large, ungainly pile of printouts avalanched off a nearby counter, and said, "*Way.*"

Long Island is having itself an earthquake, he mused; who would have ever thought? It took a moment or two for him to realize it was over, and when he did he wiggled his bottom on the chair to quiet the tingling. He gave a little laugh of surprise and wonder, turned his state-of-the-art computer on, laced the fingers of both hands together, and then pushed them toward the screen, cracking his knuckles loudly, and worked the mouse and keyboard like Daniel Barenboim. He went surfing, seeking, searching. He found plenty of noise about the world's everyday political, cultural, and financial convulsions, and within a very short time began to pick up spikes of immediate hyper yodels and yells about the earthquake . . . or earth*quakes.*

Apparently the tremor had been like a gigantic ripple, coursing across the country and the globe like a bad itch under the skin. Not bad enough to kill, mostly, but certainly intense enough to be felt — felt, acknowledged, and wondered at. One tremor, or series of tremors, that had been felt by people in every corner of the earth at the same time. Unprecedented, he thought, unheard of, no wonder the media channels were going crazy.

He sat back in his custom-designed and -built chair, stroked his beard with his right hand, and stared at the rivers of information and communication that ran before his eyes. He had another, more specific thing in common now with John Jameson in Indiana. The religious aspect of things, out there in the world. There was something there. He had stumbled across some information recently, and it intrigued him, bothered him actually, and it bothered him more because he didn't know why it *should* bother him. Religion, the faiths, the churches, sure — they were part of history, part of the historic world and today's world. Yes, he would certainly acknowledge, the different religions had played a major part in shaping our present world, and in many aspects continued to do so. He still believed religion was only an abstract part of real power. Real power being money, of course.

But millions of people spent their actual working days and nights living as if their religion were a very real part of life. So who was he to say they were wrong? It really wasn't a big issue with him. His parents had belonged to a moderate neighborhood Christian church, Methodist, easy. He grew up there, accepted the teachings as a child, and thought it was all pretty harmless. Scripted, again. Once he left high school and entered college, though, he found himself wondering what all the fuss was about. It was clearly all nonsense. Karl Marx and his opiate of the masses seemed based on clear reasoning to him then; and he was actually entertained to see how sweaty and caught up in it all some people became. He did not dishonor his parents, though, never really argued with them about it, and he and Iris were actually married in the same church where his mother and father had exchanged vows. No big deal.

He stroked his beard slowly, took a long, slow breath, and thought. But there is something . . . something. One of the women he had recently dated had mentioned some stuff she had learned in an adult Bible-study class. All about the end of the world, tribulation, Judgment Day, how it would all play out. He found it intellectually stimulating, but was still glad to learn later that night that the teachings had not diminished the woman's enthusiasm for life.

A few days after their date, almost in response to her obvious thrill at having the inside scoop, he spent an afternoon driving through various information sites having to do with different religious matters. He had chided himself for acting like one of those people who crave tabloid stuff — searching for the demeaning stories, the lascivious tales of errant priests, dishonest preachers,

DUI rabbis, and mullahs who immersed themselves in the fleshpots of Europe. The usual hypocrisy and foolishness, he had snorted. But there was something — too many references, too many events. Like the earthquake. Were there more earthquakes? Were there other signs? He came across different hints about secret religious societies similar to the Illuminati; he found quotes from respected scholars — Christian and Jewish — who seemed to be saying, "Get ready."

Get ready for what? he wondered. During his deepest digging, as he was weaving through many layers of info from intricate sites abstractly connected, he came across something that made him pause. The thing that worried him and he didn't know why. Now, as he sat bathed in the light of computer monitors, the flickering and flashing television screens, he read what was on the different sites on what should have been a quiet Sunday morning. He dug back into it. He chewed his lip as he worked the keyboard, his eyes narrowed, his concentration total.

The various stories, essays, and commentaries showed him a world in tumult and upheaval. There was great speculation about the apparent building of a new world power. Alliances were formed on blood-soaked borders, creating what one pundit called a "new empire." It was made up of Eastern European countries, including Russia, which had become a restless, uncontrolled wild beast of a country, a place of near anarchy, a lawless and immoral society bent first on survival, then conquest. If the old USSR failed, said the young, tough, hungry new Russians, it was because it tried to get along with the rest of the world. The driving hunger and unrest swept down from the Balkans, all the way to the Middle Eastern states, smothering reason and faith with the urgent weight of desire. Arabs joined with Serbs, with French, Germans, and Basques.

Oil still equaled money, and the power of money crushed religious identity and statehood together. Money equaled power, and power equaled food, as the earth actually began producing less food than it had one hundred years before. Hunger, combined with anger, shouldered spiritual promise aside. Muslims, Christians, and Jews became less interested in their future, more focused on today. As needs and desires became more base, simpler thoughts and pursuits became passions. Intellectuals, scholars, spiritual leaders, churches, universities . . . these became less important, tolerated but ridiculed by activists, and more often ignored altogether.

The complexities of law, especially regarding the laughable subject of human rights, demanded too much thought, reason, and recognition of cultural diversity. The many small countries of the globe became like rabid hyenas running in dangerous packs, often turning on one another, devouring their own body parts, gnawing on each other and anything that could not defend itself. It was a hateful and harmful clash of armed cultures, but until recently, fragmented, leaderless.

Until the arrival of one Azul Dante, thought Thomas Church as he scanned the info rolling before him. Now *there* is a story, he mused, a positive one for a change. Dante had appeared out of nowhere, originally a minor politician or union representative from northern France, and he could eventually be the right man in the right place at the right time. He was rapidly becoming a popular personage on the world stage; people who came into contact with him *believed* in him, apparently. There were even a few reports stating that the United Nations was courting him to act as some type of roving ambassador, to be used in the role of mediator. But Dante was not what Thomas Church searched for now. Perhaps Dante had some connection to it, but it was too early to tell. Besides, he wasn't even sure what *it* was. Finally, after several minutes, he found it again. One simple reference to what had to be some kind of code name or . . . *something*. One simple reference, but cross-indexed to various religious sites all over the place. He looked at the screen, scratched his jaw, and said to the quiet room, "So what in the world is the 'Prodigal Project'?"

The battered, faded yellow-and-white school bus rumbled along the littoral, the coast road. The road traversed the Pacific edge of Central America, somewhere in the region of El Salvador. For years now, of course, the borders in that part of the world had become blurred. El Salvador, Nicaragua, Honduras, Guatemala, Costa Rica, each had become a largely unidentifiable place of sadness and despair. Again the gun ruled when government failed, and people who spent almost every ounce of energy on basic survival needs had none to spare for the niceties of debate or order. Still, some tried to make life passable.

They came as missionaries, among them nuns from various Catholic orders with a long history in the region. They focused on the children, providing basic hygiene and education, working to instill dignity, self-esteem, and hope in those who represented the future.

Most locals knew the old bus, and smiled at it if they smiled at all. It was always filled with children, singing, laughing, making their way from one town to another. The nuns on board — strong, no-nonsense women with simple clothes, weathered skin, knowing eyes, and fluent Spanish — made sure their charges were fed, bathed, clothed, educated, and introduced to the Word. No one bothered the bus, or the nuns. Various armed groups fought for control of the roads, water, power plants, farms, ports, and towns. Squads of men guarded compounds, bridges, fuel depots, and the few remaining hotels and restaurants. Constant ambushes, firefights, and night attacks broke out, with no room for prisoners, no facilities for the wounded, and no rules of war. Atrocities were committed regularly, with no official sanction and very little news coverage. Killing led to more killing, revenge reaped revenge, and only a fool thought life could be lived without concern.

The nuns were not fools, but they had worked for many years in the region without being targeted by one side or the other. With one or two notorious exceptions they were allowed to go about their business with at least passive approval from whatever armed group controlled the area at the time. On this day the nuns on the bus were aware of the fighting that had taken place along the littoral in the past few days, knew that those who traveled the road were vulnerable, but made their way emboldened by their shredded faith in their fellow man, and a strong faith in God.

The driver, the youngest of the nuns, slowed and fought the shift into a lower gear as the bus came to a curving incline. The bus groaned and slowed, the engine chugged and backfired, and the children laughed as one of the older nuns rolled her eyes, made a face, and crossed herself in an exaggerated manner. In that instant the inside of the bus exploded in a firestorm of shrapnel and bullets. Smoke, dust, and blood formed a thick haze, and the roar of rifle, machine-gun, and rocket fire consumed all other sound. It took only a few seconds for the bus to become a shredded, twisted, blackened hulk of wreckage tilted into the ditch on the ocean side of the littoral. All the children, and the nuns, died in those few seconds. The words "Madre de Dios" escaped from the lips of one of the nuns, but they were torn away by the fire.

Oddly, the earth's tremors rippled through the region at that exact moment, but were not felt by those who formed the kill zone. The noise died out as the firing staggered to a ragged and reluctant stop, the quiet broken by an almost manic laugh that escaped from the mouth of one of the soldiers hiding along the ridge on the high side of the road. Then, one by one, the men stood and moved toward the horror they had created. They were young, dirty, and dressed in ragtag bits and pieces of old uniforms. Some were barefoot. Only their weapons appeared cared for.

They were led by an older man, sour, thin and dark, his lean face pocked and sanded with beard. He carried an assault rifle, and pointed at the bus with it as his command came out of their hiding places and approached the wreckage. He knew his men might be disappointed in the attack. They didn't care about ambushing the bus and killing all those in it — children or not — but they wanted the nuns alive for their entertainment. It had been discussed among them. Too bad, he thought, but not this time. This time he was driven — he would not have been able to explain it to anyone — he was simply *driven* to attack the bus and kill them all. No more, no less. He watched as his men drew close to the carnage, saw the small movement from someone somehow still alive inside, and turned away as his men lifted their weapons and fired again, until there was no more movement. And so it was done.

"Did you feel the earth move just now, newspaper girl?" asked the big cop. He was dark and muscular, with black hair, dark eyes, and a knowing smile. He looked fit and deadly in his blue uniform, and his cologne said something about the morning after.

"Yes . . . I did," replied Catherine Early with a quick nod of her head. She immediately wished she could have those words back. She knew what would come next from the Latino cop she had met before.

"Oh, yeah. You felt the earth move just standing next to me, you hot thing," he said in a purr. "Imagine what you'd feel if you and I . . ."

"It was an earthquake, or a tremor from one, you hormone-driven jerk," responded Catherine with a smile. "So get your picante breath off my neck and go try to impress some cop groupie who still *is* impressionable." She added with a frown, "This is a crime scene, you know. You could show some respect."

The cop turned to walk out of the small house, and said over his shoulder, "You're right, Early, it's a crime scene. But respect? Respect don't live here no more." He let go of the tattered screen door, and it shuddered against the warped frame. Then he added, his confident grin back in place, "But my girl, everybody knows you've dated cops before. You must like *something* we got."

Catherine Early — since elementary school she had been simply "Cat" — had several replies on the tip of her tongue, but she just shook her head and turned back to the task at hand.

A crime reporter for the *Herald*, Miami's biggest paper, Cat knew she worked a beat where many famous print journalists had made their bones, where it really was the big leagues, where a reporter saw *life* happening every day and could write about it . . . could tell about it. It had the grit, the dirt, the passion, the blood, all the cover-jacket stuff she had dreamed of in college. But she had been at it long enough now to know they left a few things off the cover jacket. Like pain, searing pain or numbing pain, the pain that comes with *loss*. And that's what we have today, folks, she thought as she slowly made her way through the cluttered house. We have loss.

She had been having coffee with a girl-friend who happened to be a traffic-homicide cop, discussing a fatal accident that had occurred the night before. Three teens had smashed into the twisted remains of a small car with a big engine, leaving all of them dead. Toxicology reports weren't available yet, but the traffic cop already had the word from one of the moms that the driver had made a big scene drinking straight from a bottle at some kid's party before they roared off to find some friends.

The traffic cop listened to her radio for a moment, then told Cat about an apparent homicide that had just been phoned in. She gave Cat the address, and Cat drove over there hoping she'd recognize a face so she could get some usable info. Through the years many of the working cops in her city had come to accept her, even if grudgingly, as a fair reporter. A newsie who knew what to say and what to hold, a newsie you could almost trust.

Several patrol cars and a couple of detectives' cars sat on the cluttered residential street in one of the poor neighborhoods. Some stripped cars cluttered the areas of sparse grass in front of the homes, along with a few mattresses, eviscerated washing machines, and old tires strewn about for effect. The house in question had a cop standing at the front door, several others leaning on the bent and ramshackle fence that defiantly marked a property line. She knew that most of the people she socialized and worked with would look upon what lay within the fence as worthless junk, the fence itself a symbol of futility. But a line had been crossed, Cat thought as she got out of her car, in spite of the fence.

She felt the looks of the patrolmen as she walked across the street and up to the front door, pen and notepad ready. She asked the tall, good-looking cop at the door if Detective Moore was on the scene, and heard Moore's booming voice call from inside the house, "She's okay, Fernandez." At that moment the whole world tilted crazily for a few seconds. Tinny objects rattled inside the house, someone cursed out in the yard. The tremor didn't last long, but long enough for everyone there to be aware of it. It tickled the soles of Cat's feet, but caused an immediate and unsettling fear in her heart. She heard someone ask, "Did you feel *that?*" and heard Moore order another detective to advise the radio dispatcher that everyone was ten-four in response to an all-channel query. The quake, or the tremor, must have been felt all over town, she thought. She made it through the living room, heard someone sobbing nearby, and turned to stand in the doorway of the bedroom, where she took in the sad tableau before her.

A lifelike doll lay twisted and broken on the bedroom floor. It was naked, had brown skin, and was anatomically correct. But it had no life — that had been smashed out of it in some kind of unimaginable rage. Sitting on the edge of a rumpled bed with soiled sheets a few feet from the tiny figure on the floor was an angular, thin woman wearing a floral-print housedress pinned to her sides by her bony elbows. She had her hands together, both thumbs pressed against her chin. She rocked back and forth and moaned,

"Lawd, Lawd . . . oh, Lawd . . ."

You're just wasting your time calling for Him, thought Cat savagely. Then she turned at the sound of the deep, melodious voice of Detective Amos Moore.

"Don't you ever get your fill of this kind of thing, Cat?" asked the large black homicide cop.

"All the news that's fit to print, Amos. And this doesn't look like the child simply fell out of bed," Early responded with more bravado than she felt.

"No," agreed the big cop quietly as he motioned Cat away from the bedroom. "We've already taken the boyfriend into custody. Crackhead, just came home from prison about a month ago. Said he was 'playing rough' with the child and dropped him. We have the mother's statement. She came in right at the end. And a ton of physical evidence in the bedroom there. But the child is dead . . . and . . ."

"And it's another beautiful day here in the city on the bay, the river, and the swamp."

Detective Amos Moore rubbed his face with one big hand, sighed, and said, "Yeah." He was in his early forties, looked ten years older, had been hospitalized twice with ulcers, and told himself he wasn't really an alcoholic because he never took his first drink until five o'clock in the afternoon. He also had six kids of his own, coached every youth sport he could, and worried that no matter what he did, one of his kids could turn out wrong.

Cat Early copied the basic information she'd need for the story and got out of there. On the way back to her office in the news building she thought about herself and her life. She was a pro, a print reporter working the crime beat in a big, energetic city that seemed always to have *something* going on. She was respected by those she worked with, her bosses finally trusted her with the important leads, and she was totally immersed in what she had dreamed of and trained for all of her young life. Well, she wasn't young anymore, would be thirty in a couple of years, but she still had some miles left on the beat. Her thoughts were interrupted by a guy in a rental car who changed lanes right in front of her. She slammed on the brakes, swerved violently, and cursed under her breath. She felt like cursing out loud and maybe employing a suitable gesture to let him know that he was number one in her book while she was at it, but this *was* Miami, after all. You could get machine-gunned for such a display.

Her thoughts took her back to the infant-homicide scene. She thought about the big cop, his knowing grin, his self-confidence. She chewed her lower lip and looked at her own eyes in the rearview mirror. The guy was a jerk, she told herself, but he had *it*. One of those men women spend time with even while every alarm bell in their head is going off. The guy was a serious hunk, and she found herself musing about how long it had been since she had felt the warm strength of a man's embrace, held on to one really tight.

"Yeah, right," she said to her eyes. "Been there, done that . . . and promised myself no more . . . no, no, no . . ." She had experienced one serious romance in her life, and had been heartbroken when the guy decided he "wasn't ready" for a commitment, even though she hadn't been asking for one. She was twenty-five at the time, and had done the bridesmaid thing for just about every one of her friends. If she never had to hear the word "taffeta" again in her life, she could die happy. She'd also grown tired of the looks she got from her friends and their families. As though a single woman nearing her thirties was to be pitied, or worse yet, that she carried some contagion, a virus that led to the disease of unhappiness. There had been other men since, of course, mostly okay guys and fun times. Problem was, they all seemed to believe in the "Make me no promises, and I'll tell you no lies" thing. She didn't feel she was too demanding, or possessive, or whatever, but the relationships had all ended in disappointment. Fine, she thought as she parked across from the news building, I'll throw myself into my work, and when I get home I'll throw myself into the crime novel I'm trying to write. And then I'll throw myself into bed, alone.

Cat's editor and boss, Bert Earnest, had sacrificed his smile to the god of terrible news long ago. He wore a constant scowl, drugstore reading glasses he bought by the handful, and a comb-over that started as a line a skosh above his left ear and was plastered carefully over his shiny round cranium. He began talking even before Cat made it into his cluttered office. "So what have you got, Early? The usual trash complaints? Bunch of stupid drunken teenagers graduated into body bags by way of their flying car? An eighteen-month-old baby beaten to death at the hands of a jealous boyfriend zonked out of his skull on crack?"

"Well, yeah, Bert. Those are two of the

stories I'm doing," replied Cat. She felt weary, grimy, and ready for a long, hot bath.

"Not gonna win a Pulitzer with that tripe," said Bert Earnest. "You need to get your bum off those mean streets, Early, and start writing about the *world*, baby." He pointed his glasses at her. "Feel the earthquake today? Big news there. Everybody felt it, emergency-management phones ringing off the hook, people screaming about evacuating the Keys. The end of the world — never been an earthquake in Florida — all the blue-haired condominium cliff dwellers having heart attacks all over the place. *Real good stuff.* And what are you working on?"

She began to answer, but he was off and running.

"Tell you something, Cat," he said, his face grim. "This world is going to Hades in a handbasket. Oh, I know, we've been hearing that since dinosaurs were in diapers, but I'm telling you, *something* is going on. World news. That's where you want to be, Cat. You need to pay attention to the huffing and puffing global scene, baby. That's where you'll find the really big news."

She couldn't help herself, and asked

sweetly, "Like what, Bert? Another princess run over by the paparazzi? The Jews and the Arabs can't get along? Unrest in Ireland? Gays, lesbians, and straights had a huge fistfight at a high-school prom? The people in Africa who aren't dismembered by machete die of starvation before they die of AIDS? There is a big argument going on at the UN about streamlining the world's monetary system? Earthquakes are becoming more frequent? The autopsy photos of that last rock star killed by a fan have been posted on the Net and different groups are suing each other over copyright? *That* kind of stuff?"

Bert Earnest blinked rapidly several times, nodded, and said, "Well . . . yeah."

"I gotta get out of here, Mr. Happy Face," Cat said with a lopsided grin. "I'm tired, and I want to go home."

"Right. Go home," said her boss. "But get those stories about dead teenagers and dead babies in the can first."

Cat Early left work and drove home an hour later. She didn't listen to the news on her car radio, and she didn't watch the news on her television. She had a bowl of soup, sat staring at nothing for a long time, then went into her bedroom, pulled a fireproof lockbox out from under her bed, punched in the code, and unlocked it. She pulled out the sheaf of papers she had examined many times; the words printed there amounted to a validation of a life, and perhaps offered an explanation of a death — the life and death of her sister, Carolyn Early.

Carolyn and Cat. Even the names suggested the differences between the two sisters. Carolyn was two years older, the dutiful oldest child. Not an overachiever, since she was blessed with so many skills, but certainly someone who could have cast a long shadow if she also weren't so supremely nice. Cat adored Carolyn and hated the inadequacy of the word "nice," but it was the one word that everyone used to describe her older sister. Along with nice came "decent," "loyal," "outgoing," and "trustworthy."

Carolyn and Cat. Sometimes more like oil and water. Carolyn was into Top 40 pop music and listening to Whitney Houston or Mary Chapin Carpenter; Cat was into punkier groups like the Dead Kennedys, The Cure. Carolyn opted for classic clothes — plaid skirts, jeans, and sweater sets, while Cat veered off into a goth phase for a short while, complete with a spiked nearly white dye job. Yet their differences seemed to bring them together rather than separate them — as though they were determined to show the world that common ground could be found if you looked past appearances.

It was only to Cat that Carolyn ever revealed her darker side — and even then only in the last year or so of her life. She was plagued by self-doubt, wondered if she had made the right choices, if law school, and a place on the fast track was the direction she should have gone. Or maybe becoming a wife and mother, perhaps even becoming a minister or another kind of teacher. She'd chosen an itinerant lifestyle, one that didn't allow for a long-term relationship, and she called Cat more than once in tears telling her about her latest heartbreak, what she perceived to be her latest failure to compromise on her values and her belief in what she always referred to as The Plan.

Everyone had expected Carolyn to join the Peace Corps, and in her career as a journalist, she'd written a lot about that organization's volunteers, about relief workers, doctors and nurses, anyone who'd done something selfless. "I feel so selfish sometimes," she had written to Cat in her final letter, "because sometimes my life is measured by the number of column inches I get in a paper or magazine. I don't judge myself and others don't judge me based on the impact of what I write, the light I may shed on an issue. I wonder sometimes what my motivations are — to do good or to be thought of as good. They're not the same thing, Cat. I marvel sometimes at the numbers of people that I see doing good works who are not necessarily good people themselves. I mean, I haven't quite figured this all out yet, but there's something going on in my head about the doer and the deed — know what I mean? Can you really do the right thing for the wrong reason?"

Cat knew that Carolyn had always felt guilty about leaving the country, leaving her younger sister with the burden of two aging parents. From time to time, Cat did feel as though she'd been unduly burdened, that "good" Carolyn had run off and done something "bad" just to escape the possibility of that burden. Now, she was willing to consider that maybe Carolyn had done it as another kind of sacrifice, opening the door for Cat to step in at this stage in her life and establish a more solid foundation with their parents. After all, with the Golden Child gone, who else was left to fill the void of her absence? Now, with both her parents dead — her mother several years ago and her father just weeks after getting news of Carolyn's passing — all those questions about good and bad and intent seemed a moot point.

All Cat knew is that she loved her sister with a devotion that she'd not experienced in any other relationship. She had felt accepted, flaws and all, and had even come to tolerate, if not completely enjoy, the avalanche of advice and guidance that her sister offered her. Cat could see now that Carolyn may have sensed that Cat was one day going to be left alone, that the two of them would suffer the loss of their mother too soon, and she didn't want Cat to be without some anchor, some means to navigate her way through whatever treacherous passages she would have to make. Cat wished that she had a better sense of what it was that Carolyn was trying to tell her. She knew that Carolyn's answer would be to pray, that the kind of celestial guidance that Cat was seeking wasn't to be found in the stars or on a navigational chart.

But in the wake of so much loss so early in her life, a beloved sister, parents with whom she'd finally established a more solid footing and something very much resembling respect, faith in God wasn't something that Cat could commit to. She knew at some level that her work as a crime reporter, seeing the worst of human misbehavior on a daily basis, was a way to fortify her belief that there was little good in the world, that there couldn't possibly be a beneficent God. After all, in the face of such overwhelming evidence to the contrary, in the world that Cat had chosen to inhabit, there wasn't much to support the kind of belief that her sister had. Perhaps though, that was what Carolyn had been trying to tell her all along — that you could go to the places in the world that seemed so far from God and find Him there, or at least find those who were doing good work in bad places.

Cat sat cross-legged on the wooden floor of her room and thought about the rantings of her editor, Bert Earnest. Maybe he knew, she mused, maybe he didn't. Either way, he sure hit close to home with his urging her to leave the local beat and apply for an international posting. That's where her sister had worked, for Reuters, but there in the middle of the *big picture*. Carolyn had reported from the thick of things in the Mideast, Europe, the Balkans, Indonesia . . . everywhere. She had been a respected, veteran journalist, fit, smart, and competent, and attractive enough to make tongues wag anytime she bunked out anywhere but home. She had broken an ankle once when a truck she was riding on crashed outside of Kabul, Afghanistan, and a few months ago she had been lightly wounded by shrapnel during a mortar attack in Africa. But she had been onto something during the last "small, bitter conflict" she had reported on in Eastern Europe.

Cat looked at a photograph of her sister, and could not help but smile. Carolyn stood on a dirt road, a small backpack at her feet, a notepad in her hand. Her funny little grin shined out from the dust that completely covered her, and in her eyes Cat could see fatigue and defiance. Cat did not even remember where the photo had been taken. She looked down at the paper in her hands, and read a draft of her sister's last submitted story:

Now at last perhaps a leader has emerged. He is a man born in mystery and mysticism, born of hunger, brutality, and war. He literally appeared out of the burning smoke and dust of battle, filmed by CNN along with a group of soldiers walking in ragged file up a steep path, the blackened and defiled ruins of an ancient city behind them. The people of the city lay in grotesque postures of violent death, including the children. The women had been violated and abused before death. This reporter (yes, I know I'm the professional, dispassionate observer, but what I saw angered me, and I was tired, and beyond caring) stood up from behind a destroyed tank, walked toward the soldiers, pointed at the ruined city behind them, and asked, "Why . . . why?" One detached himself from the group, a leader of some sort, his eyes alight, his voice firm. "Their men stand," he said with contempt, "but do not accept, submit, or follow. The children are simply in the way. The women are but beasts of burden, and temporary vessels for men who wish to use them. They are unimportant. As are you."

This reporter asked no more questions of them or of him. Later that same day a colleague told me that the one I had spoken with was admired by his men because he was their leader, and rather than give orders from a position of safety, always fought in front with his men. He was known as a ferocious and unmerciful fighter, not above partaking of the spoils of war. I was told that the soldier's name was Noc. Its origin is not certain, but it could have come from a dialect of one of the Slavic languages. Rare is the soldier who embraces war. . . . He is the spawn of darkness.

Cat read the dispatch once again, then looked at the photo. Carolyn Early, her sister, had been killed in a hail of machine-gun fire the evening she had filed her last report. The story had not been printed, as far as Cat could determine, and within what seemed a few days Cat suspected that no one even remembered Carolyn Early's name. The circumstances of her death, as reported by colleagues who witnessed it, made Cat think that it was an assassination and not a random act. Carolyn wasn't just in the wrong place at the wrong time. A man had sought her out, left a message at her hotel, said that he could give her the truth. He was a soldier with an insider's knowledge. Of course, Carolyn couldn't refuse. Another casualty of war. The soldier's name sounded oriental to Cat; odd and sinister, regardless. She laid the papers and photo on the floor, rubbed her eyes angrily, and stretched her arms, fingers splayed, over her head. She wished, as she had so many times before this night, that she could have been with Carolyn, or spoken to her at least *one more time.* There was more to that last report, Carolyn's last story — of that, Cat was positive. She looked down at the paper near her right hip, and saw the ink scribble on the lower margin of the page. Written there were the words, perhaps the last ones her sister had ever written: "Prodigal Project . . . might be a good thing for the world." Cat bit her lip for a moment, then locked everything away again, took a long hot shower, and went to bed.

Chapter Three

Paint peeled from the clapboard-sided church like the bark from a silver maple tree. Paint chips fell like snow, as if the preacher's thundered words had rattled the church's eaves. Instead, it was the very ground, the rock the church had been built on, that had convulsed. He felt it and knew everyone in his small congregation felt it too. "Brothers and sisters. *Hear* the Word, *feel* the Word," he said from the wooden pulpit, its sides polished from the oil of so many hands gripping it, placed center front before the pews. "That's right" and "Amen, amen" came back to him from his listeners.

"Any man or woman who doesn't believe He will return," he said quietly, "anyone who doesn't *believe* in a day of judgment, a day of divine *happening*" — he paused to enjoy the sounds of his voice as it swelled and rose — "they are simple ignorant *fools* who have turned away from the *truth*, turned away from the *Word*." He reached a deep crescendo. "For it is written" — he held up his old Bible, the pages fallen open like the white wings of a dove edged in gold — "it is written here in *this Book*. Not some other book . . . no . . . it is written in the only book we have that we can *believe*." A few more voices responded from the congregation with "Lawd, Lawd" and "Tell it, Reverend."

"There will *be* a second coming, says the Book," whispered the Reverend Henderson Smith as he gazed out on his small but enthusiastic flock. He stood preaching in a small community church with long ties to the families in the area on the outskirts of Selma, Alabama. The pews were filled mostly with women, dressed in colorful severity, many wearing hats. Scattered among them were fidgeting children, and a few men wearing coats, ties, and dutiful expressions. There were no heavy eyelids, though. No one slept through one of the Reverend Henderson Smith's sermons. The reverend's voice began to swell to fullness again: "This Book tells us in, oh . . . many places . . . like Thessalonians. It *tells* us He will return. He will come back to us, and those who are saved will be taken. . . . They will be *caught up* to be with Him."

He cast his eyes upon everyone gathered there, nodded at each in turn, and smiled.

When, Reverend Smith, *when* will it happen, so we can be ready?

He let his eyes sweep again over the faces of his listeners, capturing each one for a moment, letting them feel his intensity. "I say to you, and *the Book* tells you . . . it could be anytime, *anytime.*"

He paused while he mopped his sweaty brow with a clean white handkerchief, then carried on, a small smile on his brown, vibrant face. "It could be anytime, and we should be ready, brothers and sisters, not ready to be ready. Not reading to be ready. Not writing to be ready. But *ready.* A moment ago while I spoke there was a tremor, was there not?"

Several of his listeners nodded, and he heard a few "Amens."

"Now I might be a prideful man and tell you that my voice and my words were so powerful that the very ground shook under this old church." The Reverend Smith paused and smiled. "But it was a natural thing, and we know it. The earth shook a moment, and that is not completely unheard of here in Alabama. I'm not saying it happens every day. It doesn't. I'm not saying it isn't rare, because it is. I'm saying it is a natural happening here in our world. A little earthquake, a tremor, or as my learned brothers and sisters would say, a temblor."

He stopped, and let his gaze sweep the pews again. He held his Bible up in front of him, and continued, "But, brothers and sisters, you-all know . . . you *know* . . . this is God's world. He created it. He *is* the natural thing, and He made the earth shake like that this morning, didn't He? And you know what? It has been happening all over the world, hasn't it? Been shakin' and quakin' up one side and down the other, all around our poor, sinful, ignorant ol' world. So in this Book it says there will be a time, we will not *know* when that time will come, but we'll be given *signs,* won't we? 'Contractions like those of a pregnant woman,' it says." He gazed on them again, and said softly, "Maybe we all experienced a sign this morning, brothers and sisters. Our Lord, our one and *only* Jesus Christ, is coming, and those of us with Him in our hearts will be *caught up.* We will be *lifted up* out of this sorry, hurtful, sinful old world . . . lifted up . . . and carried away." He held his Bible close beside the left side of his head, his brow wet, his eyes shining, and added quietly, "Let us pray now, brothers and sisters, let us pray now for that coming, for *His* coming."

The sermon ended a half hour later, and most of the congregation left tired, happy, and full of the Word.

The Reverend Henderson Smith stood on the steps of the Mount Olive Gospel Church, shaking hands, hugging, speaking with, offering comfort and encouragement to the members as they filed out. He kept his confident smile in place, his handshake firm, his gaze direct. He was tall and thin, with mahogany skin, close-cropped black hair, and a face radiant with the light of his eyes. He had been preaching since he was a teenager, caught up in the Gospel, given strength by the promise of a new world, a *just* world.

He learned about the Bible from his mother, and from an old man everyone in his neighborhood called "Preacher." Preacher's real name was Tiller Long, and he made a living caring for the lawns of the white people on the other side of town. Sometimes young Henderson worked Saturdays or part of the summer for Preacher, and it bothered him to see the old man — strong, vibrant, respected on the pulpit — act like Stepin Fetchit around the whites who paid him to cut their grass. The whites would call Preacher "Tilley" and he would smile and say, "Yassirrr . . ." But

Preacher knew in his heart it would all even out someday, uh-huh, someday there would be a reckoning, and those with the least would have the most. It was in the Book, he'd tell young Henderson.

Henderson Smith had been in one real fight in his life. It had taken place in high school, where the whites and blacks most of the time either tried too hard to get along or simply ignored each other. It was actually a black kid that started it, making fun of Henderson because he always carried his Bible, even in class. Then there were more boys surrounding him in the parking lot, and soon it was "Hey, *boy*" and "Yo . . . Henny . . . your mama make you read that book?"

Henderson Smith, who took quiet pride in the fact that his family lived in Selma — where the modern empowerment of African Americans began — did not play basketball with the other black kids. He did not play basketball with the white kids, either, or baseball or football. He had no trouble mingling and mixing at Bible study groups or the occasional retreat his church put on, but that was it. He knew in his early years that he was different. He had a purpose, a mission, and he studied his Bible and searched for truth.

On that day in the parking lot, however, surrounded and taunted by a mixed group of "tough" kids, he acted. He carefully placed his Bible on top of his books on the ground, straightened, looked at the group staring at him, and said evenly, "Don't call me Henny. My name is Henderson Smith. And don't *ever* call me boy." Then he threw his first punch, and it began. When it was over, he and two other boys had to be treated at the emergency room, the police were called to the campus, and he and four others were suspended for fighting.

Henderson worked as an auto mechanic while he attended a Bible college. After graduation he came home, married a girl he had known as a child, and became assistant manager of an auto garage and tire shop. He began as assistant preacher too, in a local church, and in what seemed like a short time he was promoted to manager of the tire shop and had his own church, where *he* was "Preacher" . . . the Reverend Henderson Smith. His wife had given him three children, and his home was a happy one. He was firm but loving with his children, and his wife, Miriam, seemed comfortable with the teaching "The man shall be the head of his household, even as Jesus is head of the church." She attended church, shared the organ duties with another woman, and was actively involved in and supportive of every church function. She was a perfect partner for Henderson Smith, and he knew it.

The Reverend Smith smiled again as he took both hands of an attractive lady into both of his and said, "God bless you on this fine day, and thank you for coming to hear the Word." The woman, who was white, wore her brown hair twisted in elaborate French braids. Smith appraised her smooth skin and her athletic figure.

She smiled back, and said as she leaned to him, "Well, we just enjoyed your sermon so much, Reverend Smith. You have a great energy and passion, and it makes me feel so uplifted somehow." The woman was with a small group of others from a neighboring church.

His congregation had been totally black when he first took over, but within a couple of years more and more whites began coming on Sundays, and a few were active members. He attributed this to the change in demographics, some changes in attitude, and his active diplomatic work within the different churches around Selma. His ears were not injured, either, when someone told him the whites came to hear his lessons because of his power and charismatic style on the pulpit. "It's not *my* energy, sister," he responded to the woman, "but the energy of the truth."

"Yes," she said, and gave him a big smile as she turned to walk off with her friends.

"Yes," he sighed, and thought, Yes. Miriam is the perfect partner for me, at home, in life, and here in my church. I am blessed, I am truly . . . blessed. Lately he found he had to remind himself he was a lucky man, a blessed man. He wished Miriam hadn't put on so much weight after the children, and then kept it on. He had tried, gently, tactfully, to suggest she should take care of herself, but she would simply smile at him, comfortable with who she was. It wasn't as if she wasn't attractive, she was, and she was groomed and carefully dressed always. She seemed to fit right in with most of the church ladies, and although they were always talking about diets and losing weight and all of that, they could cook up some *serious* church dinners, and eat it all up with laughter and appreciation. No, it was *him*, and he knew it. Within the last couple of years he had found himself beset with what he'd come to call longings. He looked at other women, he daydreamed about being with a woman who was not his wife, just to experience it. The longings were almost gentle at first, idle thoughts, but over the course of many months they had intensified. Miriam noticed something in him, he knew. She had watched his face recently, held it between her soft palms, furrowed her brow, and said, "Sometimes, Henderson, you seem a bit too on edge for a man who has Jesus in his heart."

He helped an old couple make their way slowly down the steps, and turned to go back inside the church to straighten up, and meet with the choir director for a moment. He paused in front of the wooden doors, and reflected. My longings *have* intensified, and they're not only about other women, no. He shook his head. He had come to terms long ago with the fact that being the man in the pulpit, even in a fairly small church, could be a very real ego stroke. His brain told him, and he told his heart to hear, that he was only a conduit, a channel for the Word of God. His reason for being on this earth was his study, recognition, and comprehension of the truth as it was clearly laid out in the Scriptures. It wasn't for his ego, the pulpit, those shiny faces in the congregation weren't there because of him, they were there to hear the *Word,* the Word of God. He was only a messenger, a man perhaps given the gift of oration, of passion, given the ability to speak with the power that would hold those listening to the Word, hold them so they would *receive* it.

But he liked the power. He liked it perhaps too much, the fact that standing up there looking down into those hungry faces made him special, made him *somebody.* It was his pulpit, his church, and they *were* there to receive the Word because he had the power to *make it simple for them.*

He longed for a bigger church. A church like one of those across town — why, there was a Baptist church over on the other side with more than a thousand members. All brown brick, polished wood, and glass it was, with a day-care center, a video library, a choir that would blow the doors off anything around, and a covey of buses to go fetch those who couldn't make it on their own. They had cassette tapes made of the sermons, committee meetings, events, and retreats. And they had a beautiful hand-carved lectern. He had actually stood behind it once during a brief visit, where the man giving the Word to his flock was standing *tall.*

He sighed. He really *did* know how to interpret the Bible, he really *did* know the truth. Given a chance, he could be at the helm of a big ship of faith, a formidable, imposing edifice of prayer and hope, and from there he'd have the power to save many more souls; it also wouldn't hurt to be recognized and admired.

Sometimes late at night, while he lay in bed beside his contentedly snoring Miriam, the Reverend Henderson Smith wondered if Satan was real, working his subtle machinations, reaching out for those foolish enough to doubt the Word. It was as if the dark one himself whispered in the chambers of his heart, telling him he walked again on earth, alive, and was testing him with longing.

She felt his fingers tremble. She held one of his hands in hers and felt the flutter of a butterfly's wing — a minute tremor, a vibration of nerve ends and warm skin against the pads of her own fingertips, so light, so gentle. "Squeeze my hand, Ronnie," she said softly. "C'mon, baby. Squeeze Mommy's hand so I can know you understand." But there was no response beyond the first tremble. She looked into his open eyes, big with question, with *awareness,* with *emotion,* by God. "I know, baby," she whispered. "Mommy knows you are in there trying so hard, trying to show me you hear me. You hear me and you understand." She fought back a sob, and said again, "Mommy knows."

For six years she had been doing the same thing in the quiet of the morning, and it *was* the quiet of the morning. A nearly total silence shrouded the house, the only sounds the kitchen clock's slow ticking, and their mingled breaths marking another kind of time. For six years she would hold him, or lie with him, or kneel beside his wheelchair, and wait.

Ivy Sloan-Underwood waited for her six-year-old son, Ronnie, to recognize her, to respond to her, to answer her or choose to ignore her or laugh at her or make a face at her or in some overt way acknowledge her existence. As a mother, she could not deny it even when the bitterness that was her other side almost completely enveloped her, she could not deny that he responded to her. The response was tactile, almost feral, his quickening when she touched him, held him, soothed him, bathed him, or carried him. Sometimes he would become upset, or act in a way they had identified as his being upset. He would arch his back, move his head from side to side, make small noises in his throat. She could go to him then, and speak to him, soothe him, rub her fingers up and down his arms or across his wet brow, and he would relax. It seemed to her, each time, that as he calmed he would look into her eyes in a different way, in a way that said, "Thank you, Mommy. Thank you for being there, thank you for loving me."

He *didn't* say it though, she thought angrily. No, he didn't say it, he didn't say anything, *ever.* He looked at her, but did he see? Did he see her, did he really know she was there? Did he know the sun came up, the earth turned on its axis, bicycles were propelled by pushing on pedals with your feet, girls were different from boys, music was caused by simple vibrations of air at varied speed and intensity, that life was energy and motion and thought and hopes and dreams and action?

"Ronnie," she said softly, looking into his face, turning her head so his eyes were aligned with hers, "Mommy loves you, Ronnie, Mommy loves you."

She leaned closer to him and continued, "And Mommy knows, Ronnie, she *knows* you live in there, inside yourself, she knows you know."

Ivy Sloan-Underwood leaned back on her heels, looked at her twisted, loose-limbed, wheelchair-bound son, his lovely face nearly always in repose, and shook her head. No, the voice told her, he doesn't know. He doesn't know. He *doesn't know.* He doesn't, and he *won't.* She sobbed, stood, and turned her back on him. She did not see the large kitchen surrounding them, did not hear the clock ticking off its horrible, elongated, lugubrious seconds. She hugged herself, stood rigid, and fought the urge to scream, or break something, or *hit someone.*

She lost it, slowly picked up a bowl of fruit — Ron's mother had given her the bowl, a stupid ceramic thing in all the wrong colors — and hurled it against the counter. It shattered, skidding across the counter and onto the floor on the other side, the pieces of fruit bouncing and rolling all around her. *Why?* she screamed, her fists bunched into stones beside her hips. But she didn't scream, not out loud. She just *felt* it, from her toes to the top of her skull, she felt it and let herself bathe in the question . . . why, why, why, why . . . why?

She was Ivy Sloan. She was a college-educated elementary-school teacher. She was a pretty fair musician, a pianist, an attractive woman with a healthy female body kept toned by jogging. She was a wife, married to Ronald Underwood, a handsome social studies prof at the local community college, and a mother to six-year-old Ronnie, their only child.

Of course, she would tell her very private self, being the mother to Ronnie pretty much negated all the other things she was supposed to be. Being Ronnie's mother meant she could teach in a real classroom only as a now-and-then substitute, and even there she had to explain patiently to each principal that, no, she did *not* prefer to work with LD kids.

Being Ronnie's mother meant she could be only part of a woman to her husband, their relationship poisoned by the toll a disabled child sometimes takes on a household, and her own churning bitterness. She took care of herself, sure, the jogging a very real escape from her jagged daily reality, but for what? She had learned to decipher the looks she got from men. She could tell sometimes they wanted her, she could see it in their eyes.

They physically wanted her, like in some hotel room or something, and she played it, sometimes. She'd feel their interest, the heat, and she'd tease them, play with them to test herself. She had come to like the sensation of danger and awareness, the way her body actually became aware, actually became sort of ready.

She hadn't been unfaithful to Ron, not technically, doubted that she ever would. She remembered a former president's statements about lusting after another person in her heart, and the distinction wasn't lost on her. But she found herself fantasizing about affairs often, and actively seeking ways to find interaction. Like at school with male teachers, or at the dumb country club Ron had joined. Ron still wanted her, in spite of everything. He desired her, loved her in his sick-puppy way, and she'd let him, now and then, hold her and be with her. But it was no good for her and so, she assumed, probably not good for him either.

She sighed, turned, and looked at her son. She was not concerned about the destruction of the fruit bowl disturbing him. It didn't. Or if it did, there was no way for him to show it. God, she wondered for the millionth time, how could it all be so wrong?

She and Ron had been like kids during their courtship and the first years of their marriage. They did *not* need some bedroom marriage how-to book. It was natural, it was fun, and it was all the time. She hugged herself and allowed a tiny smile to force its way across her dry lips as she remembered the time . . . first week in this house near the central coast of California . . . when she had insisted they "make it official" in every room. Ron had surprised them both, chasing her from room to room, both of them laughing and holding tight to each other.

Ivy Sloan-Underwood laughed, a dry cough of a laugh, a dismissal. "Yeah, right," she said to the kitchen. She bent to pick up the pieces of fruit, and thought about how they'd gotten to this point. Originally she had been the one who wanted a child, she acknowledged, acknowledged *again*. Yes, it had been her idea, her desire, her wish. She had wanted to get pregnant. She had wanted to have babies, to be a mom with a family.

Ron had resisted. He liked them as a couple, he said. They were still getting settled, still building a financial base, he had argued. Why not wait a few years, then try to get pregnant. No way, she had said, she wanted a baby. She was ready, she told him, they were ready, and she wanted it.

She could make him do what she wished, of course, even then. She controlled it, and them, and in the bedroom she controlled it.

She held a bruised peach in her right hand, ran her thumb over the dented felt smooth skin, and stared out the window. The morning outside remained unseen by her eyes, which saw only memory. She'd experienced an easy pregnancy. She glowed, people cooed, Ron strutted. Life was easy, loving, and everything it was supposed to be. Her pregnancy proceeded normally, all the way through, smiling doctors, smiling nurses, smiling ultrasound operators. "Yep, we're talking boy here. . . . See that right there, Ivy? That's a boy all right." Then the night they had waited for, then the pain, the mother's pain, the very special pain reserved only for those who give birth, and she had welcomed it, wanting it all, wanting every bit of being a mother and birthing her child. And she had got what she wanted. And then some.

Odd how their faces changed, she remembered, their voices, the tone in the room. All these things had changed, and she knew immediately that something was wrong. Then there were other doctors, more nurses, people doing things, more voices telling her it was all right, it was all right. Ron's face hovered behind the people leaning into her, his voice lost in the others' as they said, "It's all right."

But it wasn't all right. It can't be all right when the newborn baby boy doesn't get enough oxygen to his brain for just long enough. Just long enough to keep him alive as he is born, but not long enough to jump-start all the intricate synapses, nerve ends, circuits, and electricity required to form the child's normal, active mind. Her baby boy was born, forever damaged, forever limited, restricted, cheated . . . *denied.* She heard a spastic tapping in the sink, and looked down to see that she had crushed the peach to wet pulp in her fist, and her knuckles beat the stainless steel in an uneven tattoo of pain, sadness, bitterness, and anger.

Then the floor moved. It rocked, tilted, shook. The broken pieces of ceramic fruit bowl tingled and tap-danced across the floor, and the breakfast dishes rattled in the sink. It could not be happening, her mind told her, but it *was.* An earthquake, strong enough to bump their house, strong enough to make the room yaw sickeningly, strong enough to make the broom-closet door bounce open and bang against a cupboard. She turned, took two wobbly steps across the kitchen floor, and reached Ronnie in his wheelchair. She knelt beside him, threw her arms around his chest and shoulders, and buried her face in the hollow of his neck, the fingers of her right hand spread through his thick curly brown hair, the exact same color and texture as hers. "Mommy's here, Ronnie, Mommy's got you," she sobbed, and hugged her son. "Mommy loves you, Ronnie. Mommy loves you. . . ."

Ronald Underwood almost fell as he hurried down the stairs from his office, a converted upstairs bedroom in their house. The tremor had already come and gone, but he couldn't be sure more wouldn't follow. He had heard the sound of crockery or something breaking, and knew Ivy and Ronnie were in the kitchen. It was Sunday morning, and Ron had been immersed in the world. World news and commentary, that is. He was an admitted multimedia total news junkie, loved following domestic and world events, and justified it with the fact that he taught the social sciences and it was part of his job. In his office he had the BBC or NPR on the radio or the local news going on the TV. He was also on-line, checking the Web, getting the real-time scoop from all the hot spots. He got images and info from the Middle East, Russia, Zaire, Eritrea, Bosnia, Japan, and Duluth. He targeted Washington, D.C., and Miami, Florida . . . Toronto, Mexico City, and Roswell, New Mexico.

If it was happening, anywhere, he was *on* it. He took pride in being knowledgeable and informed, of course, but was more proud of the fact that he was intellectual enough to understand and endorse several opinions on different subjects or events at any given time. He cared not for "fluff," pretty news faces excitedly talking about nonevents, or making obvious errors as they reported on some occurrence. He liked the hard news, given in no-nonsense terms, and if a talking head had an opinion, he expected that talking head to back it up with well-researched facts.

He was respected at his college, and did not mind when other instructors, or students, used him as a source. He was comfortable in the world, aware of what was happening and usually of why those events were taking place. He understood politics, power, and money, and was becoming more aware of how religion figured into all three. Even though he didn't travel much, he felt in many ways like a citizen of the world. He knew it, and understood it.

The only place in this world he was not comfortable, the one place where he did not know enough and understood less, was his own home. The situation hadn't always been that way.

He stumbled at the landing of the stairs, straightened his glasses — Ivy called them his "Buddy Holly" glasses — and turned to look into the kitchen. He saw his wife, his Ivy, the girl he had fallen in love with the first time she grinned at him, the girl he still saw as the only girl in the world for him, ever. She hugged their son, Ronnie, who sat impassively in his wheelchair while his mother hugged him and sobbed quietly. Ron caught his breath. He knew it wasn't the tremor that made her cry.

He had watched her before, caught her unaware as she looked at their son. He watched her face show all of her bitterness, sadness, anger, frustration, pain. He had seen it, he knew what it was, and it made his heart ache. Why can't we be like other couples with a special-needs child? he asked himself once again. He had forced Ivy to go with him to a couple of support-group meetings about three years ago, meetings where other parents with disabled children met, discussed common problems, gave advice, shared info. All good stuff. They had even attended a picnic where all the parents brought their kids, and everyone played and ate hot dogs and talked about their beautiful children.

Ivy had hated the day. Her response frustrated him; he could not understand how she could not see the positive things about it. What struck him most about the other parents was their attitude, their perspective. Sure, he understood they created many of their feelings — and their outlook — to protect themselves from pain that simply could not be handled any other way that he saw.

That didn't matter. What mattered to him was how they clearly loved their children, those other parents, and how they honestly accepted their children's disabilities as meaningful, as having reason. Those parents seemed genuinely happy to have their child, no matter what kind of challenges he or she faced. They possessed a simple, unconditional kind of love and commitment, and he wanted Ivy to see that love, learn from it, and perhaps change the way she looked at their situation, so her life could be better somehow.

Ivy had not, of course. He remembered their terrible fight on the way home from the picnic. Ivy had been in conversation with a woman whose child — a little girl — sat in her specially designed wheelchair exactly the way Ronnie did. The woman had said something about how she felt her daughter was "God's gift" to them, how they could see Jesus in their daughter's eyes, how their faith had been strengthened by having such a wondrous child of God in their home, in their lives. As Ivy shook her head, her eyes flat and cold, the woman said something about the way Ronnie looked at her little girl . . . maybe someday they could be friends.

"How did Ronnie look at their little girl, Ron?" Ivy had said through clenched teeth a few minutes into the ride home. "Did he make goo-goo eyes at her? Did he raise one eyebrow and whisper sweet nothings in her ear?"

"Ivy," Ron had said quietly, "stop it."

"No, I won't stop, Ron," Ivy had spit back. "You were the one with this big idea to go to a stupid picnic with a bunch of people stuck in the same boat we are. Well, I did it, okay. And I'll react to things I saw and heard any way I want to, okay? 'God's gift,' said the thankful mom. What a crock. What kind of gift is that? She could see the eyes of Jesus in her daughter's eyes? You have got to be kidding me, Ron. Those people are at the very least clearly delusional. They cannot accept what is right before their eyes, they cannot accept *fact*, they cannot handle their own God-given *truth*."

"And what truth is that, Ivy?" he had stupidly ventured.

His wife had sat quietly for several long moments, staring out the window as they drove down the side streets in their pretty neighborhood with its nice homes and well-maintained lawns. Finally, almost under her breath, she had responded. "Their truth is like ours, Ron. They played the pregnancy lottery, and lost. They experienced the joy of childbirth, but there was no joy, was there? They got damaged goods, that's all. And they can either spend the rest of their sorry lives taking care of what they created, or they can" — flustered, Ivy waved her hands in front of her face as though the car's interior were filled with smoke — "find some other way to deal with it, okay? If there is God-given meaning, if there is *reason* associated with the way their children are equipped to live in this charming world, then it sure as shooting escapes *me*."

She had turned to him then, and grabbed his right arm so hard it made him wince. She had leaned close, and whispered, "They've got their special-needs children, and we've got Ronnie, okay? They can deal with their problems any way they must, but don't you ask *me* to find solace or support there. I *know* what we've got. I *accept* what we've got. . . . And I'll *deal* with what we've got." She had turned away from him then, and they finished the ride home in silence.

Ron looked at his wife and son now, the ache in his heart a solid thing. Their lives were getting worse, not better. What bothered him most in recent months was how Ivy reacted to *his* behavior with Ronnie. He understood those other parents, somehow. Oh, he most definitely understood Ivy's bitterness, but he also understood the simple, pure joy of being a father — of having a child he had helped create.

He actually agreed with Ivy regarding the religious aspect of it. He was a secular kind of intellectual, putting more faith in the evolution of man as intelligent being than in man the creation of some unseen and undefined deity. Too many people used the whole God thing — no matter what name they put on it — as a crutch, a way to explain the basically unexplainable. This was a cruel and capricious world they inhabited, a physical world, a biological world.

He would admit there was that major intangible . . . love, a force very real but never really broken down into identifiable components. He knew love, knew it existed, knew its power, and he accepted it as part of man's capabilities.

He knew love when he looked at his son.

He liked to sit with Ronnie. Sometimes he would bring Ronnie's chair up to his office, then go back and carry the boy up, and watch the news or surf the Web. He found comfort in having Ronnie there, and he would talk to his son, explaining world events, sounding off about some blowhard on the TV, giving Ronnie his opinion on various things. He felt Ronnie knew him, was aware of him.

Recently, though, he found he had to be careful with Ronnie around Ivy. They would be in the kitchen, or out in the yard or someplace, and he'd make a joke for Ronnie, or ask Ronnie about something and then answer for him, and he'd see how

Ivy stared at him, her face a mask. He knew, even if she didn't say it, he knew she was asking him, "Why are you wasting your time? Do you actually think Ronnie *understands* you, Ron?" He would stop then, and turn away from her eyes.

Thank God for routine, he thought. Daily routine made their lives livable. Their house had Monday through Friday mornings and evenings, and it had weekends, and if they stayed with the routine, life was okay. They managed, they lived, got along, acted as family. The days Ivy did some part-time teaching were pretty good. Ron would take Ronnie to the special school, where they knew he was cared for, was in good hands. Then Ivy was sort of free. She could head off into the world, work with others in her field, mix and mingle and talk of things outside of their house, their little world with Ronnie. He had even tried to get her to enroll Ronnie for *more* time at his special school, but she had resisted. Money was her first reason. They couldn't afford it. Well, money was tough, and Ronnie's needs were expensive, but he took all the extra hours he could, filling in for other teachers when the need arose, and he did the freelance editing for textbooks and trade journals. Ivy said it was a money thing, but there was more, he knew. He sensed it was almost masochistic, the way she refused more help with Ronnie. She had created him, and she would care for him, she seemed to be saying. "This is all my fault, and I'll handle it."

He had it made, perhaps. He *had* to leave Ronnie and the house every day . . . off to his job, off to a place where he was liked and respected, where he was Professor Ron Underwood.

He looked at his wife as she stood and turned to him, her face wet with tears. She sniffed, rubbed her eyes, and asked, "Did you feel that tremor, Ron?"

"Yes, I did," he replied. "How is Ronnie? Did it bother him at all?"

"He's fine, Ron."

"I . . . I heard something break."

"It was that fruit bowl your mother gave us a couple of years ago. I guess I had it too close to the edge of the counter, and it wobbled off."

He looked at the pieces scattered all the way across the floor, some out into the hallway. "Oh," he said. What else does she lie about? he wondered. He was frightened for her lately — what had started within the last couple of years had now intensified to the point that he was frightened for *them*. He had seen how she flirted, saw the way she dressed when she went out with the girls occasionally. He had even had one of his poker buddies make some reference to her behavior at a party a couple of months ago, something about how he'd better think about taking care of business before some other guy decided to handle it for him.

He understood her actions weren't about sex. They were about escape, and he worried that they were essentially self-destructive. She had some kind of inner conflict going on, perhaps just a simple rebelling against her fate, her lot. He sighed. He was the head of a disjointed little family, he thought; all the pieces were there — mom, dad, child, careers, income, the house, and love . . . love among all three members of the little family, each of the three loving the other two. It was all there, but it was fractured, out of line, and he wondered what he could do to put it right.

He stepped closer to his son and, feeling Ivy's eyes on him, asked pleasantly, "Wow, that was some shaking tremor there, wasn't it, Ronnie? You bet it was, I know you felt it. Bet you thought you'd all of a sudden go rolling right across the kitchen there, didn't you? Sure you did. Well, it's over for now, Ronnie my boy, so just sit tight and relax. We've got a nice little Sunday morning going on here, don't we? You bet we do, Ronnie my boy."

Chapter Four

John Jameson went on-line to check his e-mail. He had circled around this task all morning, somehow knowing even as he woke, while the world remained quiet and near dark, knowing the message would come today. Several times he had actually walked past the computer, stared at it, then quickly turned away. The kids were back in school after the weekend, and Sylvia was engrossed in preparing some talk she was to give to her church study group. He had made them both coffee, and sat near the front window in their living room, staring out at the morning.

Sylvia liked it when he sat near her, even if they didn't speak. She just liked having him near. Even though they were alone together in one room, a third figure sat with them, silent and brooding. Waiting. While Sylvia made notes on a legal pad, a flood of memories returned him to the night, the night he had turned his back on someone knowing she would die. She *did* die. She did die, he thought bitterly, and Agent John Jameson per his training, had simply had to walk away without looking back.

Death was all part of the game, his supervisors had intoned in the debriefing. The informant knew the risks, they said, the informant knew that the information she passed to him would save lives, would help prevent another terrorist act being committed against innocent people, and she knew she might have to pay a heavy price for ratting out the rats she used to work with.

But we could have saved her, he told himself again, as he had *already* told himself countless times before. He told his supervisors, too. She could have been brought out. We could have saved her. No way, his bosses replied, and they reminded him that he *knew* there was no way. If she had been taken out of there with him, they hypothesized, the terrorist cell she belonged to would immediately have "sanitized" every connection to her, effectively negating the value of what she gave up with her sacrifice.

You need a rest, his supervisors told him; clearly he had allowed emotion to get in the way of the job. She was a criminal anyway, they reminded him, and she slept with the head of the terror cell. She was certainly no Girl Scout, Jameson, so get over it, they said. He knew he would not get over it, because he knew there was more to the girl, the *informant.* Even now he felt a disquiet in his stomach, thinking of her in these terms. Not as a name, not as a person, but as a role, a function, more tool than human being. She had turned away from her group. Not only had she tried to get away from what they were and did, she had decided to actively help destroy them if she could.

And she had trusted Agent John Jameson, trusted him enough to put herself in grave danger in order to pass on names, dates, locations, account numbers, all good info. Jameson had seen something in her eyes, he remembered, something that gave him pause during their last meeting. She knew. She knew she would die, and she was . . . okay with that.

His supervisors had paraded his own actions before him, illustrating their point about his getting too close, about his needing time off. He should have been on that first chopper out. The extraction point was set, the time window locked in. He had actually been at the site with minutes to spare, but even as the thud of helicopter blades beat the hot air above the ravaged town, he had turned away.

He knew the extraction team would

hover for thirty seconds, make one rotation, hover for another thirty, then depart. They had prearranged a fallback lift point also, and they'd be over that in thirteen minutes. He remembered gritting his teeth against the futility of it even as he ran through the dark alleys and narrow streets searching for her. He had found her, her face almost childlike in the forever slumber of death, a trickle of blood behind one ear. He had almost made it to the fallback lift point when he heard the *crump thump* of mortar fire. Then the missiles rained down. Ours, theirs, hers, mine, he thought, the mortar fire could have come from any or all of the combatants. It didn't matter. One of the explosions had lifted him as he ran. It threw him into a collapsing wall of dried mud bricks. He had managed to pull himself out, stunned and limping, and got one arm and his other hand on the harness even as the chopper pulled up into the night sky and clattered away from the fire and dust, with him dangling below, racked with pain and anger.

He sighed now as he waited for the computer screen to show his incoming mail. There was one new message, dated that day, routed so it looked as if it came from the U.S. Customs office in Norfolk. "Contact Office of Personnel ASAP regarding insurance policy problems," it stated. He rubbed his eyes with the flat of each hand, let out a deep sigh — part relief, part resignation. He pushed back from the desk, leaned over, and picked up his cell phone. He punched in the numbers, pictured the offices of his organization nestled among a heavily forested part of northern Virginia, and listened. "Thirteen," a soft female voice soothed. A pause lengthened, then the voice said again, "Thirteen." He was mildly surprised, not by the message, but by how rock steady his own voice was in response.

Sylvia Jameson looked up at her husband as he came downstairs from the office he'd converted one of the bedrooms into. She saw his troubled look, put down her pen, and waited. Though she'd played this scene many times, the variations of it still held her attention, quickened her pulse.

"Gotta go back, honey," said Jameson quietly.

"When, John?"

"Now."

Sylvia stood, and embraced her husband as he came to her. They needed no words; they simply held tight to each other for a moment. With her face against his chest she said, "The kids will be home in less than an hour."

"I know," replied Jameson. "I'll pack slow . . . give 'em both a hug before I go."

She smiled at his lie. He was already packed, he was *always* ready to go. It came with his job, with his life.

"Good," she said. After a moment she asked tentatively, "John . . . can I, can we . . . say a brief prayer?"

John Jameson smiled down at the top of his wife's head. God, he loved her, and he loved his kids. "Let's say one together," he said.

Cat Early sat at her desk at the *Herald* building in downtown Miami. She looked out one of the windows on the east side of the offices and was rewarded with a spectacular view of Biscayne Bay. The masts of yachts and sailboats in the harbor clicked back and forth like metronomes. In the distance the hotels of Miami Beach sat bathing in the sun. She allowed herself this momentary distraction before she focused her mind again. She had read the morning paper, not off her computer screen, but the actual printed paper she took from her editor's desk. She scanned the "World News" section. It contained the usual litany of strife and hardship.

"Mysterious Crash of Mercy Airlift in Old Russia — 150 Known Dead"

"China Denies Mental Torture of Religious Dissidents"

"Homicide Bomber Kills 20 During Jerusalem Prayer Vigil"

"Judge Suspends Basque Separatist Party"

"Health Forces Pontiff to Cancel Philippines Visit"

"United Nations Called 'Toothless,' Asked to Investigate Nigerian Ethnic/Religious Clashes"

"UN Considers Azul Dante to Head European Coalition"

The last one caught her eye and held it. Another attempt at a coalition? Two people could barely learn to live together, let alone nations. She chewed her lip for a moment, then leaned forward and quickly typed a message to her editor. "Bert, you win. I want that international assignment," she e-mailed her boss. "Will you help me get it, or point me in the right direction at least? Thanks, Cat."

She received his message a few minutes later. "Cat, I have second thoughts about my advice. I don't want to lose you. I wish I had never mentioned it. Stay here. Don't go. Take me with you. Oh, of course I'll help. Reluctantly . . . Bert."

Shannon Carpenter watched Doug Mann's face carefully. For a fleeting moment as her boss spoke, telling her about a meeting with one of their biggest clients, she could have sworn she saw fear in his eyes. Certainly hesitation, concern, distress. She saw these emotions ripple across his usually smooth and composed countenance, but there was also fear. Seeing it on his face, in his eyes, unsettled her.

"But, Doug," she ventured softly, "you said it was good news."

He turned his chair toward the corner window of his large office, giving her his profile, and responded, "Oh, it's the *good news*, all right, Shannon. The good news that our churchgoing clients have been preaching about, or warning about, for years." He paused, then continued, "I'm still not sure if I was supposed to hear it, or if they *wanted* me to hear it."

Doug Mann had called for her the moment he returned to his office from the morning meeting that had taken place at the gigantic glass cathedral on the edge of

Lake Erie. She had not been surprised at the summons, since she had been working with him on the church accounts and cases for some time now. As senior partner, Doug represented three of the largest churches in the region, in addition to a consortium made up of various congregations for the purposes of investment, the acquisition of real estate, two retirement centers, and three schools.

Handling their affairs was a "plush fix," to use Doug Mann's term — lots of billing hours, straightforward legal work, and very few problems or confrontations. The members of the church hierarchy included savvy businesspeople who were dedicated to keeping the church organizations solvent and capable, and they put up with no funny business. If they acted smug and sanctimonious on occasion, Doug Mann and his partners indulged them — just as they would any other important client. Mann usually returned from a meeting with the church "Finance and Legal Committee" with stories and asides for Shannon. He often made a little fun at the expense of the "tight-bottomed holy rollers" who opened the meetings with a prayer, and punctuated them with "Praise God this" and "Thank you Jesus that."

But not today. He continued to stare out the window for several moments while Shannon waited in silence. Finally he let out a long sigh, as if he had made a decision, and without turning his head said to her, "You know what they've asked me to do, right? For the last two years, I've been consolidating some of their holdings, liquidating others, moving funds into easily accessible accounts so they could be 'put in hand' on a moment's notice. And so we have done as our clients asked, covering all the legal demands as we did. Good. There was a 'project,' we were told, something coming that would benefit the church." He looked at her now, his eyes grim. "Remember how I joked around with you, about how excited, almost giddy, they were? Like a bunch of schoolkids they were, had a big secret, made them all sweaty and giggly just mentioning it. Remember?"

"Yes," she replied, her mouth suddenly dry. Sounded like her husband, Billy. Because his company did construction jobs for his church and a couple of others in the region, he was privy to church insider news, gossip, and business.

"Well, today they were barely contained," said Doug Mann. "Gave me a short laundry list of things they wanted done pronto, then sat there buzzing and ticking like a cheap watch."

"Because their 'project' is going well, Doug?" asked Shannon.

"Because their 'project' is about to actually *happen*," he answered quietly. " 'It's time,' they kept saying. 'It's *time*.' "

"Time for what?"

Doug Mann turned away from Shannon Carpenter again, his face toward the window. Several long moments passed, and while they did she could see he was undergoing some inner struggle. Finally he pinched the bridge of his nose and said, "I don't know. They wouldn't tell me exactly. Just asked me if I'd accepted Jesus into my heart."

"That's so strange. After all this time working for them, to ask you that now."

He didn't answer.

"Mr. Mann. Doug," implored Shannon. "What is it? What did you hear that's got you so . . . shaken?"

"Do you know the Bible story about the prodigal son, Shannon?" asked Doug Mann softly. "The *return* of the prodigal son? We all know your husband, Billy. We like him, he's a good guy. But he's heavily into the church, isn't he? Sure, and I'm sure you've heard all the Bible stories, and you've seen how they believe in them, how *literally* they take the Scriptures."

"Yes," Shannon replied cautiously.

"They told me that story." He turned his chair to face her now, and leaned forward, his face wet and intense. "Said that for someone like me especially this story was relevant. In the light of upcoming events."

"Like you?" Shannon said under her breath, trying to make light of something that clearly was way beyond anything she was prepared for.

"The prodigal son, Shannon." Mann raked his hand through his salt-and-pepper hair. "Prepare for the end. Doomsday is near."

Shannon joined in his laughter. "C'mon, Doug. . . . Let's get busy making up signs, hit the sidewalk and march back and forth chanting 'Prepare, prepare' and 'Repent, repent,' " chided Shannon. Even as she spoke the words, she saw that Mann's laughter was a facade. She wished Billy were there. She shut her eyes and pinched the bridge of her nose, felt her heart pounding, and still trying to dismiss it, asked, "Which son was it, anyway?"

It took a long time before Doug Mann answered, and when he did it was in a voice barely audible. "*The* prodigal son, baby." His eyes went far away, and a strained smile crawled against his teeth. He added, "Ladies and gentlemen, Elvis will *definitely* be in the building." He said nothing more, and after a few minutes she let herself out of his office and quietly closed the door behind her.

Her heart told her something of tremendous import was indeed happening. Her head, always pragmatic and skeptical, told her to find out everything she could. Perhaps Doug Mann was going through some personal crisis that had him jumping at shadows. She'd never seen him acting so strange. She knew he hadn't been drinking, but that seemed the most plausible explanation for his behavior. Shannon felt as though she'd watched the bitter and frightened cross-examination of a middle-aged lawyer with faith only in his manipulation of the law, and money. She shook her head and thought perhaps the church people had gotten ol' Doug Mann back for making fun of them. They had spooked him for sure. The man had actually seemed frightened.

She tried to shake off a feeling of uncertainty as she walked briskly back to her own office. "Elvis is *dead,* baby," she said as she picked up her cell phone to call her husband.

In the morning mists the long lines of soldiers embraced the earth, their weapons pulled close, and waited. They looked like soldiers have looked for thousands of years, mud brown and gray, armed men on the brink of movement — movement that would propel them into a series of horrific acts made honorable by time and the histories of the triumphant. Their eyes scanned the mountains to their north, the place where their enemy lay. Earlier they had faced Mecca, bowed in prayer, surrendered themselves to Allah.

They were told, like all soldiers, that their cause was just, and necessary. Like most soldiers, they were told that God was on their side, that in fact this battle was to fight for God, to destroy those who had perverted the truth for their own reasons. These men were members of the Harakar ul-Mujahideen, Lashkar-e-Taiba, and Jaish-e-Muhammad. Once a loose conglomeration of Muslims from around the world, they were now united under the leadership of one man and one cause. They wanted to defeat the Hindus of India, wrest Kashmir from its control, free their brother Muslims and join them on their journey to conquest.

Many had been trained to fight the Soviets in Afghanistan. Their confidence bolstered by that unlikeliest of victories, they'd sought other conflicts, traveling to Pakistan, Chechnya, and the Philippines, wherever a call to arms was sounded. Now they were amassed on the Line of Control in Kashmir, nearly a million strong. Following the assassination of the beloved leader of the Jammu-Kashmir Liberation Front, they'd become all too willing to accept the *new* good word from that organization's new leader. The old good word had failed them, had become a mockery, he had taught, an ineffective fossil passed on from one generation to the next with nothing to back it up. Now, growing almost daily, came their new faith, a new understanding of what must be done.

On one front, they would wage war on the Pakistanis. Though they shared the same faith, they did not share the same vision. For too long Pakistan's leadership had threatened India but had not acted. Its demonstrations of force, its nuclear arsenal, meant nothing, were mere pretense. They would demonstrate force, they would show them what men of action could do.

On the other border, it was India. The Indians had a long history of barbaric acts against themselves, but always banded together to repel any outside threat. The government of India simply did not believe that the mujahideen or their leader posed a real threat. The Indians had no interest in merging for oil, food, or ideology, and accepted the coming war as inevitable. The mujahideen leaders began massing their troops along the rugged border, and prepared their troops for invasion . . . promising them whatever spoils of war came along, and the chance to rid the new world of an "old world parasite."

Now as the soldiers rose at the whispered signal and leaned forward as they lunged toward the enemy lines, the mists seemed to shroud them like tattered cloaks. There had been no artillery or air prep, which had been standard military attack doctrine for at least a hundred years. No, the mujahideen made their charge first, knowing that the artillery concentrations would come rumbling over their shoulders just as their lead elements reached the first enemy positions. Artillery prep signaled an attack, and the supreme mujahideen leader would not have it. This tactic created a very powerful and immediate one-two punch, and usually had devastating results on the forward enemy positions. That it caused "friendly" casualties because the lead ground elements were often ripped by their own artillery fire did not deter the mujahideen leader. His troops piled on, so even if the lead elements suffered losses, there came many behind to finish the job. The soldiers accepted it in the same two ways all soldiers always accepted their leaders' orders — if they died, they went to heaven for fighting the good fight, and it wouldn't be *them* that got hit, it was always the *other* guy.

A mujahideen sergeant leading a squad against a position on the Pakistani border looked to his left at one of his men — a boy, really, pudgy and dirty, but with an easy smile stuck on his face. The smile made him look even more frightened than the sergeant knew he had to be, but at least the kid was moving forward. Suddenly one or two ragged volleys of fire came from their front as they traversed what might have been a plowed field. The sergeant could hear the almost soft rushing of air above their heads now as the artillery arced over them, and within seconds a series of crushing explosions ripped along the entire front.

The sergeant let out a guttural yell, fired his assault rifle toward the enemy positions a few yards away, and felt the buffeting and tearing of hot metal as it screamed outward from the many explosions. He looked again to his left, and saw the boy with the pudgy face disappear in a red mist, his rifle, still gripped by white-knuckled hands, cartwheeling into the next man in the line. That soldier screamed, fired a long burst from his light machine gun, and went down kicking with a bullet in his throat. The tracer fire from the enemy positions tore through the formations at knee level, cutting down many of the mujahideen within yards of the crest of the hill they sought. The sergeant felt a tug on his right pant leg but ignored it, still firing, still charging. He fell facedown at the edge of the Pakistani position, and felt the roar of an artillery blast rock the ground beneath him. He sucked in a breath and lunged forward again, sensing the movement of his troops around him.

Now, he thought as he leaped over torn sandbags and into a trench that connected several fighting positions. Much of the hill had been pulverized by the artillery fire, but many of the Pakistanis still lived, still fought, so the sergeant slammed another magazine into his weapon and began advancing through the connecting trench. He did not need to look up to know that the artillery was shifting to enemy positions farther back now — he could hear it. He didn't care about the artillery now anyway. Now it was time for the killing. As they advanced, the sergeant and his men fired into both the living and the dead they encountered. The dead made no protest. The living often threw their weapons down in the face of overwhelming odds, hoping for a soldier's mercy. But the mujahideen gave none.

The sergeant, his chest heaving, the blood of the enemy and his own men on his hands and clothing, hesitated each time he encountered an enemy soldier. He did not hesitate because of indecision or mercy. Instead, he wanted the enemy to see him, to see his eyes, to watch him bring the barrel of his weapon up into his enemy's face. He wanted his enemies to see him as the deliverer of death. The ones who fell to their knees, their empty hands pawing at the dirty air in supplication, he lingered over. He let their howls wash against his ears, let their meaningless tears leave tracks through the filth on their lying cheeks. Then he would fire one shot into them.

They found a few women among the enemy troops. This was common, even in the Muslim ranks. The older ones were shot out of hand; the younger ones — those who had not managed to blow themselves up with the grenade they carried for that specific purpose — were grabbed by the sergeants' men, tied, and made to follow along. If they died during the fighting, too bad. If they lived, they would die in little bits and pieces during the next few nights, brutally used by the soldiers as their right. One was brought to the sergeant by another soldier down the line. The man owed the sergeant, and presented him now with a childlike waif of a girl huddled in a filthy uniform much too big for her. She fought the battle against her tears, and lost. The sergeant looked her over grimly, nodded at the other soldier, and gave her to one of his men for watching.

He scanned the battlefield, and noted the advance was going well. The Pakistani troops were falling back in waves, abandoning their positions and their wounded in a near rout in their attempt to flee from the mujahideen. The sergeant nodded. It was good. A radioman knelt beside the sergeant, waiting. He had already reported to the sergeant the information that the units were advancing well all along the line. The enemy fell back in droves, leaving their equipment and their wounded behind. The radioman looked at the sergeant while he scanned the battlefield, and shuddered.

The sergeant had a coldness about him, a feral cunning, and a total absence of fear. It was as if the man knew he could not be killed. At that moment the sergeant turned to the radioman, his eyes on fire, his lips pulled back into a grimace against his teeth. With his right hand he pointed to the front, and in a quiet voice he said, "You wonder about me, soldier? You have heard I have no past, I simply am, and I lead you and the others in battle? Look around. Do you see the work of *war?* Do you see the death, hear the screams of the damned, *smell* it . . . the rotting flesh of mortal, foolish men? She is my mistress, do you understand, soldier? War is my mistress, my mother, the food for my soul. I love her." He turned away and added, "Waging war in this body of flesh is a good thing, a righteous thing, a feast."

"Within days," wrote Cat Early in one of her first dispatches from the front, the mujahideen have pushed the Pakistani forces to and into the trade city of Multan, leaving only death in their wake. Clearly, it is a rout, and observers question the effectiveness of the Pakistani leaders in Islamabad who have hesitated simply to surrender in order to save their people from certain destruction. The president of Pakistan appealed to the United Nations, and that body fired off several "protests" to the leadership of the mujahideen.

The Pakistanis also petitioned the United States for help, and were rewarded with a reminder from the White House of how Pakistan failed the American people only a few short years ago. Oddly, Pakistan has not deployed any nuclear or weapon-of-mass-destruction devices so far — something it had promised to do prior to open warfare breaking out. Most observers agree that now it is only a matter of time. Izbek Noir, leader of the mujahideen, issued a statement saying he deplored the waste of human life caused by needless conflict, and called on the Pakistani people, soldiers and civilians, to rise up against their leaders, destroy them, and join the "peaceful union of men that is the Harakar ul-Mujahideen." One unconfirmed report given to this correspondent indicates that that may already be happening. The report states that the Pakistani president was caught attempting to board his private jet with "bags of old-issue cash" and his family. They were seized by his own palace guards, and are reportedly being held in a warehouse near the airport.

On the Indian offensive, the front line of the invading mujahideen is on the outskirts of Jaipur, already south of Delhi. Reports from the front indicate that the Indian army is fighting ferociously. One correspondent reported, "The Indian army has seized the traditions of the British fighting troops of long ago. They stand and fight, stand and die, with pride." Again, pleas to the UN and the United States have been met with promises, but no real action. Again, India has not used its nuclear capability against the invading forces, and it is not clear why. It is felt that the government of India must see the handwriting on the wall, but perhaps "going nuclear" is such an irrevocable step that no government can implement it, even in the face of its own destruction. In a recent conversation with me, Rahi Singdal, a long-respected member of the Indian Parliament known for his support of peace with the mujahideen, stated, "Sadly, the face of war has revealed the hideous death mask beneath the benign countenance of Izbek Noir and his troops. I see now my strenuous efforts to avoid conflict were the products of deceit. I love peace, I hate war, but I feel peace at any price may be a fallacy. We might have made peace with the mujahideen leadership, but we would have been sleeping with the devil. To arms now, people of India . . . to arms." Rahi Singdal's death in a car bombing shortly afterward has already been widely reported. The statement decrying his death issued by Mr. Noir must be seen as either the height of irony, or chutzpah.

Cat Early read over the dispatch, then at the rocket her new editor had e-mailed her. "Your job is to report the war as you observe it, not to have an opinion. You are still a new kid, so knock off telling us what has irony or chutzpah . . . capish?" She knew that the editor referred to that last

135

line, and knew that if the story was printed or used, the offending line would not be included. Okay, she thought, I'm a new kid, spank me if you want, but I'm still going to write it as I see it. She had learned a lot in the past few days, about the world, about people, about her sister, and about herself. After her first day in the field she began to understand why her sister, Carolyn, had pursued her career on the international beat. It was intoxicating to feel yourself swept along by the powerful winds and tides of change; millions of people were affected, lives changed in dramatic ways, and she was there to witness it and report back. To report back meant to *tell*, to describe for the people at home just what was taking place, to put a human face on these global events and convulsions.

That said, she told herself, this new assignment she had managed to wriggle into through the help of her old bosses — and maybe a little talent and solid journalistic background — came with a price. At home she was charged with taking the death of a child, flesh and blood, hopes, dreams, and potential, and giving that death, that loss, a voice through her reporter's words. Each word the tolling of the bell, she had told herself, each word a candle's flame signifying dignity and worth. The value of a child's life, tell us about it, journalist.

Now her words represented untold thousands, the lives and deaths of soldiers and "noncombatants" — the elderly, the infirm, the women, the children. Her words spoke out for them, and spoke out for the *truth*. But therein lies the rub, she thought now. She could report the truth as she saw it all she wanted, but her words would not be read, would not be heard, until they were filtered through the editing process — thus diluted, diminished, less impacting and effective.

Too bad, she thought, Rahi Singdal had been an eloquent voice for peace, a discerning leader who had tried to do his best for his countrymen, and had had the courage to speak the truth. To her, when she sat with him in the interview, his words were clear. He smelled a rat. He wanted peace for India, peace with the rapidly conquering mujahideen, but something gave him pause, something about the mujahideen leader worried him. Then he began voicing his concerns, and died in his car, shredded and burned, his dreams of peace mingled with the billowing gasoline funeral pyre.

"Hey, Cat Early?" Her thoughts were interrupted by a skinny young guy in khakis, leaning out of the driver's side of a battered Humvee.

"Yes," she responded as she stood on the side of the partially destroyed road less than a kilometer from last night's front lines, "I'm Cat Early. Are you my ride to the front?"

"Pile in," said the young man with a grin, "and join this little gang of reprobates."

Cat struggled into the backseat, stuffing her backpack against her feet, balancing her laptop on her thighs. She nodded at the three other people, two men, and a woman, all reporters, judging from their gear.

"I'm Slim," said the driver as he slued the Humvee onto the cratered road and accelerated wildly. "No, that's my name, silly!"

The two other men rolled their eyes, and the woman shrugged. She was even thinner than Slim, her cadaverous body topped with a long, mournful face, painted-on eyebrows, and spiky hair the color of straw. She had a thin brown cigarette in the corner of her mouth, and it stuck to her top lip when she spoke. "Eva," she said with a gravelly voice, "*Le Monde*."

"I'm Cat," responded Cat, "Trib Group."

The painted eyebrows shot up in twin arcs as the woman said, "Le Group Tribulacion? How odd."

"Tribune Group, Eva," said one of the men from the front seat. "Remember the old *Tribune* from the States?"

The woman took a long drag on her cigarette and stared out the window.

The driver spoke again. "You ever have family in this business, Cat? Your name is familiar."

"My sister, Carolyn," responded Cat. "She worked the international stuff. I . . . I did the crime beat for a big daily at home."

The driver did not reply, but she saw him looking at her in the cracked rearview mirror.

"Some war, huh?" said the man in the front seat. "The whole face of the globe is changing even as we report it. Man, the world is goin' through some serious changes, and diplomacy is definitely takin' a backseat to war." He paused a moment as the Humvee rattled over a washboard series of ruts in the road, then went on. "I'm gonna do a follow-up on some info we got from a source in the Presidential Building in Islamabad. Remember that 'peace delegation' Noir sent in to try to stop the war at the last minute? They were all killed in their quarters, so Noir had his green light and the shooting began. Our source says it was one of the mujahideen delegation's assistants that killed them, then killed herself as the Pakistani palace guards broke down the door. Pakistan was blamed, and the more they protested, the worse they sounded. Noir and his troops are on some kind of fast track toward being one of the big three superpowers, know what I mean? That guy has got it goin' on, and anybody on this continent that doesn't like it better get a gun, quick."

"Not that having a gun is going to help them, poor sods," opined the other man, older, with the sad jowls and red-rimmed eyes of a bloodhound, weary. "Making war against the mujas seems like a bad decision, based on what we've been seeing. Noir has the charisma, it can't be denied. He has managed to bring an incredibly diverse group into line with his thinking, and it is a formidable machine."

"Power and money, money and power," replied the other reporter. "He's offering stability, wealth, oil, food, and power to millions of people who have seen themselves on the short end of the stick for generations now. I keep hearing reports about how he's so amazing because he can get the various Islamic sects to work together, and now he's singing to the Israelis. But I don't think he cares what they believe in. This whole thing is about power, and Noir has it."

"What do you think, Slim?" asked the older man.

"I'm just a photographer," answered the young guy after a moment. "I see things through the lens . . . digital, or my trusty ol' thirty-five. Nobody asks me what I think, don't have no editor rewording my text, it's all captured image to me."

Cat pulled her eyes from the devastated landscape they drove through and asked, "You remember an old novel called *Delcorso's Gallery*, Slim?"

He glanced at her in the mirror again as he answered. "Sure. Combat photog convinced he can capture such horrific images of war, when they are shown to the public they will have such an impact that all wars will cease, forever."

"Is that you, Slim?" asked Cat, and then surprised herself by adding, "Or are you just another mercenary gore-lover?"

Slim did not answer her at first, his attention focused on battling the steering wheel as they crossed a stream. Before them lay the remains of a bridge, twisted and broken. He studied the water for a moment, pulled down onto the embankment beside the bridge, and drove through the water, the Humvee rocking and groaning over the rocky bottom. He accelerated up the far embankment and maneuvered past a wrecked column of vehicles made up of three large trucks and two tanks. All of the vehicles had been destroyed, ruptured and charred by explosions. Many bodies lay in twisted and grotesque postures of death, blackened and burned.

With the Humvee up on the road once more, the young driver made eye contact with Cat in the mirror, and said evenly, "I capture images, and I sell them. The images are for the people to decipher, to comprehend. It's a living, it's not noble, okay?" He paused, began to slow the vehicle as he approached a roadblock manned by armed mujahideen, and added just for her, "Sometimes I get to shoot beautiful things, uh, beautiful people standing for a moment in the filth of war."

Cat remembered the last photograph she had of Carolyn standing at the edge of a road in some godforsaken place, and she knew. "Yes," she said with a small smile.

Eva, the cadaverous reporter in the backseat next to Cat, sucked on her brown cigarette until over an inch of ash hung improbably in front of her grim mouth. It fell in a light cascade as she said, "It's about religion, you fools."

The entire sky over the battlefield — the killing field — is the color of blood. The sun hangs there, embarrassed, diffused by the haze of cordite and smoke of civilization burned beyond recognition. It is early afternoon, sultry hot, and already the stench of death is palpable. It is everywhere, the smell, cloying and clinging, leaving a greasy smear on my cheek when I rub my eyes. It seems to be partially cleansed by tears, and as I walk the path of the morning's battle I see that other observers have also discovered the value of tears. The mujahideen troops met our Humvee at a roadblock earlier and, after some wrangling, agreed to let us spend some time here. They were boastful, proud of their victory, and wanted us to see the power of their advance. So we see.

Visions of dead soldiers, from Gettysburg to Flanders to Normandy to Chosin to Khe San to Kuwait, never change. They lie in sweet repose, or violently wrenched postures of death. Their stillness is complete, unimpeachable. Whatever they were in life has now departed, leaving behind pathetic lumps of flesh, truncated frameworks of bone and gristle, puddles and splashes of blood. At first I walked the battlefield with the eye of a forensic anthropologist reconstructing the progress of battle through the path of bodies, seeing first the mujahideen troops, facing forward, even in death. Then, within a few yards, the bodies of the vanquished Pakistanis, lying back, their arms thrown over their heads, falling in lines like trees in the face of an unyielding gale. Then, the first time I — as a journalist new to war — began to see Pakistani soldiers who had clearly been executed. Some seemed to have been in the posture of prayer, or total supplication as they were shot point-blank in the face. I was cautioned by those who observed it with me — it is a part of this war, they said, there is a "take no prisoners" mandate given to the mujahideen troops, and they embrace it; but it spoke to me of cowardice, deceit, and shame.

Soon we came to another by-product of this war, the dead noncombatants. No longer in a forensic mind-set, I stopped the first time I came upon what appeared to be a pile of old rags in the back of a blown-up truck. The rags were wrapped around the bodies of children, of course, children who had been herded into the truck, then massacred. An old woman, her face lifted in silent scream, clung to the rear panel of the truck as if crucified. It was apparent she had attempted to stop what was coming, and was simply machine-gunned along with the rest. With me was a combat photographer, and I watched in silence as he carefully captured her image on his cameras. I wanted to tell him to leave her alone, but before the words came he turned to me and said, "See how her eyes seem to be seeking God as she turned her face to the heavens? Perhaps He couldn't see her through the fire and haze." I left him to his work.

A few meters from the truck we came upon what might have been a kindergarten class on its way to a picnic. Almost twenty children lay along the edge of a sad ditch, holding hands, one before the other. At their head was a young woman, another at the end of their little chain. Both women had been shot in the head, their clothing in disarray. One can only guess why children were left so close to the front lines. Perhaps the Pakistanis never thought it would really happen, or perhaps the Pakistanis had read the old war stories that contained meaningless and contrived words like honor and chivalry. There is no nobility here, no dignity, no victory. Nothing good can come of this.

The victorious troops strut like bullies, preen like hyenas, steal like vultures. They boast of conquering the rabble army of unbelievers, and declare that their mission is difficult, but necessary to a better world. They are rapacious and cowardly, and if this army represents its leader, the whole world should take another look at what he is.

Cat Early, Trib Group Correspondent.

"No way," said Slim, the photographer,

as he looked over Cat's shoulder at what she had written.

"What?"

"No way your bosses at the Trib Group will print your story," explained Slim. "They'll print your observations, your descriptions of the battlefield, the advance of the troops and all that, but when you begin putting your o-*pinion* in there, they will flush it."

"As has already been demonstrated," Cat agreed ruefully. She blew a puff of air, looked up at Slim, and said, "But I've written it, and I'm sending it. They can roll it into a little ball and —"

"Now, now, Cat. Let's remain ladylike and professional, even in this rustic and basically messed-up setting."

She grinned at him, and shrugged again.

"Heads up," he said then, but he was not grinning.

One of the mujahideen soldiers approached and pointed one grimy finger at Cat. She stood, and he crooked the finger, indicating she should follow him.

"What's this?" asked Slim.

"I asked to speak with the company sergeant in charge when we left the roadblock earlier. Looks like my wish is being granted," answered Cat quietly. She stepped toward the soldier. As she did, the photographer grabbed her bag and his, and moved to her side. The soldier pointed his assault rifle at him and shook his head, but Slim said easily,

"Just carrying her bags, old boy, not to worry, I've been her valet for years now, so pip-pip and so forth." The soldier scowled for a moment, rubbed his thick stubble of beard in indecision, and finally shrugged and turned away. Cat and Slim followed along.

They walked through a large, open bivouac area where many mujahideen soldiers cooked over small fires, cleaned their weapons, dozed, or spoke quietly in clusters. Many stared at Cat and Slim as they made their way toward a group of command vehicles in a line on an elevated road. Most stared at Cat, and she became unsettled by their open looks and leers. "Steady on," she heard Slim whisper behind her. As they approached the command vehicles, a man disengaged from a tight group of officers examining a map and walked toward them. He was dark and dirty, but his uniform fit well and his weapons were clean. He had gunpowder, mud, and the copper sheen of dried blood on his face and hands. His eyes appeared bright against his sweaty cheeks, his thin lips compressed in anger. Before the escorting soldier could speak, the man waved him away. He stood with his hands on his hips, shoulders square, and stared at Cat. She had never seen anyone with such menacingly dark eyes. They reminded Cat of the charred remains of a campfire; like those embers, something seemed to smolder and flare up.

"You could not come alone, woman reporter?" asked dark eyes.

"I . . . I was afraid," replied Cat, sensing immediately that the man would be comfortable only with a woman who knew her place. "This is a man I work with, and I asked him to accompany me. Thank you for taking the time to speak with me."

He studied her face a moment, glanced at Slim, who said nothing and tried to appear uninterested, and said, "No matter. What is it I can tell you?"

"Did you find the Pakistani defenses as formidable as expected?" Cat asked. "And are you still on your hoped-for timetable?"

"There is no timetable," dark eyes answered and waved for them to follow him. He began walking down the road, away from the command vehicles. "Anywhere troops stand in defiance of the mujahideen, the clock is ticking. From the moment they resist, the sands beginning running out for them, yes?"

"It appeared, from our inspection of the battlefield, that many of your own troops were killed by your artillery fire that fell on your advance," ventured Cat, wanting to rattle this man, wanting to get to him. "Was that a mistake? Isn't it a wasteful way to use your frontline soldiers?"

"There is no waste in war, journalist . . . especially in victory," he said without breaking stride. "You were able to inspect the battlefield because the battle was *done*, understand? The enemy slime died or fled, leaving their precious land, their women and children, their comrades. You stood on ground now part of a new world. Is that wasteful?"

Dark eyes stopped on a low berm that looked down on a smaller camp area made up of perhaps a dozen tents. He proceeded no farther, but clearly had brought them there so they could see. They saw. This was a makeshift "rest and relaxation" area. To Cat it appeared that most of the soldiers in and around the tents were sergeants or officers; the others there were young girls. Most of the girls were in varying stages of undress, and huddled together in shame and fear.

Cat, angered by what she saw and the fact that he wanted her to see it, said, "I saw many Pakistani soldiers who appeared to have been executed. They were shot in the face, as if summarily killed even as they attempted to surrender. I saw women killed, and children. I ask you as a member of a conquering army, is that what you are? Is that the foundation for your 'new world'?"

Slim watched the man's face harden as Cat's words fell against it. He readied himself, not knowing exactly what he could do. He simply prepared to protect Cat if he could.

The soldier searched Cat's face for a long moment, then said quietly, "I will say to you words I heard my leader say once to a journalist about the enemy. 'Their men stand, but do not submit, the children and old people are simply in the way, and the girls are vessels to be used by those who still stand after the battle.' "

Cat's mouth went suddenly dry as she heard his words, knowing she had seen them, read them, before. Before she could respond there was a commotion below them. An officer had approached a huddle of young girls, grabbed one by her hair, and pulled her to her feet. As he did, another one — very young, with big eyes, and hair that reached to the small of her back — left the huddle and began walking quickly toward where Cat, Slim, and the sergeant stood.

Without hesitation, Cat asked, "May I speak with that girl?" The sergeant recognized the girl as the "gift" given to him that morning by one of his troops. He watched her approach, looked at Cat, hesitated, and said, "Please. Be my guest, woman reporter. You wish to speak with a perfect example of the enemy's weaker vessels? You will learn nothing of import from her." He walked a few feet away and lit a cigarette. He watched from that distance with a tight grin cut across his face.

"Warning, warning," whispered Slim out of the side of his mouth. "Cat, what are you doin'? Why don't you just kick that poster child for war criminals in the crotch and be done with it? Girl, you are goin' to get us killed."

Cat did not answer him, but kept her eyes on the young girl, who came to within a few feet and then stopped, her eyes downcast. The girl's hands were hidden in the folds of a blanket draped over her small shoulders. Cat did not think the girl was more than twelve or thirteen years old. So, journalist, she asked herself, what questions do you have for *this* participant in war? She ran her tongue over her lips, glanced at Slim, then at the girl, and asked quietly, "Yes, child . . . will you speak with us?"

The girl smiled shyly, her teeth white against her lips, and answered in a small voice, "We all agreed, my sisters and my friends, we agreed before last night that we would die before we were captured or allowed these men to *use* us. I . . . I wished, we all wished, to save ourselves for the husband we might someday have. But we had heard the stories, what happened to other girls who were taken." She stood about ten feet away, and moved her left hand so it showed under the blanket. In her hand she held a grenade. Cat sucked in her breath, and from the corner of her eye felt the soldier looking at them.

The girl smiled sweetly, her voice childlike as she continued. "I could not do it. I saw my sisters die. I saw my friends die, some before they had a chance to do it themselves. One of my sisters was taken by the soldiers even as she took her last breath. But I could not do it. I was afraid. I am still afraid. . . . But now there is no choice. I have watched all day, I have seen what they do. I know I am to be used by that one." She nodded toward the sergeant. "I hoped you were foreign reporters when I saw you. So you could see, so you could *tell*."

"See what?" asked Cat, already knowing the answer. "You don't have to do it. You can survive him, and survive whatever he does to you. You can —"

The girl shook her head, her smile deepening. "I no longer wish to be here. If there is something more, as we have been taught by our learned old men, then I wish to be there . . . not here."

The soldier was already moving toward them. He threw the cigarette down and said tersely, "Enough chatter. This is foolish. Time to go back with your team, woman journalist, time for this little sweet to come with me."

Cat felt Slim grab her right arm above the elbow and pull her back a step as the girl turned toward the man, made a movement under the blanket with her hands, and stepped toward the man. The soldier continued, "You have seen enough now, woman journalist? You can report about this army, how it will crush all those who resist, how it will take what it wants?"

Cat managed to say, "No," as she reached out toward the girl with her left arm. The girl flung herself at the soldier, her arms wrapped around his chest as she clung tightly to him. In reflex the man moved his assault rifle to his side, one arm across her back, and lifted her feet off the ground. He had an evil grin on his face.

The soldier's evil, somehow knowing grin was the last thing Cat registered before the world exploded around them. She and Slim were tumbled down and back together, rolling off the berm in a tangled embrace. She felt blood in her mouth, and heard Slim grunt as the roar of the grenade going off filled their senses. After a moment of disorientation, she got to her hands and knees, then regained her feet. Slim came up beside her, rubbing his ears, his face covered with dirt. They saw everyone in the small camp looking toward them, some pointing, then looked to where the sergeant and the girl had embraced. The blanket enveloped what remained of the girl, and the soldier lay sprawled and bloody a few feet away. Cat reached out for Slim and gagged.

She expected the officers and others in the encampment to come running, but they did not. It seemed to her that they saw what had happened, determined the action was over, then dismissed it and them. She leaned down to look at the girl, and felt the pull of Slim trying to stop her. She brushed the long hair away from the girl's sleeping face, studied her peaceful look a moment, and was startled by a harsh laugh. She looked at the soldier, saw him pull himself to one knee, pick up his assault rifle, and stand slowly. His right hand was bloodied, and his right pant leg was torn in several places. The right side of his head was blackened, his right ear crimson. The man looked into her eyes, spit, and laughed again. "Stupid Paki twit," he said in a low growl. "She thought she could kill me with her little hand grenade. What about that, woman reporter?"

Cat and Slim were frozen in place, not sure of what they had just observed. Slim actually rubbed his eyes as he stared at the man, who could not have been standing there after the blast, but was. Slim swallowed, and said evenly, "Well, look at the time. We really must be going, Cat."

The soldier began to say something, then turned his head quickly at the sound of whistles being blown in the distance. A voice squawked on a radio, and the man reached for his belt, then looked around until he found the handheld device lying in the dirt a few feet away. He picked it up, spoke into it, received a quick reply, and clipped it to his belt. "You see how they fight, woman reporter?" he asked with a scowl as he pointed at the dead girl under the blanket. "You ask me about 'executions,' about the deaths of women and children? This is *war*, understand? When countries stand against the new world, we will wage war. And a ferocious undertaking it will be." He heard another squawk on the radio, and began walking quickly toward the line of command vehicles in the distance. "Go now, if you can find your way back." He flicked the back of one hand at Cat as he passed them. "You, I will see again."

"One last thing," Cat said, her voice defiant. "How should I refer to you? What's your name?"

Without turning to speak to her, he said, "Nacht." Slim and Cat exchanged questioning looks.

Thirty minutes later the pair stood near the front of his battered Humvee as they waited for the other journalists to join them. Cat had felt sick to her stomach, realized she hadn't eaten all day, shared some rations with Slim, and promptly threw up. She washed her mouth out with water, and felt better after sipping on a warm can of soda Slim had found under one of the Humvee's seats.

"Cat," said Slim tentatively, "uh . . . before the others get back, I . . . uh . . ." He rubbed his face with both hands. Cat expected him to say something about the death of the young girl they had just witnessed, but he blurted out, "Listen. I knew Carolyn, okay? I knew your sister."

"You took the last picture of her, didn't you, Slim?" asked Cat with a smile. "Where she's standing beside a road, her bag at her feet."

"Yep."

"I think it's great that she knew someone like you, Slim," said Cat. "Were you, um . . . you know . . . I mean, Carolyn rarely told me about her love life, or boyfriends . . . or stuff like that."

Slim watched her eyes for a moment, then replied, "No. We were like really close friends, and as you can see, being out in these places, tough places where bad things happen . . . Well, it will bring you together. We were friends and colleagues, that's all. I wanted to, ah . . . I let her know I wouldn't mind bunking out with her and all, but she told me the time would come in her life for that, and the time wasn't now, I mean then. Anyway, she trusted me, and I miss her." He looked down, and to Cat's amusement actually scuffed one foot on the gravel roadbed.

"I'm glad you were her friend, Slim," said Cat. "And who knows . . . another time, another place?"

"Yeah," he responded. He looked at her a moment, then asked, "Did Carolyn ever mention the old priest to you, Cat?" He saw Cat shake her head. "She never told you about wanting to go to a small town in northern Italy, where she was supposed to meet with the old priest who could tell her a 'great and frightening secret'?"

Cat remembered looking through Carolyn's papers in her bedroom at home, and a feeling of dread settled in the pit of her stomach. "No," she said.

"She trusted me, Cat," said Slim as he saw the other journalists approaching, "like I said." He went to the driver's side of the Humvee, reached under the front seat, and pulled out a battered leather knapsack. He handed it to her, and as he did she saw the letters "CE" written in Magic Marker on the flap. "It's some of her papers, private stuff. Couple of photos and letters from you, actually. I've been lugging it around since she was . . . since she died. So it's yours now." He grinned, and his face became young again. "Hey, it's already got your initials on it, and all."

Cat reached out and took the bag, then slowly hugged it to her chest. "Thank you, Slim. I mean it."

A few minutes later they were all back in the Humvee and careening down the cratered road. Slim drove, the other three chattered about things they had seen and heard on the battlefield, and Cat sat quietly, staring out the window. I always wanted to go to Italy, she thought.

Chapter Five

"It's in the Scripture, Reverend Smith, but we got it wrong." The Reverend Henderson Smith looked at the man who spoke those words, and did not respond. He was, in fact, speechless. That this man, this representative from one of the largest Southern fundamentalist congregations in the country, would make such a statement was impossible. Smith leaned back in his old leather chair in his small office behind his church and looked the man over. Mid-forties, florid and porcine, with carefully blow-dried cotton-candy hair, a linen suit, a fat tie embellished with little golden crosses, the man looked almost cartoonish to Smith. He had called to make an appointment, using the name of his organization, and informed Smith it had to be quickly and "hush-hush." The Reverend Henderson Smith knew of the organization, of course, and had attended a few of their huge conventions, the last one in Gatlinburg. But he did not recognize the man's name, Andrew Nuit (rhymes with "sweet," he told everyone he met), even though his business card identified him as

"Outreach Coordinator." Nuit seemed to fill Smith's small office with his bulk, and he leaned forward as he spoke, his hard little eyes and sweaty brow evidence of his intensity.

"I can see how you are looking at me, Reverend Smith," said Nuit with an easy smile. "You're sitting there hearing a fundamentalist church mouthpiece admitting we can't read the Scripture, and you might be right on the edge of either launching into a thunderous sermon — I've heard you can bring down those Jericho walls with your zeal — or simply throwing me out the door. I understand, believe me." He leaned even closer across Smith's scarred desk and added, "But indulge me for a few moments, and perhaps you'll look at me differently. These next few moments could be the first step in a flat-out meteoric ascension in your career."

"I told you on the phone, Mr. . . . . Nuit" — Smith tried to work some moisture into his suddenly dry mouth — "I've got my church, I've got my flock, and it's growin' every day. My church isn't about me, anyway. It's about spreading the gospel. I don't need no 'meteoric ascension' to spread the gospel." Smith hoped he sounded convincing. When he had got the phone call from Nuit his heart had begun pounding. Nuit's organization represented the big leagues, with the resources to make his dreams come true.

"Of course," said Nuit. "And we knew how you would respond. But let me ask you this: Isn't it more effective if you spread the good Word to *thousands,* rather than a few hundred here and there?"

Henderson Smith pursed his lips and nodded, not trusting himself to speak.

"It's time for the new good news, Reverend Smith," continued Nuit, "news that will carry this sorry world out of darkness and into a light only imagined by our fathers. We need voices to help spread the Word, powerful, respected voices, the voices of intelligent and godly men who know their Bible . . . know it and are spiritual enough to get down in there amongst its words and find the *truth.*"

"With all due respect," said Smith, measuring his words, "you are skirtin' right on the edge of pride, arrogance, and intelligence. I am not a scholar, of course." Smith paused, waiting for the laugh that didn't come. "I don't fault them for their search. Tryin' to peel apart every nuance of each written sentence, caught up in the intellectual pursuit of complex and complicated truths so they can explain the sometimes unexplainable. The truth is there, plain and simple, been there for a couple of thousand years now for us to read and know. You start talkin' about a 'new' gospel, you gonna find yourself labeled a 'cult' before you can get through your first sermon." He shook his head, his fingers a steeple in front of his face, "No sir, I preach the truth as my sweet Lord has it written out for me. I don't need to go messin' with it."

Nuit's round pink face broke into a huge grin, exposing his large teeth. "Bravo, Reverend Smith, bravo. I told my boss you were not a man to be trifled with. I told him you would brook no nonsense, would not sit for anyone to start messin' with the gospel as you learned it." He sat back and studied the large diamond ring on the sausage-like pinkie finger of his right hand. He looked into Smith's eyes, and went on. "But my boss told me you were a man with God in your heart, solid in your faith, and that you'd hear me out because you did not fear false prophets."

Henderson Smith found the words "What's in it for me?" on the tip of his tongue, and the thought frightened him. His heart was pounding against his chest;

part of him wanted to leap out of his chair and run from the room and this sweaty, heaving bulk of a seducer as fast as his skinny legs could carry him. Instead, he crossed his arms over his chest and said, "So give me an example of what we're talkin' about here."

"What is God?" asked Nuit.

"God is love," replied Smith.

"Paul," said Nuit, "in Philippians, what did he call the Bible?"

"A group of love letters."

"*Love* letters, Reverend Smith," said the big man quietly. "He is love, we are His children. He is mercy, and forgiveness."

"Yes?"

"Reconcile that with Revelation Six, sixteen, the 'wrath of the Lamb.' "

"Those who fail . . . those who fall," offered Smith tentatively, "nonbelievers and charlatans . . . they will suffer His wrath."

"How can a loving God and the Lamb be wrathful? The 'wrath of the Lamb'? How can that be?" asked Nuit.

"Tough love," answered Smith, more confident now, "like a father to a child. He gave us free will, but he also gave us the Word. When the end times come — like it *clearly* spells out in Revelation — there will be hell to pay for those who have not taken

Him, sweet Lamb or wrathful Lamb, into their hearts. Tough love and challenge, that's what the Scriptures spell out for us. There is salvation, we will be taken up with Him, but woe unto those who turn away from His truth."

"Millions will die?" asked Nuit. "Suffer untold miseries during the tribulations? Our world, *created* by Him for us as a beautiful place to live, learn, and grow. He will destroy it? All of His 'errant' children, too?"

"C'mon, Mr. Nuit," answered Henderson Smith. "You are asking the childlike question man has been asking all along: 'How could a loving God allow this to happen to me, this cancer, this car accident, this death of my child?' Some things, especially about human suffering, *we just might never understand.* You go to Romans, go to Thessalonians and read about the rapture, to Ezekiel, all of Revelation . . . man, it is laid out step by step. You are so far out of line I don't know why I'm wasting my time."

"So you can show me the word 'rapture' in there, Reverend Smith?" asked Nuit with a small grin.

Smith made a dismissive gesture with one hand, and replied, "Don't play those kinda games with me, Nuit. Rapture, the lifting up, those left behind, it's there, okay?"

"Tribulation? Pain? Suffering of untold scores of souls? Burning forever in lakes of molten sulfur?"

"It's there, Mr. Nuit," said Reverend Smith. "You know it, and any student of the Bible knows it."

"First Thessalonians Five? '. . . we do not need to write to you about *times* and *dates*.' . . . We will not know when it will happen, right?" pressed Andrew Nuit with a deepening intensity. "First Thessalonians Five, twenty-four . . . 'The one who calls you is faithful and he will do it.' "

What about Second Thessalonians 2:3, thought Smith as he struggled to control his desires, struggled against Nuit's corrupting siren song. What about the Man of Lawlessness?

"What if the loving God decided to change any part of it?" asked Nuit. "What if He has free will even as He has given it to us? What if there was a chance He would *bypass* all that suffering. He offered Revelation to us to warn us. What if He — ?"

" 'What if, what if?' " replied Smith. "Man, I've had better discussions in Sunday school."

"Who is the prodigal son, Reverend Smith?"

"C'mon, man."

"Who is the prodigal son, and when will he show up to lead us . . . *here* . . . on Earth?"

Smith said nothing, but placed his hands together as if in prayer, kissing his thumbs.

"You may have heard we are building, right now, and it is happening fast, a new cathedral," said Nuit quietly. "It will be the biggest, most beautiful church in this part of the country. It will have all the electronic bells and whistles so the Word can be broadcast to the multitudes. Its own radio and television channels, of course, huge Sunday school programs, a choir to rival any, a gigantic staff and support system, and a pulpit demanding a voice."

Henderson Smith waited, perfectly still; he took no breath, and thought even his heart stopped beating.

"We have been searching for a voice, Reverend Smith," continued Nuit. "A voice rich in Biblical knowledge, faith, and timbre, a voice that will be heard by the multicultural masses who are thirsty for a gospel that speaks to them." He stopped, motionless.

Henderson Smith fought it, but he could

not keep his head from slowly turning until finally his eyes were held by the bright and brittle eyes of the temptation incarnate sitting a few feet away. The eyes were black, ice and fire, alive and dancing with a force that pulled at Smith's very core. "You could be that voice, Henderson," said the big man. "You could preach the new gospel and not in any way pervert or subvert the gospel as you already know it. You could bring salvation and comfort to thousands with your voice, with the message that He has come — come quietly and without trumpets and burning chariots — that the world can receive the returning son, the *first* son, now. We want you to be our voice, to tell the masses about the Good News, and we want you to stand tall in the respect you will be given. Stand tall in a pulpit of grace, splendor, and promise."

The Reverend Henderson Smith heard his own breath, in and out, heard the clattering of the rickety wall air-conditioning unit in his office. He tore his eyes away from Nuit's knowing, smiling face, saw the peeling paint on the old wooden walls of his office, the antiquated printer, the dust, the *smallness* of it all. He glanced out of the window next to his desk, across the gravel parking lot to the faded redbrick sign that said "Mount Olive Gospel Church," with his name in amateurish hand-painted lettering underneath.

"What shall I tell my boss, Reverend Smith?" asked Nuit quietly as his eyes pulled Smith's back to his with an irresistible force.

Help me, Lord, thought Henderson Smith as he stared into the abyss.

It was a pastel world, drawn by a loving hand with life's chalk. The sky was a gentle pink, streaked with white, and the light that brought soft color to the earth held a serene orange-gold glow. Small birds darted about, their song given in hushed and playful tones. A comforting stillness seemed to hold everything in place — the narrow, rutted road, the twisted and gnarled old tree, the town with its tiny chapel in the distance, the dust that hung in the air. The branches of the tree reached out in the same direction, over a crooked wooden bench, and partially shadowing the road. On the bench sat the old man, his shoulders rounded by time, his head down, chin on his chest. He might have been dozing.

Cat Early stood and looked at the scene

before her. It was as if she gazed upon a painting by one of the masters from two centuries ago, and she distinctly felt that she could simply step into it, be held in that timeless moment, and know peace. She sighed. She had followed the directions in her sister's journal, and found the village a few kilometers outside of Milan. Leaving a war-ravaged area and traveling through northern Italy had been intoxicating and disorienting. Her eyes were thirsty for color and texture, her heart hungry for normal days, quiet nights.

She stood for a moment a few feet from the bench under the reaching branches, and studied the old man. If he dozed, it was with his eyes open. He seemed to be staring at his feet, his hands locked in a ball in front of his stomach, and he rocked back and forth slowly, perhaps humming. He was a small man, his olive skin creased and shadowed, with the dust of his world shading the color and highlighting the various curves and edges of him as he sat. He wore a simple suit, which had once been black, and a clean white shirt buttoned at the throat. She was content to stand there and watch him breathe; but after a moment his eyelids fluttered, he licked his lips, and spoke without turning his head.

"So," he said in a surprisingly firm voice, "you are the young innocent, come to hear the confession of this timid and nondescript old man, a priest, no less."

"I am far from being a young innocent," answered Cat quietly. "I am Cat . . . Catherine."

"You are closer to being the young innocent than you could know, child," replied the old man in a gentle tone, turning his face to look at her.

Cat said nothing, but met his gaze. She saw strength and sadness in the dark pools of his eyes.

"You are Cat, sister of Carolyn, both of you daughters and receivers of God's Word." He smiled. "Thank you for coming to see me. Please come sit beside me." He patted the bench. "Many heavy bottoms of gossiping women have worn the wood smooth, and perhaps absorbed any splinters there might have been." He pointed toward the village in the distance. "I live and work in that tiny house of God now, waiting for His call, knowing it will be soon. I have reverted back — life is indeed a circle, my child — back to what I first was, a peasant priest saying his prayers in a small and loving church attended by people who kneel and try to understand."

He shrugged. "For many years I had other work. I attended to the needs of some of the leaders of the Church. I, a barely educated working man who heard God's command one pristine morning while laboring in the quarry. I traveled, attended conferences, visited important and busy places." He shook his head, his face wrinkled in amusement. "Who would believe it? Not I. Many times through the years I have asked God if He had picked the right man, and in His infinite wisdom He always responded with, 'Why don't you pray on it?' So I prayed, and I tried to do my duty, and be of . . . value."

She liked his smile, and decided it was his overall patina of sadness that made his smile so appealing. She watched him, and waited.

"I read a short article your sister wrote, in one of the international newspapers," he said, looking at his hands now. "One of my jobs was to quickly scan various reports every morning to see if there was something that might affect the Church in one way or another. I had my own collection of colored markers to better assist those I served in their search for information. She chose her words carefully, your sister, and I found myself — it is called 'reading between the lines,' I think — hearing her. After that I actually searched for her pieces, and found them to be generated from the heart." He shrugged again, took a deep breath, let it out slowly, and went on. "Then she was on the world news one evening. I knew it was her from the voice, even before I glanced at the television set. She was lovely, like you, with her chin out, eyes looking straight into mine as she spoke her words. Words that cleanly and clearly described the horrific and degrading acts visited upon man by man."

A church bell tolled in the distance, a soft footfall with a deepening resonance as it traveled across the dusty golden ground. Cat was sure the bell had sounded the same for centuries, felt embraced by it, and wished she could sit in that moment forever.

The old priest listened, then said, "My song. The lyrics have a sameness to them, but the beat is steady, no?" He smiled at her. "Yes?"

"Yes."

"So. Your sister," continued the priest, "I liked her, and more important, I knew she was one I could trust with a little bit of a larger truth." He hesitated, straightened his shoulders, then said almost to himself,

"I know what I saw. . . ."

"You saw something you wanted to tell my sister about?" asked Cat. "Is that your confession, Father?"

He nodded, his face glum. He looked at her, then away, and after a moment he spoke. "I had decided . . . being first the man that God had created almost eighty years ago . . . that if I were young and had not found the calling, I would have made my way to whatever place your sister was, and I would . . . be with her." He smiled again, comfortable with himself and her. "That said, I felt compelled, driven perhaps, to tell Carolyn Early, the reporter, what I had learned. She was in the snake pit, at the end, and I do not know what she knew or what she saw. And *look,* she reported from very very dangerous places, no? Yes? So she was killed, gunned down, 'caught in a crossfire,' I believe they said. May God have mercy on her soul, which *of course* He will." He stopped, and after a moment she heard him breathing, and felt him rocking back and forth slightly.

"Carolyn was killed, Father," ventured Cat, "and you had not shared what you had learned. Then you heard about me, about my coming behind her in the same work. Is that why you were not surprised when I contacted you?"

"Yes."

Cat waited.

The old priest sighed, crossed himself, and began: "It so clearly warns us about false prophets, usurpers, pretenders to the throne. It is written, we study it, we intone the words solemnly to our poor flock. It is lovely in our mother tongue, businesslike and straightforward in yours. We teach the gospel as it has been given to us by our heavenly Father. But we are men, afraid and distrustful, always looking for a sign, always looking for a guarantee we can seize with our clutching hands. Faith alone — and *we should be* faith-based in all things — is sometimes not enough, apparently. So when we see something we can recognize, something or someone we can *relate* to, we are quick to grant it validation, to call it genuine. Your sister spoke of one who seemed to be gaining in power and popularity, a new conqueror, a man who was not only more than he appeared, but appeared ready to save the world from itself." He turned to face her, one finger held in front of her eyes. "And I met that man, was in the same room with him. Oh yes, he was invited to a secret meeting. May the Lord forgive those well-meaning fools who represent our new and learned leadership. He wanted our support, he needed our help because we could reach out to so many, and what he said was so generally accepted as . . . good, and . . . truthful. I was not permitted to remain in the room the entire time, Catherine Early, so I didn't hear all that was discussed. And perhaps I am an old man of feeble mind who smells conspiracies under every cloak and can no longer tell from garlic or clove." He stopped, took her hands in his, and asked, "Do you know the one I speak of?"

"Yes, Father," responded Cat, all of her senses tuned to his every nuance.

"You have heard of this Prodigal Project? Know of it, know of him?"

"Yes —"

"Then I say this to you, child. Go back to the Scripture, and it will tell you what to beware of. This one who comes . . . this one who says with confidence and without hesitation how he can change the world, he is *not*. Foul cannot be blessed, darkness cannot be light, evil cannot be salvation." He turned his head as a sudden gust of wind blew the dust on the road before it. It seemed to come out of nowhere, the gust, and it rattled away with the leaves after a few seconds. The dust it had lifted covered them both, and the old priest rubbed his eyes. He looked all around him, then up into the sky, and grinned. "It is good that you came quickly, Cat Early." He squeezed her hands and went on. "That part of me that is still the young man sweating in the quarry would like to stay right here holding hands and staring into your eyes. You are lovely, with a good heart, and perhaps if I was that young man we might have found other things to think about. But I must return home now, and pray for strength and forgiveness. Walk with the truth in your heart, child, and do not be afraid to expose the lie when it comes." He stood, still holding her hands. "Good-bye, Cat Early."

She did not want the meeting to end, but saw his resolution. She leaned forward and kissed him on his right cheek, squeezed his hands, and said, "Ciao, then, Father. Until we meet again."

"Thank you, child," he said with a sad smile as he turned to walk down the road. "But it is simply good-bye."

She watched him go, a simple man simply clothed, his shoulders rounded by his years and the things he had carried through them. Little puffs of dust followed his steps, and as they fell they covered his footprints, leaving no sign.

Ivy Sloan-Underwood looked at herself in the dressing-room mirror. She wore shorts and a halter top that showed her belly button. She was in the mall, at an up-scale clothing store that catered to the younger set. She was living what she called "one of Ivy's little lies." This lie was the one she had told her husband, Ron, when they went to bed last night. She had told him she had to go to one of the elementary schools to discuss part-time teaching with the principal. Ron would have to use their van with its hydraulic wheelchair lift to carry Ronnie to his school and therapy center. She would take their Honda, run a few errands after the meeting, and probably be gone most of the day. Her husband, predictably, had agreed. No problem. His college teaching schedule for that day was open, she had already checked, and she knew he tried hard to give her whatever time she needed. She had given him a peck on the cheek as his reward this morning as he was loading Ronnie into the van.

She turned this way and that, looking at her reflection in the mirror. She liked the way her body looked, still fit, toned, with athletic arms and legs, a rounded bottom, okay on top. She frowned. This little outfit with the exposed belly button might be on the edge of *too* young for her, but she knew if she wore it anywhere she'd get more than a few glances of appraisal. She felt a thrill as she remembered the dream from last night.

In the dream, she had been seated at a restaurant, a little French café kind of place. There was a sprig of purple flowers on the table, and a basket with fresh-baked bread. She was resigned to having her lunch alone, but after a moment she was approached by a man wearing dark slacks, black shoes and belt, and a charcoal shirt with matching tie. He was over six feet tall, supremely fit and tightly muscled, and possessed an easy smile. His long fingers were carefully manicured. His thick head of black hair was brushed back off his forehead, and his cologne was male and subtle. His face was angular and strong, with deep black eyes, a straight nose, and sensual, full lips. Whoa, she thought in her dream, of all the men I've flirted with, all the times I've thought about actually fooling around with a man who was not my husband, this has got to be the one. The man stood beside the table for a moment, looking into her eyes; then he leaned down slightly and said in a whisper, "I'm in the middle of one of my little lies." He reached out and took her left hand in his, and his skin felt smooth and warm. "Mind if I join you in yours?" She did not hear herself speak in the dream, but she must have said okay, because the next part had him leaning over the table, with her hands in his, his eyes glowing, as he said, "You want to. I want to. Let's get out of here." Then they were in another room, looking into a mirror. He stood close behind her, looking over her shoulder. With his shirt off she could see that his chest, shoulders, and arms were tanned and muscular. She felt him hug her tightly as he said quietly, "Take off that pretty outfit, I want to see you." Then she woke up, her heart pounding, her body warm with a pleasant anticipation.

She stared at herself in the dressing-room mirror now, and tried to push the dream out of her mind while she decided whether to buy the outfit she had on. Then, with a clarity that caused her to flinch, he stood behind her, his forearms crossed over her tummy, his chest tight against her back. She stared into the mirror, and saw the easy smile on his good-looking face. "Yes," she heard herself say, and then he was gone. She hugged herself, looked away from the mirror, then back, and saw only herself.

She left the new outfit in the dressing room as she hurried from the store.

After a few minutes she calmed down, thought about the dream from last night and the flash in the dressing room, and laughed at herself. You are having yourself a day, she reminded herself, don't waste it. She decided to take herself to lunch, and a few minutes later a waiter held the chair for her as she sat in a small French café. She was one at a table for two, close to the front windows, which looked out over a pretty tree-lined boulevard. She ordered a glass of chilled white wine, blew a puff of air, and tried to relax. The waiter brought a basket of warm bread when he came with her wine, and as he walked away she saw the sprig of purple flowers in the center of the table. Suddenly thirsty, she took a long sip of the wine. . . . It was cold and good.

The waiter took her order for soup and salad, and bustled away. She was looking out the window at the people walking by when she heard a man say quietly, "I'm sorry to disturb you, but I am compelled to ask you a question." She turned her head slowly, already knowing it would be him, and it was. Tall, darkly handsome, wearing the charcoal shirt with matching tie, his hair brushed back, his eyes glowing, his sensual lips curved into a friendly smile. The scent of his cologne was familiar.

"Yes?" she managed.

"Aren't you a teacher? I know I've seen you before. . . . How could I forget?"

"Yes," she said again, wanting to gulp her wine, but not trusting it.

"Ivy? Ivy . . . right?" he continued. "I don't remember your last name, but Ivy I do." He put his right hand out. "I'm Thad. I know that sounds like a mournful person with a lisp, but it's shortened from something much worse, believe me."

"Yes," she said again, then straightened and added, "Um, yes . . . I'm Ivy . . . Thad. Nice to meet you." She shook his offered hand, and the feel of his skin caused a tremor to course through her chest.

"May I join you?" asked Thad.

No. No. No. No. No, thought Ivy, but she said with a smile, "Of course."

Thad sat across from Ivy, and the waiter appeared and took his order, which duplicated hers. After a moment he leaned slightly across the table and said, "I'm actually being a bad boy today. Supposed to be making my rounds — I represent a research center — and just didn't feel like it, if you know what I mean."

Ivy nodded.

"Truth be told," Thad went on, "you were on my list anyway, so I guess this little rendezvous is okay."

She looked at him, sipped her wine, and said, "Your list?"

"Of people I might speak with, about something my firm is doing now."

Ivy felt confused and disoriented looking at him as he spoke. She didn't know what was happening to her, but she was quite sure that if he told her she was on his list to go right now to a no-tell mo-tel and dive into bed she'd say *okay*. She licked her lips, took a breath, and said, "I'm sorry, uh, Thad . . . I don't understand." Trying to regroup, she asked, "Do you have a last name?"

"My last name is Night, but this is about your son, Ronnie, Ivy," he said quietly. "That's why I was supposed to try to arrange a meeting with you."

She was dumbstruck. Ronnie was the last thing on her mind at that moment.

"I'll tell you honestly, though," he confided, "spending any time at all with you, no matter what we discuss, is a gift to me. You are lovely, and if I'm out of line saying so, so be it."

She sat up in her chair, placed her hands palms down on the white linen tablecloth, and said, "Listen. Yes, I'm Ivy. Yes, I'm Ronnie's mother. I'm glad you find me to be lovely and I don't mind your saying so, but what are you doing? What is this all about?"

He sat back, one hand with splayed fingers on the table in front of him, and said, "I'm on two tracks here, Ivy. The first track is my assignment, which is to talk to you about something concerning Ronnie's well-being. The other is I'm a man, I've seen you before, and if I thought I could somehow, you know . . . perhaps spend a little time with you . . . um, outside of other commitments, well . . . I would."

He had her attention on both counts.

They sat staring at each other as the waiter placed their lunch on the table and withdrew.

"I hope you don't think me too obtuse, or rude." Thad broke open a piece of bread and offered her a piece.

"No," responded Ivy, "but you understand that both 'tracks' you are on are unsettling to me."

He waited.

"Ronnie first," she said, ignoring the food on the table. "You apparently already

185

know he is a seriously disabled child, permanent neurological, okay? We, his father and I, have exhausted all medical avenues. We know what to expect, we understand there is nothing we can do to make him . . . better, and we *accept* it, okay? We accept it." She found her napkin balled up in her fist, took a breath, and relaxed her grip on it.

"I guess that's the hardest part," he replied without guile. "The acceptance of what is, and what can't be changed."

She just looked at him, then went on. "So. Ronnie is what Ronnie is. And he is my son, Ronald, and I love him, and I am raising him and caring for him and cleaning him and feeding him and doing all the things I must do to keep him —"

"Do you pray for him, Ivy?"

She stared into his eyes, a flutter of fear falling through her like dead leaves. "I don't pray anymore," she replied quietly.

"Of course," he said. The expression on his face was one of concern.

She tried to regroup. She patted her brow with her napkin, leaned closer to him, and said, "Look, Thad. If I get into a mom mode, if I get wired up talking about Ronnie, my feelings about him, about our . . . situation . . . you can stop thinking

186

about that other 'track' you spoke of. Sure, I'm a mom . . . and a wife too, okay? But I can tell you already know I'm having a little day for myself, a little escape, okay? So if you want to play those kind of games . . . let's play. But we can't do both."

He watched her for a moment, nodded in agreement, and said, "Yes. You are right, of course, but I must say I have hopes we can work on the difficult problem first, then perhaps explore variations on a theme."

"I'm still not sure I understand what you are all about, Thad," said Ivy. "And I'm not sure why I don't just get up and walk away from you right now."

"Perhaps you should," he said. "But then you'd never know about what I can do for Ronnie, or about what we . . . might be."

She emptied her wineglass, surprised the wine was gone already. "So talk to me about Ronnie," she said.

His demeanor changed. He straightened, squared his shoulders, his hands bunched into fists, and his eyes widened, as if he searched inside himself as he spoke. "He can be whole . . . if you wish."

A four-letter word Ivy never used burst out of her mouth. She pushed her chair back with her hips and prepared to stand.

"That's it," she said in a tight voice.

He took her right wrist in his left hand, squeezed, and looked into her eyes. "No, Ivy," he said, his eyes pulling her, "don't run from the possibility. Listen to me. Hear me. Then decide."

She slowly settled into her chair, the waiter approached in query, and Thad motioned him away.

"You know of wondrous advances in medical research, Ivy," he said as his eyes held hers. "Stem-cell, cloning, transplants, artificial skin, electronic assistance devices . . . the list is endless, marvelous, and ongoing. Ronnie was born complete, but something happened during his birth that apparently forever damaged him, right?"

She said nothing.

"You have heard of experiments with the regeneration of cells . . . procedures designed to reattach severed spinal-cord nerves, that type of thing? Good. What if I told you the company I represent, my . . . boss, has the capabilities to join all the triumphs of modern medical research with a previously untapped, or rarely tapped, source, a source of power, of natural energy and potential that can alter the state of a human condition? Are you okay with potential, with possibility?"

"I'm okay with potential," responded Ivy. "I'm *not* okay with medical fraud, new-age foolishness, or hucksters who prey on the desperate and vulnerable."

He smiled, and she liked his smile in spite of the conversation. "I'm smiling because I told my boss how you'd react, told him you were nobody's fool, even if you do love Ronnie and want only that he gets a chance at anything that might make him . . . right." He paused, then went on. "We can, within maybe a week's time, bring Ronnie's physical body back to the stage of a normal six-year-old boy. Certainly the muscles, though he's been in constant therapy, will need time to grow and strengthen, but I'm describing a complete regeneration."

"His mind?" asked Ivy in a hoarse whisper. "His mind, his memory, his . . . personality?"

"All good, all there," replied Thad breezily. "Again, he will need tutoring, lots of help reading and doing shapes and colors and basic numbers and all those things he'd be doing in kindergarten or the first grade." His smile broadened as he squeezed her hand and added, "And you're a *teacher*, Ivy. I think you could handle all of that."

She looked at her hand in his, and the words rocked her soul. Ronnie could be whole, normal, a six-year-old boy running, laughing, hugging his mom, living life. "If something is too good to be true," she said, "it . . ."

He nodded. "Probably is." He let his eyes explore her face for a moment, then said, "Maybe it is too good to be true, Ivy. Maybe I'm full of beans and I've got personal motives, perhaps as base as simply *wanting* you. So? What have you got to lose? What has Ronnie got to lose, except perhaps . . . never knowing?"

"You are one lousy piece of work, Thad Night," she replied, "if you are toying with me."

"This is no game, Ivy," he said.

There was another question she had to ask. She stared into his eyes a moment, collecting herself.

"The cost," said Ivy. "The price. No firm, or company . . . whoever your 'boss' is, no one will perform a miracle with Ronnie or anyone else without being paid for it. What is the price?"

He did not say a word, but held her eyes within his. His pupils darkened, and became deep pools, pulling her gently into their depth. He did not say a word, but held her with his small, knowing smile, and as he did, she learned all she needed to learn about who he was, what he represented. Of course, she heard herself say . . . of course.

"Nonnegotiable," he said.

"Of course," she responded. A terrible battle raged in her heart. You are his mother, intoned a voice, committed to Ronnie's life. He is your son, you bore him, you brought him into this world, you *forced* Ron to make it happen even though he had some kind of premonition or something. Ronnie is your responsibility, Ivy Sloan-Underwood, he is given into your arms, your care. Now you have a chance to make him whole, to give him a shot at a real *life*.

Sure, whispered another voice, act like this is about Ronnie, when we really know it's all about *Ivy*, don't we? What kind of life does Ivy have because of her damaged son? What kind of marriage does Ivy have? What kind of love life, adventure life, professional life? What kind of life does Ivy have? If Ronnie were a normal boy, what kind of life would Ivy have? Without warning, her thoughts shot off on a tangent. She saw Thad standing behind her in the mirror, the charcoal shirt fell away, his hands were on her bare shoulders. His lips formed a knowing smile. Hers was one of hunger. . . . Then his hands moved, and she turned her face toward his.

Ivy came back to the now, her hands gripping the sides of the table, the gentle sounds of the restaurant coming back to her ears. Thad still sat across from her, watching. "When do you need my answer?" asked Ivy in a husky voice, her lips quivering.

"The answer has always been there, Ivy," said Thad. "All of what we have discussed will become so when my boss says, 'Make it so.' " He stood, touched her cheek gently with the fingers of his left hand, and walked out of the restaurant.

Ivy reached for her wineglass, sipped the crisp, cold liquid, and wondered when the waiter had come back to refill it. And why was it now red?

Chapter Six

The small border town of Figuig, Algeria, was a place where dust, poverty, and secrets shared equal space on its crowded streets. So many languages, dialects, and combinations of ancient and modern slang could be heard in the narrow back alleys of the market district, it was as if the bricks from the Tower of Babel had been used for the foundation of the city. It was a place populated by anger and intrigue, its residents possessing as many loyalties and faiths as languages. It was third world, though, with poor roads, capricious water and power supplies, and a tangled communications network. Like most places, panic was the norm on the day of the disappearance.

John Jameson found himself running at full stride through the back alleys of another chaotic and dangerous town. He couldn't believe it. First there had been all this weirdness locally, stories of people "disappearing," rioting in the streets, police and militia shooting into the mobs, and occasionally gunning down members in their own ranks. Trucks and wagons were overturned at intersections, their contents looted, drivers beaten or killed if they interfered, then the vehicles set ablaze. That was bad enough, but now his watch-sensor had been activated, alerting him to an immediate extraction.

After over two years of patient work, putting agents in place, reading reports, melding intelligence tidbits gathered here and there, Jameson's team was very close to infiltrating a seriously nasty terrorist group that danced between Libya and Algeria, with both governments acting as if it didn't exist. With the destruction of the *Mercy Ark*, fingers had been pointed in their direction, but no direct links could be established. All those hours, all that work, two informants dead — one skinned alive, the other simply hanged — to come down to this morning, and an emergency signal that would blow the whole thing away. Like hyenas, terrorists kept their noses to the wind, constantly on the alert for even the faintest hint of danger. The arrival of helicopters, even if unmarked, over Figuig, armed men running through the alleys amid the chaos, would cause these hyenas to run for cover without taking even one second to ask who, what, or why. Any meeting with their local leader — Jameson was to act as a weapons broker from Belgium — would simply not take place.

Jameson gritted his teeth as he jumped over the bodies of two young women sprawled in the dirt. The weapons he would have supplied in his role as arms rep had micro signaling devices buried in them, and could be tracked by satellite wherever they were taken. All that work, all that money. A huddle of dirty and bloody people turned and looked at him as he sprinted the last few yards toward Lift Point Alpha. One of the group pointed an assault rifle at Jameson, thinking perhaps that the big foreigner was coming to take what they struggled over. Jameson saw the barrel of the weapon aimed at him, saw the panic in the man's eyes, and fired his automatic pistol twice, his slugs impacting the man's lower legs, twisting him down into the dust, the assault rifle flung aside. As Jameson ran past them he saw they fought over two or three loaves of bread and some canned goods. He turned his back on the hurricane of dust as the chopper floated two feet above a large brick wall that surrounded a mosque, then jumped into the cabin through the open side door, hitting the deck hard and grabbing for a handhold as the helicopter lifted and banked sharply in its ascent. Jameson sat up, returned the door gunner's "Okay?" hand signal, and looked below at the outskirts of the tormented town. Where are all the kids? he wondered.

He put the offered headset on, snugged the cups over his ears, and heard the chopper pilot say, "Sir?"

"Go ahead."

"We are out of Algeria, inbound Morocco . . . Marrakesh. It's a Zulu-Zulu, copy?"

"Copy."

"Sir, do you have global capabilities on your person?" asked the pilot. He hoped Jameson had either a radio or a cell phone.

"Roger, son. We didn't build it, but it works most of the time," responded Jameson. He never entered a hostile environment with any equipment that would link him with the home team. "My wife want me to check in?" He meant it as a joke, but he saw the pilot's eyes as the young man turned toward him, and knew he wasn't laughing.

"It's a Zulu-Zulu, sir," said the young man, his voice quavering through the headphones. Jameson couldn't tell if it was fright or the vibration of the chopper. The pilot added, "But, sir, it's a Zulu-Zulu like nothin' you've ever *seen*. It's worldwide, and it is totally weird. You are to contact your Delta Six."

"Roger dodger, over and out wilco." Jameson hoped his over-the-top response would make the guy relax. It didn't work, and it didn't make him feel any better either.

"Sorry, sir," Jameson heard through his cell phone earpiece five minutes later, "still no response at your home number."

Jameson pulled the helicopter intercom headset off his ears and pressed his fingers against the left side of his head, trying to hear better. They were still a long way out of Marrakesh, where he would meet a team jet, and he was trying to come to terms with what the operations boss at his headquarters comm center told him. Thousands, maybe millions *missing?* Gone, like . . . disappeared. A cold lump of leaden disquiet lay in the pit of his stomach. All the children, the voice had intoned, no rhyme or reason to any of it, but for sure the children. All the children around the world? Gone? Who says what is a child? How old until you're not a child? Voices crashed inside his head, thirsting for answer and explanation. He realized he was very afraid.

"Okay, wait one," Jameson radioed. He forced himself to concentrate for a moment, then told the comm guy, "Go to casual, number five local." The operator referenced Jameson's callout info. He heard the comm operator acknowledge that the transmission was not agency cleared, and in a moment heard a frantic voice. In his earpiece it sounded tinny and faraway. It was.

"Hello? Hello . . . yes?" squawked Conner Eagan, Jameson's golfing friend in town.

"Conner? Conner, can you hear me?" spoke Jameson into the small transmitter; he knew Eagan was on his cell phone. "Conner, it's me, John Jameson."

"John?" answered Eagan. "*John?* Is that you? I can't believe it. Where are you, do you know what's going on, is it Iraq, is it . . . *What is going on?* You should see what's happening here, man, it is *crazy*. . . . Everything is screwed up, people are missing, people are crying and stuff . . . man . . . it is bad."

"Conner."

"Some cop shot a guy who drove his car into the Piggly Wiggly over on Ridge Road, then the crowd, there was like this mob, they beat up the cop and the store manager, and . . . man . . . there are cars parked everywhere, people standing in the street crying and stuff. . . . I guess the governor or somebody called out the National Guard, but a lot of 'em wouldn't show up, but the ones that did are guarding the banks and stuff and it's a real —"

"Conner."

"I'm sorry, John," said Eagan, and Jameson thought he heard the man sob. "I'm just freaked out and —"

"My family, Conner," said Jameson. "I can't get through to them. I need you to check on them."

"Oh, man, I was just going to your house because I thought you might know what was going on, I mean, I knew you were out of town and all but I . . . hold on, I'm on your street."

Jameson listened to the hiss of static in the earphone. The chopper beat its way through the hot sky. The pilot said something to his copilot. The door gunner fingered a crucifix.

"John? John . . . I'm at your house, I'm *in* your house. . . . The neighbor lady was already here, the front door is open and she's inside. Hold on." Fifteen seconds, fifteen years, of cold, empty static hiss. "John . . . uh . . . I don't know, man . . . uh . . . wait. . . . I'm on the phone with him *now*. . . . Yes

. . . John? Uh . . . it looks like they're gone
. . . uh, Sylvia . . . Sylvia and the kids . . .
wait . . . yeah, okay. John, they're gone disappeared like the others. The neighbor
lady says Sylvia's Bible is open on the bed.
Looks like maybe she and the kids were all
together. . . . What . . . yeah . . . they were
all in the same bed, uh, your upstairs bedroom, John, but they are gone now. The
neighbor lady says her kids too, and her father who lived with 'em. Hey, John . . . all
my ex-wives, everybody in my crowd made
it. . . . I mean, I didn't lose anybody . . . uh,
so far, uh, that I know of —"

"Conner," said Jameson, his voice tight
and cold, "tell the neighbor I've been ad-
vised. Lock the door, and leave it. Leave
the house. I'll contact you in a day or so,
okay?"

"Yeah, John, we'll lock it up and all.
What is this, John? Is it the end of the
world or somethin'? John? John?"

Jameson listened to the static hiss, which
seemed comforting now. Then it was re-
placed with a droning roar in his ears, his
head felt cottony, and he became very
alone within the confines of the helicopter
cabin. No, he thought. No. Not them, not
my Sylvia, not my Sonia, my Johnny. Sonia
is not a child anyway, she's a new teenager.

200

. . . All children . . . okay, Sonia is not a child. No. No. Not them. Not them.

He stared out of the cabin at the flat blue forever sky. Not them, he thought. Sylvia was smart enough to get out there when any trouble started. They'd discussed it. Then had a plan. But he knew. He knew with a clear certainty, and suspected he already understood the how, and the why Sylvia had talked about it. Had told him to be prepared. But how could he have believed her? A man who lived his life on the line only on the basis of the most sophisticated and comprehensive communications and intelligence-gathering capabilities couldn't believe in intuition and interpretation. It made no sense. Until now. With this evidence, he could begin to understand, but he couldn't accept.

Sylvia had told him. His kids had believed her. Still he stared out, and thought. Not them.

So there came to pass — in a linear world measured in the ticking of a clock — a moment out of time, a window of seconds or minutes measured by the roll of the earth as it spun around the sun, that suddenly could not be measured. The universe seemed to hold its breath; all motion ceased while the earth lay cupped in the hands of an all-encompassing power. It was as if during the sparrow's fall an unseen wind momentarily held it suspended above the leaves, then let it go. As the tiny wings collapsed into the loam, one or two feathers that hung improbably above went on with their descent, leaving no trail, no sound, no impression.

In the absence of any other markers, the people of time and space living on earth during that expanded or compressed window of heartbeats were certain in the knowledge that *something* had happened, but exactly what it was they could not describe or recognize. Somewhere beyond the blink of an eye, perhaps, less than a whispered sigh, the absolutes of past and future were stilled, and for a moment there *were* no moments.

John Jameson, crouched in the shadows of a mosque somewhere in Algeria, and Shannon Carpenter in Ohio, sensed it, knew it, thought for an ethereal moment that a choir of a million souls had joyfully cried out, then were lost in silence. Henderson Smith, in Alabama, heard his wife whisper, "Oh," and then he lay in the darkness of his bedroom, listening for the children. Cat Early dozed in the shadow of an overturned truck a few kilometers from Islamabad, and woke with a start, while Thomas Church, in New York, thought he heard someone call his name, but was mistaken. Ivy Sloan-Underwood sat in a window seat in her son Ronnie's bedroom, staring out at the branches of an old tree that reached awkwardly into the evening sky.

Ivy let the shadows come into the room unhindered by any lights while Ronnie slept peacefully in his wheelchair a few feet away. Ivy had the impression that there was a momentary wrinkle in the sky, and the branches of the reaching tree flexed, then relaxed. Behind her in the soft gloom of the darkened room Ivy heard her son say, "Mommy?" but she was afraid to turn her face to his, afraid once again to be disappointed.

The moment passed.

It was absolute, and terrifying, at once random and comprehensive, immediate, and in its aftermath, unimpeachable. Yet there seemed to be a certain gentleness about it, the act resolute and certain, not arbitrary or cruel. Of course chaos and panic ensued, a visceral and collective reaction, the limits of man's understanding diminished even further by shock. But for those able to put their emotions in check, those discerning enough to observe the event in global terms, the faint outlines of intent began to pattern the hard capriciousness of it like fine lace. Those discerning enough were few. A reason existed, but it was obscured by a real and primal fear.

Around the earth, in countries large and small, in the ice, the desert sands, the oceans, tangled jungles, ancient villages, huge grids of steel, glass, and concrete that form the sprawling cities, people were taken. They were, and then they weren't, and for those around them who witnessed it, minds railed at the impossibility of what had just occurred. For each individual soul taken, each of the millions worldwide, there seemed to be an epiphany, a sudden movement toward repose. Those sleeping changed not. They were, and then they weren't. Those going through their living day or night turned their face, slipped to the ground, relaxed, and were gone. Those in movement stopped. People affected who were passengers in any vehicle became quiet, relaxed, and were no more. Millions left this world, this earth, with sudden and swift certainty, leaving millions of souls in turmoil, despair, and confusion.

"Wake the president," said the chief of staff.

"Sir?" responded the Secret Service agent in charge of White House security. "Uh, just so you are aware, sir, before the president and first lady retired for the evening he sort of jokingly told me in no uncertain terms to, uh, not disturb him unless we reached national security threat level five." The agent cleared his throat and went on. "Something about not having slept good for over two weeks, sir —"

"Stop." The chief of staff shut his eyes for a moment. "I don't even know how to categorize this threat level, do you understand? Just wake him, for Pete's sake."

Less than one minute later the agent called the chief of staff. "Sir," he said breathlessly, "the president and his wife are gone. I mean, they did not leave the building through any of the level-one or covert exits, there was absolutely no disturbance reported by the security teams, but they are both gone."

"This can't be." The chief of staff, already aware of the reports billowing in from all over the world, felt his heartrate quicken and his throat constrict. "This can't be."

"We went in," continued the agent, "and you could see they had been there. We conducted a quick search, and the teams are initiating Containment Alpha, but we can't find —" The agent fumbled with his earpiece. "What? Uh, hold on a minute, sir. Uh, sir . . . several of my teams are reporting agents missing also. . . . What the heck is going on? Sir? Sir?"

The chief of staff said again, "Stop." When he heard the agent breathing into the phone, he said, "Kick it up to full alert. Initiate Zulu-Zulu. Get a head count going, find out who you've got with their feet on the ground, get 'em armed and on duty. Do it now."

"Yes, sir."

On the northern outskirts of Jacksonville, Florida, under a bridge that crossed the Turtle River, the grass grew thick in the mud at the water's edge. It thinned slightly as it carpeted the embankment up to the road, and gave way completely to the packed dirt directly under the bridge overhang on the south side. It was comfortable under there, though, with enough breeze to keep the bugs out, and sheets of cardboard down in layers providing a bit of cushion from the hard ground. The small fire fueled by broken pieces of wooden packing crates and sections of discarded furniture created a dancing yellow glow, and the transient community that bedded down within it felt snug and secure. The hard camaraderie of the homeless and hopeless took the edge off of lonely, and the people under the bridge talked, argued, sang, and dreamed the night away.

One of them, Hubcap Conner, held the wine bottle for his friend, Quiet Stan. They had known each other for several years, had met in a jail somewhere in southern Georgia and formed an informal bond as they traveled through the South panhandling, working day labor, or doing what they could to get by. Quiet Stan was a Vietnam vet — that's all Hubcap knew about him. They were both old men, shaggy, rugged.

Hubcap held the wine bottle out, and said in his gravelly voice, "C'mon, Stan. My left arm's gettin' tired here. Shoot, man, I know you don't drink the wine like the rest of us — hah, more for me — but you'll take a sip for sport, won't ya?" Hubcap leaned forward toward Stan's bedroll. "Stan? Stan?" He looked around at the others. "Anybody see where Stan went?"

"Maybe he went to see a man about a horse, Hubcap. Shut up and pass the grape, you old fool."

"Hey, guys. Sally's gone too. She was layin' right over here a minute ago. . . . Hey, her stuff's still here. Look, she left that old picture of her kids that drowned back when she was a wife an' all."

"Maybe Sally and Quiet Stan snuck out while we was tellin' lies, and they is playin' hiding out over in the bushes."

"Oh, man, that's not it. Look. They were here, and now they are *not* here."

Hubcap Conner took a long pull on the bottle of wine, wiped his nose, and began to cry.

Less than a mile away, an Amtrak train headed northbound crossed the Turtle River trestle and began to lose speed. This section of track was long and straight, with the next major stop scheduled in Savannah. Normally the trains kept a good pace through the area, up to speed before they left the limits of Jacksonville, two or three locomotives powered up and holding. The interior of the drive locomotive basked in a red glow from the instruments, and rocked gently with the motion of steel on steel.

The assistant engineer, a young man

with big hands, big ears, and a big appetite, glanced at the gauges and looked out the side window at the world going by. He felt it first, then quickly looked to the power settings to confirm his assessment. The engineer, on the other side of the cabin, had begun to slow the train. He hadn't said anything to the assistant engineer, and there had been no mechanical warning, track warning, or radio instruction. Something was wrong. The assistant looked forward down the track, saw no sign of trouble, and scanned everything in the cabin again.

"You okay, boss?" he yelled to the engineer, who seemed to have slumped against the cabin wall. "Boss?" he said. "Boss?" The Amtrak train came safely to a stop, and the engineer was gone, along with more than thirty of the eighty-three souls on board.

"Nathan," said Captain Fowler, master of the large container ship *Sinclair Victory*.

"Sir?" responded the first mate.

"Ship is safe and secure, and you have the outer channel buoy for the Liverpool Turn, Nathan?"

"Aye, sir," answered Nathan, glancing at the Bible the captain had carried with him through the night and into the morning. "An' the lads will be happy to see those docks, I'm guessing."

"Good, Nathan. I'm off the bridge, then. You have her."

"Sir?" replied the first mate with some alarm. It would be a rare thing for a captain to be off the bridge when his ship came into port. Especially this one. "We won't have much of a channel run before we're ready to —"

"You have her, Nathan," said the captain gently. "Good luck, and God bless." He turned, opened the door to his sea cabin, and went inside.

The first mate called his section heads — they were already at their stations in anticipation of the call — and brought the ship to full-duty crew. Two chiefs called within a minute, both advising that they had men missing; and then one of the chiefs didn't answer his radio.

The first mate told the helmsman, "Steady on, you know the drill," chewed his lip for a moment, and said, "No way." He knocked on the captain's sea-cabin door, waited, knocked again, then pushed it open. The captain was gone, his Bible lying on the deck beside his bunk with the pages spilled open. "Captain?" the first mate asked the emptiness. "Captain Fowler?"

During that wondrous and terrifying moment of time later called "the disappearance" by almost all the peoples of the earth, many automobiles, trucks, and other vehicles traveled on highways and city streets, back roads and country roads, dirt roads, tunnels, bridges, and pathways too numerous to count. On each and every one, no matter if it was a tanker truck at maximum speed on the autobahn in Germany, a battered pickup on a washboard gravel road in Arizona, a sleek Porsche challenging the winding roads through the Alps, a train of grocery trucks passing a dusty settlement in the Australian outback, taxicabs, police cars, limousines, family Volvos, or the ubiquitous Hondas and Toyotas scattered throughout every nook and cranny of the planet, it happened in a strangely controlled way.

The drivers of the vehicles, men and women, young and old, professional or private, seemed to relax; a sense of calm surrounded them and then they were simply gone. Accidents occurred, most caused by other drivers not ready for the vehicle in front of them to slow or stop. Fatalities occurred worldwide, but certainly no more than during any other twenty-four-hour period.

Many instances of minor accidents, road rage, gridlock, and frustration occurred everywhere at once because of the sheer number of vehicles on the world's roadways at any given time. Thousands upon thousands of cars and trucks suddenly stopped on highways, in the middle of intersections, on the side streets, and in tunnels and parking lots all over, and those vehicles still under the control of a driver often had no place to go in the snarl.

In Manila Bay, a large ferry jammed with passengers, their goods, and some livestock began circling, out of control, until several of the deck crew looked in the wheelhouse to find the captain and the mate — both of whom knew how to operate the vessel — gone. Three fishing vessels were run down and sunk by the huge ferry as two or three crew members and passengers fought over control of the helm, and it finally came to rest after running aground on a muddy beach on the west side of the island.

A Liberian tanker with a Dutch crew swung sideways in the Panama Canal, driving its huge flared bow against one side of the canal while the stern swung wildly until the big props dug into the bottom on the other. Two other ships narrowly missed colliding during the turmoil.

An observer seeking evidence of a controlling force during the disappearance might have found the most compelling clue in how the many hundreds of aircraft in the skies above the earth at that moment were affected. Crashes and deaths resulted, but they were relatively few.

Fatalities in airplanes occurred in France, at the Charles de Gaulle Airport, and in Buenos Aires. In both instances the ground controllers disappeared, which caused aircraft to collide on the taxiways or runway thresholds. For the many passenger airliners above the earth at that moment, a curious pattern formed. If the entire crew was gone — which happened on only two aircraft — the plane made a slight deviation from course, proceeded to the nearest airport with long enough runways, and landed safely. The disappearance of the crew was determined only after the plane sat without moving, engines spooling down, at the end of the runway, and attendants, passengers and cabin finally were frightened, curious, and determined enough to break into the cockpit to find the empty seats.

In all the other planes in the skies during the disappearance, there remained at least one crew member capable of piloting the aircraft to a safe landing at a major airport. In one instance an inexperienced copilot "landed long," and the huge plane skidded off the end of the runway and across a perimeter road, and came to a stop in a grassy area adjoining a highway. There were some injuries, none serious. In another, the pilot suffered a heart attack after his flight engineer and copilot were both taken while he dozed, but he managed a hard landing with the assistance of the chief flight attendant on board. The aircraft was damaged, several passengers were injured, and the pilot died a few hours later in ICU.

There were many instances during that wrinkle in time when aircraft came to unscheduled, but safe, landings at airports they were not originally routed to. When some or all of the passengers and/or crew members disappeared, within a few minutes the aircraft was parked without further incident *wherever* it landed; the most commonly used phrase to describe what occurred was "the plane seemed to be guided by an unseen hand" or "unseen force."

These indicators of *order* went for the

most part unnoticed during the first hours and days after the happening. First came fear, then panic, then chaos. The *scope* of the thing shocked most people. To find your wife, who a moment ago was lying in bed beside you, suddenly and inexplicably gone, disappeared, taken, consumed, destroyed, vaporized, was terrifying. To run outside in turmoil and dismay, blindly seeking help, only to discover your neighbors out there, wailing and crying and screaming that *their* loved ones were gone too, was mind-numbing and crazy.

To turn on the radio or TV to hear and see the first confused, then confirming reports of similar occurrences all around the world was cause for panic — immobilizing, primal, spit-stealing, nerve-jangling instant nightmares that transcended any horror story ever known — and raw, visceral fear. Whatever it was, it was *bad.* And after the initial reaction, many people all over the world spasmodically activated their traditional emergency plans — get all the cash out of the bank, *now.* Where banks were open, this meant storming the teller windows even as the managers — if any were working — tried desperately to calm the rush or simply lock the doors. Locked doors were smashed apart, in more than one case with a vehicle; bank employees were beaten, many killed outright if they didn't move fast enough.

Where it was night, the ATM machines came under assault. Riots ignited around them, people were killed and brutalized if they stood a moment too long trying to remember their PINs, and hundreds of ATMs were simply ripped out of the walls with trucks and chains and set upon by mobs feral and insane.

The other parts of traditional emergency plans revolved around weapons and food. Those with guns foraged through their closets seeking ammunition. Survivalists who had stockpiled weapons, food, and ammo for years came under attack. Not by rogue federal agents, Commie hordes, or cunning terrorists, as had been hypothesized, but by their neighbors who knew of the stash. Shoot-outs erupted in thousands of places around the globe, and the orderly and law-abiding residential areas of the United States were the scenes of many acts of violence, with trickling streams of blood merging into sad coppery rivers within a few hours. The desire to gather food in the emergency manifested itself in basic riot form.

Grocery stores in every country were set

upon, forced open, and looted, again with loss of life as people fought over a few cans of beans. Pillagers were disemboweled amid scattered piles of rice, bludgeoned while struggling for torn loaves of bread, or shot and killed while loaded down with baby formula. Blind mob mentality created convulsing beasts of people who, stripped of reason, decency, morality, and respect for the law and their brother by the fear storming through their heads, violated every law of common decency and human rights with many acts of horrifying ferocity. The diverse populations of our world writhed and convulsed in a primitive orgy of lawlessness.

News organizations, their ranks reduced by the disappearance, jumped on the biggest story in the history of man. A few managed to report the facts, but most, staying with a format that had worked for years, began describing the more gruesome and sensational pieces — an embarrassment of riches — and let their "news personalities" initiate speculation. No one really knew what had taken place, but that didn't stop most news stations from trotting out talking-head experts who spoke in fervent and learned tones about what was actually occurring. Some stated with bulging eyes and sweaty brows that those taken during the disappearance had been seized by aliens. Somewhere just beyond our array of satellites and the space station, giant alien warcraft drifted silently through the freezing nothingness of outer space, gasped these experts. The aliens orbiting our rich and fertile planet were either destroying us in numbers with some type of weapon as yet not invented by man — a "particle beam molecule deconstructor" had a nice ring to it, and was bandied about on several channels — or in some sinister way lifting us bodily from the earth. Those thus taken were brought aboard the alien craft to be added to their army of slaves, or to be experimented on or eaten.

Other pundits stated with confidence that a secret military weapon had been used for the first time. Only "industrial-medical-military" organizations, covertly backed by their governments, would have the minds and resources capable of creating such a weapon. Within a few hours, however, when the people of the world learned that there were victims of the disappearance *everywhere*, this argument seemed harder to sell.

People and governments immediately

turned to their lists of the usual suspects. If it was the Russians, ad hoc panelists asked one another, why had they taken so many of their own? China? Well, perhaps the Chinese were capable of destroying thousands of their own citizens because they had so many, or to get rid of dissidents, or something. Muslims, then. Maybe the Muslims had acquired a weapon of mass destruction no one could have imagined, and were out to destroy any culture that they considered infidel.

This possibility seemed so plausible, and identified such a clear and accessible enemy, that it caused shock waves to course out from government and media centers. Muslims worldwide were attacked, countries declared war, fuel stores everywhere became coveted, and the remaining world hovered on the brink of theological self-destruction. India, already engaged in battle with Pakistan over Kashmir, actually launched a nuclear missile toward Islamabad. Their weapons technology lagged behind their aggression, however, and the atomic blast that resulted was a "low-order" detonation that ravaged several miles of largely unpopulated desert. The people of the world had their finger on the trigger, and in every latitude and longitude of the globe man stood poised to kill his fellow man.

Pacifist speculators, members of the academia for the most part, suggested we stop looking for enemies to kill, and study the disappearance as if it were the ignition of some type of unknown virus. Spontaneous human combustion was cited as an example of a "natural chemical-biological occurrence" that could make a body disappear. It was a clumsy example, granted, and most with this opinion quickly moved on to theories about superaggressive, rapidly multiplying megaviruses that had been actuated by some confluence of forces or powers within the earth . . . triggered by UV rays from the sun, perhaps. Here and there a voice rose momentarily above the cacophony to suggest that what had occurred was actually a Biblical event.

Those who tried to connect the worldwide loss of human life, and the swelling sea of grief that came with it, to religion were largely shouted down or ignored . . . at first. Rabid "fringe" representatives of any group always make for more colorful and contentious interviews than the mainstream, and this holds true for religion also. Many television "news " shows had as guest commentators people who stared into the camera shouting disjointed dogma and interpretation of various scriptures, warning of the end of the world, and usually adding that the only way those remaining could be "saved" was to believe what *they* would teach.

A minority of the more shrill voices smirked and said that everyone still on the earth was going to hell, Satan had won, and, again, only *they* had the ear of the devil himself, and might intercede for anyone who groveled before them. Here and there educated, confident, calming voices implored people to return to their family Bible. In that family Bible, they stated, were words that would comfort and explain. Study it, they suggested, reflect, listen to your heart, and perhaps all was not lost. This was *not*, said the few men and women with this message, not the time to lose faith, to give up on faith, to revert to a primitive, finite being trapped in flesh. On televised news panels where others participated, these voices were usually shouted down before they could finish a complete sentence. The most common rebuttal: You are still talking about *God*, you fool? How could any God let this happen to us?

★ ★ ★

"It is, in fact, dust," said famed forensic pathologist-anthropologist Dr. Myron Bern. His head was still spinning from the events that had ripped him at breakneck speed from his office in Quantico, Virginia, to this large bedroom in the White House. He, like most people, had been reeling as he tried to make sense of what had happened to the world over the last twelve hours, and then a Secret Service team had literally grabbed him and rushed him into the president's bedroom.

"Dust," repeated the vice president, a small-boned black woman named Clara Reese.

"Dust like the president's bedroom needs to be cleaned," asked the chief of staff with an edge to his voice, "or dust like evidence, or as a result of —"

"Both," replied Dr. Myron Bern, who did not like the chief of staff's impatient tone.

"Please, Dr. Bern," said Vice President Reese soothingly. "We are frightened, this is obviously a matter of global import and national security, and we are searching for answers. The president and his wife have been taken, as have so many, and we must decide very quickly if we as a nation are under some type of attack or terrorist action. My chief of staff does not mean to appear rude, we are simply —"

"I understand," responded Dr. Bern, who like everyone else in the room had clearly heard the "My," and who happened to feel that the country was in good hands at that moment. "Let me explain what I mean." He leaned across the bed again, gently moving the sheets with his gloved hands. He managed to collect a small sample of the sandy residue, and examined it with some type of magnifying device. He took his gloves off and rubbed some of the material between his fingers, then held those fingers under his nose for a moment, breathing in their scent. "As I'm sure you know, Madam Vice President, I am one of the world's most experienced and knowledgeable pathologists. Because forensics is my specialty, I spend most of my time conducting postmortem exams of crime victims, seeking cause of death or clues to the killer — especially of those in the advanced state of decomposition. In addition, I am occasionally asked to examine remains found in ancient digs, burial mounds, or the like."

"I remember you were one of the team that attempted to solve the murder of King

Tut, isn't that right, Dr. Bern?" asked the vice president.

"Indeed," Bern responded, pleased to be recognized. "The reason I'm predicating my initial and informal opinion on *this* situation with a little of my voluminous résumé is to help validate it."

"And what is your opinion, Dr. Bern?" asked the chief of staff, which earned him a glare from the vice president.

"This dust," answered the doctor, pointedly speaking only to Clara Reese, "is the dust that one finds after the almost total decomposition of the human body. 'Ashes to ashes, dust to dust' ring a bell? In my experience, this dust is identical to that which might be found in an ancient tomb. I must qualify my findings, of course. To be more convinced I must take these samples back to my office and lab, where I can —"

"Of course, Dr. Bern," said the vice president. "We know we're forcing you to give us a quick opinion, but we value it."

"Once the life force leaves the human body, marvelous temple of flesh that it is," continued Dr. Bern, "the skin, bone, muscle, and fluids begin to break down almost immediately. Through the many years of investigation and records keeping, we have learned with what rapidity this occurs, given modifiers such as clothing, moisture content, temperature, environmental factors. We can examine a body *in situ,* or in a facility, and make a fairly accurate determination of how long the body has been there." He waved one hand in front of his face, as if impatient with his own discourse. "What I'm saying is this: This dust is what remains after the almost total — and natural — decomposition of a human body occurs. If a body lost its life force while lying on this bed last night, and that is what you have told me, then this, to me, this dust is a sign that the body decomposed naturally." He held up both hands, palms out, to ward off the coming protests, and continued. "The body decomposed naturally, but the process was somehow *very rapidly accelerated.*" He enjoyed their faces as they distilled and wrestled with what he had said; then he added as an aside, "I have heard serious discussions regarding this phenomenon as applied to the body of Jesus Christ after He was laid out in His tomb, and what was found three days later —"

"So you're saying this is a *natural* apparatus," said the vice president. "Is it possible for someone, a person, to use a machine, or an energy, to kill and then *cause* this unnatural acceleration?"

"Like some kind of twisted laser-beam apparatus, or something like that?" asked the chief of staff excitedly. "Like the Russians or Muslims or some group has this thing, and they aim it at our president, and then his body just breaks down to dust just like it would anyway but way faster and all there is left is this dust?"

But Dr. Myron Bern was finished answering questions for the leaders of the free world, or anyone else. He nodded distractedly, his eyes turned inward, and he became very solemn and quiet.

Chapter Seven

Shannon Carpenter knew the very moment she woke from a troubled sleep. The quiet unsettled her. The house was filled with a surreal silence, a palpable emptiness, and she lay on her back, listening to the strong, rhythmic thumping of her heart, somehow aware that she was the only living soul there. *It is irrational,* she told herself, *you don't know, it's your stupid imagination.* But she lay paralyzed by doubt and the absolute fear that if she moved she would find out she was *right.* A few inches from her left shoulder was her husband, Billy. That's where he slept, his part of the bed, on the door side of the room. He was a few inches away, and all she had to do was turn her head, and he'd be right there, grinning at her. She turned her head. The bedcovers were there, the pillow with the soft crater in the center where his head would rest. She moved her left arm so her hand, fingers splayed, slid across the cool sheets. She felt a fine grit, like beach sand. That was all.

With one motion she threw off the bedcovers, twisted, stood up from bed.

"Billy?" she called to the empty house. She hurried down the hall, into Matt's room. She knew her youngest would be sprawled almost sideways across his "big-boy" bed, no crib, but still with side rails. His blankets would be jammed against the footboard, and he would have one arm flung across either Barney, Woody, or Mickey Mouse. His hair would be tousled, his face the face of an angel in repose. He was not there, and she said in a throaty whisper, "Oh, Matt . . . did you climb out of bed again and wander into your brother's room?" She almost ran across the hall to the room of her oldest son, Billy. Matt was not curled on the floor beside his brother's bed, and Billy was gone too.

"No," said Shannon as she stumbled in her hurry toward Laura's room. Her daughter was only six, but her husband had built three extra bedrooms into the house, somehow knowing that one of his children would be a girl, and a girl ought to have her own room. Laura's room, a study in pink and purple, with a myriad of stuffed toys and dolls, posters, shoes, and toys, had everything in it but a child. Only the stuffed toys stared at Shannon as she ran to the bed and pulled back the covers. "Laura," she said. "Laura?" She flattened her hand, palm down, and leaned forward to feel the sheets, then hesitated. She bit her lip, sobbed, and quickly ran her fingers across the fabric. More beach sand. "No," she said angrily. "No sir . . . no sir . . ."

She ran then from room to room until she checked everyplace upstairs. Each empty room she checked, including the bathrooms and closets, she said, "No." She glanced at her husband's work boots in passing, her daughter's blouse she had ironed the night before, both boys' scuffed and battered sneakers, and knew. She slid and almost fell in her haste to get downstairs, then did the same thing in each room on the ground floor. Everything was neat and orderly, the way Billy liked it; everything was in place and ready for a busy family to wake up, get dressed, come downstairs for a good healthy breakfast, and make their way off to work, school, and day care after being kissed on the cheek by their wife and mom. Perfect. Orderly. Empty. The house felt cold, and each room seemed emptier than the next — a cumulative emptiness — cold, and mocking her.

She opened the door from the kitchen to the garage. She looked at her small SUV and Billy's dusty pickup truck. Their headlights looked back, their grilles grim and silent. She slammed the door. She stood for a moment in the kitchen, her stomach tumbled, and she gagged.

Wait, she thought. They're not gone, I mean, they're not here but there is an explanation. . . . So you have this "feeling." . . . So get over it, settle down, think, try to figure out why Billy would get up and take the kids with him without telling you. She put her fists against the side of her head and pressed hard against her skull. Sure, you idiot . . . Billy took the kids but none of them wore shoes, and he left without driving his truck, which he takes everywhere. *"No!"* she yelled at the empty house. She ran to the front door, struggled with the dead bolt that Billy insisted they always lock, and flung it open. The paper was not on the lawn. That was odd, but even worse, several of her neighbors were outside, one or two huddled together, others alone, looking this way and that. She heard someone sobbing, another calling out, "Marge? *Marge!* Enough of this nonsense. Get in here and fix my oatmeal or I'll be late." She slammed the door.

Less than one hour later Shannon Carpenter was in her car, headed for the office. She had showered. She was sure she'd step out of the shower and her family would be in the throes of a typical morning's histrionics. She'd watched the shrill and disjointed news coverage of the unbelievable global event on the TV, and had made several phone calls. Billy's cell phone rang as it lay on the dresser with his wallet and truck keys when she dialed his number. There was no answer at her mom's, or Billy's, no answer at the law office, and the rest of her calls were met with the strident busy signal. She stopped only long enough to vomit into the bathroom toilet, then rinsed out her mouth in the sink, grabbed her car keys, and headed out.

She drove through what appeared to be the filming of one of those disaster movies . . . like the ones about the aftermath of a nuclear war. She saw several auto accidents, many people simply wandering the sidewalks, ambulances wailing up and down the roads, helicopters circling in the skies above the schools and malls. She passed what looked like a riot in front of her bank, saw a large woman sprawled in the parking lot, her blue dress pushed up around her waist, pale skin blotched with blood and bruises. Mosaics of broken glass and twisted metal sat in the intersections, and when she stopped for a red light once, a man with wild eyes threw himself across her windshield. He was screaming something at her, and his spit left a messy trail as he careened off when she jammed her foot onto the gas pedal and sped away. She had to swerve around a police squad car sitting at one intersection, its engine running. The officer was not behind the wheel, and on the ragged edge of panic and hysteria, she giggled, "Just look for the little pile of sand on the seat, Chief."

She finally pulled into the small lot in front of the law office, parked, and hurried inside. Behind the curved polished-wood reception desk sat Gail, the young, leggy, surgically enhanced, pretty girl well on her way to targeting a successful lawyer for the purposes of securing a big ring, fine car, plush home, country club membership, and marriage if necessary. When Shannon hurried in, Gail gave her a thousand-watt smile with lips that looked as if lipstick had been applied while she drove down the railroad tracks. "Good *morning,* Mrs. Carpenter," she said brightly. "And it *is* a good morning, right? I mean, it's a *normal* morning here at our law office, right, Mrs. Carpenter? I mean, the attorneys are here. I'm here. You're here. And I'm going to lunch today with Doug. . . . Mr. *Mann* is what I meant. Right? Right . . . Mrs. Carpenter?" She stopped at the sound of a punchy, muted bang, which came from a large office down the hall. "Gee . . . that sounded weird, didn't it, Mrs. Carpenter?" asked Gail, but Shannon had already turned away.

She found her boss, the successful attorney Doug Mann, sitting in his large leather chair behind his impressive redwood desk. Mann looked uncomfortable with his head thrown back, chin stuck up, bloody mouth wide open in a silent scream. His right hand lay against his chest, the crimson fingers grasping a tiny automatic pistol. The back of Mann's skull was misshapen and wet, the silk wallpaper behind him spattered with fat drops of something, and in the quiet she heard a steady dripping. The room had a sickly coppery smell, mixed with firecracker. Shannon did not sense Gail behind her until the young woman said with a knowing sarcasm, "Well so much for our lunch date." Shannon turned and brushed past her, did not look in any of the other offices, hurried to her car, and left.

She drove straight to Billy's church, Cuyahoga Christian, over off Lakewind

Road. Cars were in the lot; small clusters of people huddled near the open front doors. Shannon parked, got out, hesitated, then walked toward the church. As she approached, people turned and looked at her, some nodding in recognition. Many of them were crying or had been, even the men. "We knew Bill would be gone," said one man, tall and sallow, with a wrinkled white shirt buttoned at his throat. His large Adam's apple struggled against it as he spoke. "And the children, of course." He paused. "We, uh, didn't know about you."

"But you're here, and welcome," said a small woman hanging on the man's arm. "You can be with us now."

Shannon did not know how to respond, so she simply nodded and walked past them to the doors. She hesitated again, then stepped across the threshold. The first thing she noticed was the light inside the building. It was soft, with a golden shade, and seemed to hug her as she entered. The next thing was the sound of sobbing. She looked up the aisle to the front, past the first smooth wooden pews, and saw a woman in a housecoat collapsed against the pulpit. Her arms reached toward the top of the lectern, her knuckles white as she grasped the edge.

"Lord," she wailed, "my sweet Lord, my only true and sweet Lord, you forgot me. You forgot one of your faithful children, Lord. Oh, God, you forgot to take me." She bent her head, sobbed with a gut-wrenching burst of tears, and continued. "Sweet Jesus, sweet, sweet Lord, don't leave me now, don't leave me here alone. *I'm afraid,* Lord. Oh, I'm afraid and alone, oh, my sweet Jesus don't leave me here like this, I'm one of *yours,* Lord, one of your children. Oh, God, please don't leave me here."

Shannon sat in a pew and looked up at the cross that dominated the front wall of the church. Billy had helped build it and finish it. She remembered how he'd worked for hours in the garage on it. He'd said that considering Joseph's trade and Jesus' early apprenticeship, it was only fitting that he use his skills to honor them. She smiled and thought of Billy and his faith, how she'd often considered his deep and abiding faith in God just another part of his simple, uncomplicated approach to life. Whenever they'd encountered a rough patch — a washer in need of repair, a bill come due, one of the kids being ill — he'd tell her the way to get through it all was to kiss it off. Keep it simple, Shannon.

How wrong she had been to assume that his faith was merely a way for him to not face the harsher realities of life, an escape. Who was the one left needing an escape now?

Shannon rifled through her purse, seized by a kind of panic that shot a jolt of adrenaline through her. She needed to feel normal, if only for a moment. She pulled out her daily planner, turned to the day's date. Today she had to get Laura to her tumbling class after school. Matt and Billy junior would want to spend the wait time at McDonald's. She could picture the two boys in the backseat, playing with whatever toy they'd gotten with their Happy Meals. A lover of irony her whole life, even Shannon couldn't manage a rueful laugh at that one.

She tried to remember the last words she'd spoken to Billy, to each of the kids. She wished she could go back in time, not just to remember those words, those actions, but to change them. In a flash of recognition, she saw herself snapping at Matthew at the dinner table last night. He wouldn't even give the green beans a try. He'd started to cry after she'd lit into him, and that had hardened her resolve. He must have sat there for two hours, haloed in the light from the fixture over the kitchen table, defiant, refusing to take even one bite. She'd sent him off to bed without a kiss good night. Keep it simple, Shannon.

She could tell that Billy was displeased with how she'd handled things. But the day had taken on a momentum of its own that she couldn't bring under control. Doug Mann's erratic behavior had only added to the usual stress load. She'd kept her back turned when she felt Billy climb into bed. She'd stayed that way when he put his hand on her shoulder and whispered his nightly "I love you." Shannon felt tears welling now, as she had last night in the face of such simple and unconditional love. She'd turned away from it then, and was this the price she'd had to pay?

Or could love ever be that simple? As simple as accepting the gestures that were offered to her? Or did it have to be something that she'd have to schedule, to plan for, make a notation on her calendar to make official? These thoughts were too much for her.

Sunlight poured through the windows and washed across the pulpit. Shannon sat in the crux of the cross's shadow, feeling the weight of what had happened to her bearing down on her. Times like this she'd grown accustomed to Billy's steadying hand, his guidance. That was gone. So much was gone.

"Might be, we could still be saved."

Shannon took her eyes off the cross and saw who had spoken to her. An elderly woman, thin, her white hair carefully in place, her dress neat, sat in the pew next to her, her hands in her lap, her composed face turned to Shannon.

"What?" asked Shannon. "What?"

"Panicking and carrying on isn't going to help us now," said the woman with a nod toward the one in front. "Several of us have tried to calm her down, but she's lost . . . lost." She managed a tiny bit of a smile. "You're Bill Carpenter's wife. Shannon, right?"

Shannon nodded.

"I'm Elaine, Elaine Hodges. You've met me a few times at different church functions, but you probably don't remember. It doesn't matter. What does matter is Bill's gone, and the children, and I guess your poor heart is just as broken as most every other heart that's still beating around here."

"Yes," said Shannon.

"Do you understand what has happened,

girl? I mean, where everybody went?"

"I . . . I think so," Shannon answered. "I'm not . . . sure. On the TV news this morning they were going on about some secret weapon that one of our enemies has. And they were saying some people thought like aliens or something from another galaxy were taking us. And a bunch of medical scientists thought it was a megavirus and the Centers for Disease Control were working on it, but —" She stopped, took a deep, ragged breath, looked at the light in the church, and added, "One person they interviewed said it was a biblical thing . . . like the end of the world, or something."

The woman leaned forward and took one of Shannon's hands in hers. Her grip was strong, her skin warm and dry. "Listen, girl. There is hope, there is reason to hope. Don't give up now."

"I'm not giving up, Mrs. Hodges," replied Shannon. "I'm just not sure what has happened, I'm frightened, and I don't know what to do."

"We're *all* frightened, Shannon," said the woman. "But there is hope for us. Yep, even those of us who were not taken. We can still be saved."

"Saved from what?"

"Saved from ourselves, silly," answered Mrs. Hodges. She leaned even closer. "Listen. Our church, and others, the church leaders, they were working on something recently, a good thing. It was like they had a hint of what was about to happen, and there was a plan in place. A plan so all would not be lost, so there might be a second chance for us."

"A good thing?" asked Shannon. Her mind flashed back to the last conversation she had had with her boss, Doug Mann. She shuddered as the image of him this morning flashed through her mind. "A second chance?"

"Prodigal Project, girl," said the woman, nodding her head energetically as if to convince herself. "You get into the Prodigal Project and there you'll see the plan. The plan, the one who will make it come true, and our salvation."

Several days after the disappearance, Air France's ticket counter at Orly Airport was nearly overrun with American tourists clamoring to be aboard the first flight home. The French authorities had let it be known that an Air France flight would leave Paris for New York, in the first attempt to ease the stress on a severely taxed

240

system. For the first three days after the disappearance, all flights had been suspended, until aviation authorities received clearance from the health ministry that no contagion had caused the disappearance. Though the evidence was not conclusive, governments worldwide were fearful of the tensions rising between foreigners and natives. In addition, they feared reprisals should something happen to Americans while on foreign soil. Though as crippled as any nation, America was still a powerful force, and no right-thinking country was prepared to do anything to slight it. The State Department had recalled all of its diplomatic corps, and urged all Americans to return to the States, further influencing the French decision.

The French government and its president, Alain Daigle, hoped to return the many Americans stuck in the City of Light. More important, they hoped to demonstrate to the rest of the world that the French, as they had through every conflict, would somehow manage to carry on. Besides, Daigle had his own citizens to worry about, and Basque separatists, always a source of conflict, were using the disruption to their full advantage.

At Orly, security appeared to be tight,

with members of the elite French military unit walking the concourse with their TK automatic weapons held in front of them, bandoliers crossing their chests. Their heads encased in Kevlar helmets, their eyes all but inscrutable, they were a strangely reassuring presence.

But the ranks of regular security personnel had been depleted, and morale was bottomed out for the rest. The hastily enacted safety procedures were a symbolic gesture at best. Who could concentrate on doing any job in the wake of such a sweeping disaster? Even the crowds of Americans jamming the ticket counters seemed strangely subdued, their impatience numbed, their glares and watch checking more of an act than a real gesture of frustration. And everywhere you looked, someone stood staring vacantly, red-eyed and tear-stained; people had grown so accustomed to public displays of mourning or fear that the grieving no longer drew much attention, no longer bothered to hide their faces.

One youngish man, clad in jeans, sandals, and a long black lightweight raincoat, should have caught someone's attention. Even the security dogs, perhaps so acutely attuned to the emotions of their distraught handlers and overwhelmed by the collective vibrations of the crowd, let him slip past them with no notice. At the boarding gate, he shouldered his way into line and then past the gate agent, his hollow-eyed stare really not much different from the expression on the faces of the previous fifty passengers to board. That he didn't have a ticket hardly seemed to matter to the gate agent — he was just one fewer American to have on French soil. Let his fellow Americans sort things out if there wasn't a seat available.

Now that the American economy was on the verge of collapse, the reason for tolerating Americans and their rudeness, the American dollar, was gone. What difference does it make? she thought. Besides, the soldiers assigned to the initial checks would have detained anyone suspicious. What she didn't know was that the soldiers were too busy searching the pretty young women to bother with one more ragged, once wealthy young American traveling on his parents' money.

Just after the plane pulled away from the gate and began rolling down the taxiway, he unbuckled his seat belt and strode down the aisle toward the cockpit. A flight attendant, a petite redhead who had been flying as a reserve prior to the disappearance, vacated her jump seat and confronted him. She waved her arms and pointed toward the rear of the cabin, but the young man kept coming toward her. Her boyfriend, who had wanted her not to fly, fearing angry passengers, the uncertainty concerning the nature of the disappearance, and his own nearly crippling fear of being alone, hadn't been able to completely dissuade her, but he had armed her with a can of Mace. When she pulled it from her pocket and showed it to the young man, she thought it odd that he smiled.

Before she could spray him, he twisted her arm behind her and produced a Glock nine-millimeter pistol that he held to her temple. The copilot, who had been watching the surveillance monitors in the cockpit, immediately radioed a Mayday to the tower. A moment later, two shots ripped through the safety door, followed a moment later by the young man. Afterward, when they were interviewed by Interpol and members of the CIA, everyone commented on the young man's steely calm, his nearly resigned disinterest in the task at hand. In precisely formal but heavily accented French, he instructed the pilot to proceed immediately to the nearest runway. The pilot did as told. Once the plane was in position for takeoff, the young man used the intercom system to tell the remainder of the flight crew to evacuate the aircraft. Though they'd wanted to activate the emergency slides to prevent the craft from taking off, the young man reminded them that he still held the captain, the engineer, the first officer, and the flight attendant hostage. To drive his point home, he fired a single shot into the navigator and had the other two members of the flight-deck crew drag him out into the galley to serve as a reminder of who was in control.

He didn't object when he saw many of the passengers carrying seat cushions to toss onto the tarmac, hoping to create a softer landing spot for themselves. Just so he wouldn't leave everyone with the impression that he was altruistic by nature, he insisted that the pilot and first officer toss their fellow officer onto the pile before anyone could jump. Once the plane was evacuated, the young man powered up and took off for an unknown destination.

NATO and French military jets had been scrambled together at the first Mayday signal, and they escorted the craft out of French airspace. Fearing the loss of additional civilian life if the plane was shot down over a heavily populated area, once the plane passed over the Mediterranean, the French recalled their fighter jets. It was a decision that was later used by various Islamic governments to claim that the West was complicit in the operation that devastated Muslims worldwide.

The pilot seemed to be deliberately avoiding large cities or any airspace that might be deemed a threat to the countries he overflew. He ignored the controllers calling him over the radios, and flew straight and level. The NATO jets were joined by Israeli warplanes. All the military commands were already on edge, and a dangerous dance was choreographed through the skies as fighter jets tried to shadow the big plane without getting too close to one another. The television news shows caught the whole thing live, and within minutes CNN had the White House press secretary giving the U.S. position on the matter. This learned personage stated with confidence that the pilot of the hijacked plane was probably an extremist supporter of the mujahideen. What his purposes were could not be determined, until the big plane was observed angling into a long, shallow dive, which dramatically increased its speed.

For a few tense moments frantic radio traffic between fighter jets and controllers from several countries considered what action to take. It looked like the pilot was going to drive straight into the ground, perhaps into the desert wastes of interior Saudi Arabia. Then an argument began over which countries' fighter jets should shoot the airliner down, if that was to be the action taken. With that much jet traffic, getting a heat-seeking missile locked on the right target would be difficult. No one wanted to be the one to fire a shot that would bring down another country's jet. Friendly fire had never been interpreted so loosely.

An Israeli pilot was seconds from firing all of his air-to-air missiles at the airliner when it impacted the Kaaba, which held the sacred Black Stone, in the Masjid al-Haram, Mecca, Saudi Arabia. Several thousand of the faithful, who had gathered at the site to pray for understanding immediately after the disappearance, died in the explosion and horrific fireball that boiled out as the huge airliner roared in nose first. The sacred structure was destroyed in the volcanic fire and crashing impact of tons of metal and fuel. The structure fell, as it had fallen many times during the early centuries. But the rock remained.

Amid the flurry of diplomatic protests, accusations, recriminations, and military threats that flew within moments of the immolative crash, one man enjoyed the news more than any other — Izbek Noir. The young pilot of the hijacked airliner, trained by the mujahideen, was a recruit from Canada, a young man who had attended the University of California at Berkeley and fallen under the spell of a liberal political science professor who'd taught a course entitled "Oil, Flexible Interventionist Policies, and the Gulf War: An American Tragedy." He'd left behind his family and friends in Toronto, taken up residence outside of Islamabad, and joined a terrorist cell within months of his arrival.

Noir's strategy was simple: by attacking the holiest of shrines and making it look like a Western nation was responsible, he hoped to make more converts to what the media had come to think of as his jihad. That it cost the lives of thousands of his fellow Muslims didn't matter to him one bit. He took pleasure in knowing that the Western media misused the word *jihad*, equating it with a holy war, knowing that the true meaning of the word, the internal struggle, was a delicious irony.

Following the attack, the UN Security Council, which had been in session nearly around the clock since the disappearance, cleared its schedule to convene another emergency session in hopes of heading off global warfare.

Thomas Church sat in his office in his house on Long Island and pondered the state of the World Wide Web. Things were a mess, just like outside. Many sites were simply not there, and his favorite search engines seemed to work sporadically at best. During the first few days, Church had gone outside once or twice, had actually considered driving into his office in the city, but it was all way too weird out there. The roadways were like some demolition derby, gangs and groups and thugs roamed the neighborhoods, and the police were besieged. With his own eyes he had seen the rioting in front of banks and food stores, and twice people had tried to stop him or open the doors on his SUV. The lines near gas stations were a battle zone — literally and figuratively. In the wake of the attack on Mecca, OPEC had stopped exports to the West. U.S. oil reserves, an issue that most Americans seldom thought of unless prices soared, suddenly became a focal point. Nonessential travel was to be curtailed, and roadblocks were established to keep private vehicles off the roadways.

In major metropolitan areas, public transportation — trains and buses — was even more jammed than usual. Church wasn't about to take any chances; he had turned his house into his personal fortress. He owned a nine-millimeter pistol and a shotgun. He loaded both, and kept them near. He was frightened, but at the same time fascinated, almost amused initially. It was all just too much for him to comprehend, and totally *unscripted*. He had awakened to the disjointed news on the TV, and had flung himself onto his computer to see what he could see. Complete craziness, the whole thing. He had tried to phone both of his kids, got nothing, and e-mailed them. The icon said "sent," but who knew for sure?

Most of the leaders of the world, good, bad, or worthless, were calling for calm. That much he learned while he stumbled through the Web sites and clicked through the channels. With his satellite feed he had been monitoring Al-Jazeera, saw celebrations in the streets throughout the Middle East and wherever else a Muslim Majority existed marking the day the West had been served its comeuppance. He was disgusted by their display, angrier than he could ever remember being; he also felt more powerless than he'd ever felt before. The only thing he could do was sit and watch or try to dig up as much information as he could to figure out the cause of the disappearance.

He couldn't really call it surfing the Web, he thought, more like jumping from one pothole to the next. He hated that part of this situation, hated his beloved PC working in fits and starts. When he did find a chat room that looked as if it would offer promising information, it was filled with babble from anyone who could get in there with a statement or opinion. He abandoned that idea and tried to stay with the established news organizations, and around the edges of their hysteria he was able to put the pieces together.

He leaned back in his chair and laughed out loud, the sound hollow in his room. What if the people in the church were right, he thought, and this is the end of the world? He laughed again, tentatively, then added with a shake of his head, Nah. On an intellectual level, he admitted to himself, of all the theorists trying to nail down the cause of these global disappearances, the talking heads who argued in favor of a biblical explanation seemed to be able to show the most evidence to back them up.

Such an explanation was totally irrational, but the thought that the Christians were right, that this was like some lock-jawed "end-times" scenario being played out in real time, really *bothered* him. He had *gone* to church in his relatively unblemished life, he had mouthed the little Christian themes, said the prayers, the whole thing. He wasn't proud to admit that his faith had never really had any *substance* to it. Church attendance was just something to do, a place to go to hear a nice story to make everybody feel better during Easter and Christmas. But he wasn't alone in that regard. He thought of people he knew in his immediate neighborhood, some of his coworkers, and he could point to those who were in his estimation worse than he was, yet many of them had been taken. Where was the justice in that? Where was the feel-good he'd come to count on? The more he thought about it, the angrier he got. Besides, he soothed himself, the hand of man was all over the Bible, any scholar could tell you that. His brow furrowed. If this whole thing *was* an act of God, then it was a hurtful thing, a wrong thing.

One thing was certain, he determined, it was easy to dismiss the "alien" theory, just as it was (though he liked it for its dramatic possibilities) the "megavirus" conjecture. Still, he knew enough of the world's machinations to not rule out any country's use of weapons of mass destruction, chemical or otherwise. For all the digging he'd done, all the information that he'd gathered from so many different sources over the last few years, all he knew for certain was that he knew very little at all.

When he thought of the impact these events would have on the world's financial markets, he was even more deeply troubled. Not at the thought of the personal losses he might suffer — he'd done enough work to insulate himself from any market failures with offshore accounts and nearly instant liquidity — but that any government could have taken these steps to destabilize the world's economy. After all, as he well knew, even at the worst of financial times, there was always the opportunity for someone to make money — usually someone who already had a lot of money. He thought of his father's constant lament that the rich got richer and the poor got poorer. The sooner he got off his own shocked butt, the sooner he might be able to move some funds around, cut his losses and make a few dollars besides.

A strange feeling hit him in the gut, and he knew then that if in fact he was not one of the saved, the source of his abandonment was not a callous or indifferent God, but his own shortsightedness. He knew that it was important to invest, to put enough away for the proverbial rainy day. If God was indeed raining down His justice from heaven, then he'd invested in all the wrong places for all the wrong reasons.

The world sorely needed strong leadership to pull what was left together. The peoples remaining on earth, throughout the four corners, still needed food, water, electricity, medical help, transportation, shipping, air flight — all the trappings of modern civilization. What was needed was cooperation, not conflict. Thus he was completely dismayed when the hijacked aircraft smashed into the mosque in Mecca. In the past he could have given two figs for the Muslims, but now he knew that everyone would begin finger-pointing immediately — and that some of the fingers would be tipped with bombs and missiles.

The United States was not the only country to lose its president, prime minister, or leader. Whole governments were decimated, and confusion and jockeying for position were the disorder of the day. He thought Vice President Clara Reese looked and sounded pretty presidential during her first, hasty speech from the Rose Garden, but he also knew she'd need a fairly complete structure of government to effectively control the country and influence the world.

He learned the fires of war had been lit all over the globe. Africa was a horror — had been for some years — and many of the cross-border conflicts were spreading with mind-numbing speed as various Muslim sects turned on one another. The Middle East was a hair trigger away from exploding, the Far East was up in arms — the Chinese could not be blamed for seizing such an opportunity, it was suggested — and Russia seemed to be under the control of madmen, with vodka and the pain of old humiliations fueling their vitriol. Suddenly their fire sale of weaponry and weapons technology heated up in a seller's market.

Where were the leaders? He bounced from one site to another, and besides the remaining well-known governmental stewards such as Clara Reese, the only name that kept appearing was some emerging warlord named Noir. A bit of research showed that this Noir seemed to have come to prominence during the India-Pakistan conflict. He was portrayed as ruthless and effective, a warrior-leader who would be king, a savage soldier who led by example and whose soldiers fought and died for him by the thousands. How he had managed to climb so quickly in rank — one source referred to him as "General" — was unclear. Hey, mused Thomas Church, now is the time that we all feared, the time when someone tough, unforgiving, maniacal, and strong enough can seize power in the right regions. Thomas Church knew that a world disrupted or a nation with a wounded ego is ripe to fall under the influence of a strong leader, and if he is "savage," so what?

His fingers danced over the keys, searching for more on Noir. There was not much about his history before becoming a soldier. He had supposedly been charged with war crimes more than once, but the charges were always unaccountably dropped. No family, no political affiliation. A Muslim, supposedly, but not an imam or a mullah. He seemed to appear at the hot spots — through the years his name was known on several battlefields, large and small. He seemed to have cut his teeth in Africa; but early reporting from there identified him as an imposing Hutu leader responsible for the slaughter of thousands of Tutsis, while later wire reports claimed he was in fact a white South African. He couldn't be both, surely, but there was no story or info clearing it up. Either way, Church learned, the guy was one incredible fighting leader. Many observers — soldiers, hospital workers, and journalists — stated with awe that Noir killed and plundered like no one had seen in a long time. He read more than one report of Noir's use and destruction of women in the various campaigns and his apparent relish of what war was. Thomas Church read one report twice, then carefully read three or four that corroborated it. The report stated that many who had fought with, or against, Noir were convinced that the man could not be killed.

This is one scary guy, thought Church as he read more and more about Noir, and he has made his appearance during scary times. He went back to the sketchy biographical material on his subject and learned his first name: Izbek. "Izbek Noir," said Thomas Church grimly to his computer screen. "What else?"

While he pondered the information he had accumulated, he received an e-mail from his daughter in Virginia. It was short and, because of his past research, not totally mystifying. He read the e-mail.

"Dad," appeared on the screen, "Mitch and I are still here, don't know if that's good or bad. Have you heard from Tommy? Mom got through to me . . . Still doesn't want me to tell you from where, but wants me to forward her message . . . same one to me: 'Go to church.' She sent that, and added, 'It is at church, look for Prodigal Project, or Prodigal One, or Person . . . like that.' Last thing in her message was 'There is hope in Dante.' I don't get it, but she wanted me to forward it, okay? We are staying on the campus for now, Mitch is afraid of 'anarchy.' Me, I'm just afraid. I love you, Dad. Lynn."

He searched his memory, remembered coming across the Prodigal Project, and guessed that the "Dante" the message referred to was Azul Dante, a respected academic who'd started as a commentator on the world political scene but soon turned his notoriety to his political advantage.

Though he'd never held official office, he was rumored to have the ear of many, particularly in the Balkans.

What did it matter? What difference could one man make? Especially if God had taken Tommy, his son? That would be a hurtful thing. Anger simmered in his heart. He read the words of his daughter, and with brutal clarity remembered each and every single time through her life with him when she had wanted to be held, hugged, or paid attention to, and he had turned away, had been too busy for a hug. He wished he could hug her, and Tommy, now.

Of all US. cities, New York suffered the most but, typically, showed it the least. With the economy on the verge of collapse, trading on Wall Street was suspended indefinitely, but not before the Dow had lost more than 500 points in the first few hours after word of the disappearance had hit the airwaves. Since then the Department of the Treasury, acting in concert with the Federal Reserve, had put a temporary freeze on every citizen's assets. Both moves did little to quell the spreading uprisings, but the newly installed president knew that a devastating economic crisis on top of what had already transpired might very well spell doom for the country — especially in light of the yen's trouncing of the dollar and the Nikkei index's Lazarus-like rise from the grave.

The *New York Post* probably captured the tenor of the town best with its headline: "Jumping Jap Cash, It's a Crash!"

A cold rain fell as Azul Dante's Ilyushin jet landed at LaGuardia. The jet was formerly the private aircraft of the premier himself, but Dante had been granted unlimited access to it in the weeks before the disappearance. Dante watched as the flashing lights of the police escort that accompanied him on the Grand Central Parkway kaleidoscoped on the dripping panes of his limousine's privacy glass. The trip was lengthy. Department of Sanitation trucks with plows attached to their front end shoved aside abandoned cars. From the Triborough Bridge, he could see the faint skyline — emergency conservation measures had most high-rise buildings dark at night, and rolling blackouts blanked parts of the city. Some long-time residents had protested, thinking that the Empire State Building and the Chrysler Building were symbolically important and should have stayed lit.

Once on the FDR heading toward midtown and the UN, their pace quickened. Crews had already removed guard rails, retaining walls, and some curbing to make it easier to push cars into the East River. Dante asked the driver to get his escorts to make a quick detour to Fifth Avenue to see the Metropolitan Museum of Art. Early in the crisis, those prescient enough to figure out that economic conditions were likely to be dire had stormed the buildings, hoping that even in this world turned upside down, some would still be willing to pay a price for works of art. As the limo slipped past the museum, a trace of a smile played on Azul Dante's lips. The building looked more like a prison now than a museum. Concrete barricades surrounded it, and a hastily constructed barbed-wire enclosure clung to it like a web of vines.

"Such beauty and splendor spoiled," Dante said to his young traveling companion. "But it can be restored. I'm certain of that." He smiled more openly, hoping to reassure her.

She pulled her gaze away from the window and regarded the man who sat across from her. He was exactly the kind of man that she hoped that she would someday marry. An accomplished scholar, a published author, a man comfortable in boardrooms and lecture halls, and a four handicapper on the links, he was the most self-possessed man she'd ever met. To say that he charmed people was an understatement; though he didn't really dazzle, he had a mesmerizing way of ingratiating himself with people, making them feel when he spoke to them as though his entire being were focused on them alone, that the rest of the world had ceased to exist.

Though in her observations of him he'd remained almost preternaturally calm regardless of the circumstances, just beneath that calm exterior beat a passionate heart. Whether it was his darting, piercing eyes, a grin that turned from rapacious to self-mocking to boyishly reluctant in a span of a few seconds, or the wedge of salt-and-pepper hair that flopped over his left eye and cast it in shadow (and against which he waged a constant battle) didn't seem to matter. Whatever the source of his power to connect with a wide array of people, he'd developed a considerable following. In interviews he was gracious in deflecting questions about his past, citing a desire to keep his family out of the limelight. Some hinted that he was the scion of a wealthy family; others speculated that he feared that exposing his humble roots would diminish his standing. Though he had not exactly appeared from nowhere, no journalist had been able to document him as a wunderkind with a pedigree to match his considerable intellect. In the aftermath of the disappearance, such questions had become irrelevant.

How Sophia Ghent had come to be his assistant seemed at times almost as much of a mystery to herself as he had at one time been to her and the rest of the world. She had been a student in a philosophy seminar that he'd led as a guest lecturer at the University of Prague. Rumor had it that he'd been influential in the negotiations that ultimately led to the formation of the Czech Republic and Slovakia; similarly, he had played a minor role in the unification of Germany while beginning his academic career in Stuttgart. Somehow she must have made an impression on him, though she hardly remembered speaking up at all. Sophia had been content to take notes as she sat as far from him as possible. Now she was with him in New York, helping him to prepare for his most important mission yet — his meeting first with the UN Security Council and then his address to the General Assembly.

Their relationship was cordially professional. She kept his calendar for him and coordinated with the young man who handled most of his correspondence, and in recent weeks she had also begun to act as his sounding board whenever he was preparing a speech. He preferred to write in French, thought it the most suitably diplomatic of languages, and though she was fluent, she was not in love with the language in the same way that many of her friends and Azul — never Mister or Monsieur — were. He counted on her to make his English sound less formal and trusted her implicitly.

"Sophia, I know that this isn't how you'd hoped to find New York," Azul began, "but you must remember, that is why we are here. This is an opportunity — one that I wish hadn't come to pass. But —" He let the word hang in the air.

"That is one way to look at it. Another is to say that if I had my choice, I would forfeit this opportunity if it would mean that what has come to pass hadn't happened."

"Understandable." Dante waited for her to continue.

"I know that Paris, London, Brussels, Geneva will all be more or less the same. I feel bad that I'm still eager to see them all

— even in their ruined state."

"New York is hardly in ruins. An altered state, perhaps. But just as a church is not a building but the community that worships there, a city is its residents. New York is the perfect place from which we can launch the Prodigal Project. Vitality still breathes here. When I stepped out of the airport I felt it."

Sophia was about to comment that he'd only taken about five steps from the terminal into the car, but thought better of it. She was still smarting from what she perceived to be a snub. She'd not yet read or heard any of the text that he was going to deliver. Like the rest of the world, she would have to wait. Unlike most of the world, she would do her waiting in the comfort of a room at the Waldorf-Astoria Hotel.

Gathered in the situation room off the Oval Office were the Joint Chiefs of Staff and the remaining members of the president's cabinet, including the secretary of state, the head of Homeland Security, the justice, treasury, and transportation secretaries, and the newly installed head of the Defense Department. To avoid the appearance of any partisan power plays, she'd also included the Senate majority leader, from North Carolina, and Gregory Davis, the maverick liberal Senate minority leader, from Massachusetts. She knew that Davis had been gathering support for a run for the presidency in the next election, but thus far no one had attempted to make political hay of the situation. She knew that wouldn't last for long.

Though on the job for only three days, Alan Clarke of the Defense Department was clearly the right man to step into the key role. An avowed policy wonk with a taste for scouring intelligence reports as though they were the box scores of his beloved Baltimore Orioles (the reports were about as reliable as the team, some office pundits liked to observe), Clarke was now finishing his report to the president on China.

"We are at the highest state of alert. NORAD is locked down, and all personnel are there for the duration. In our estimation, China poses the single greatest threat."

General David McNally looked to Benjamin Carter of the CIA and smiled. Though he was senior to Carter by nearly two decades, he deferred to the younger man.

"Madam President" — Carter looked around the room to make eye contact with everyone — "as you all know, we've been tracking the activities of Izbek Noir and the mujahideen for some time. Our operatives tell us that since the attack on Mecca, his status in the Arab world has risen immeasurably. While China has and remains a clear nuclear threat, we can't dismiss the India-Pakistan conflict as a not-in-my-backyard scuffle."

"Mr. Carter," said the chief of staff, still trying to get his tongue comfortable with the words, "it seems we have another situation developing. You're forgetting that Madam President attended every meeting concerning him or was briefed very thoroughly about Noir."

"Michael," Reese said, "I don't need you to speak on my behalf, nor do I need anyone to pull any punches for me. Mr. Carter's point is well taken. The Chinese situation is reasonably under control."

"Precisely, Madam President." Carter took off his glasses. Without them, he seemed weaker, more vulnerable, and he knew it. "If Noir is able to get the Pakistanis and the Indians to unite in their opposition to the West, American vital interests are sure to fall."

"Proceed, Mr. Carter. You've got the floor."

"As you know, Madam President, at first it was fairly easy to dismiss Noir as a warlord run amok. We now know that he's much smarter than that. Not only is he wreaking havoc on the citizenry, he's also shown some fairly remarkable organizational skills. These" — Carter pointed to the latest satellite photos arrayed on the table — "show vital pipelines being attacked and rendered inoperable in Saudi Arabia. Same with refineries."

"You can link him directly to these? He's been operating in Pakistan and India," Clarke interjected.

"With the mujahideen it's always difficult to find direct links, but we've been monitoring transmissions throughout the region. Saudi Arabia seems the most susceptible. Especially in light of what happened in Mecca. Since the eighties, oil prices have dropped. Unemployment among those in their twenties is skyrocketing. They're not enamored of the strict Sharia laws. He's fomented unrest there, and they've got a convenient scapegoat in the West."

"And the Saudis are about to cut us off?" Reese turned to her secretary of state, Robert Butler.

"Correction. Have."

"What about our friends in Venezuela, are we still making nice with them?" Reese felt a sharp pang of sadness on looking at Butler. He'd lost his first wife to a terrorist attack when he was ambassador to Greece. Several years ago, she'd attended his wedding to a much younger woman. Usually a May-December romance caused a scandal in D.C., but she knew that the couple were very much in love. She also knew that Butler had lost his second wife and his young son and daughter to the disappearance. It couldn't have been easy for him to carry on, but here he was, looking even more hang-dog than he usually did. No wonder everyone referred to him behind his back as "the Bull Dog."

"So far. They plan to continue to export oil to us, but we can't be sure for how long or at what price. They're in the driver's seat, so to speak, Madam President. Who knows how long they can remain stable. After all, early estimates show that they've lost the greatest percentage of their population of any of the Latin American countries."

"Explanation?" Reese looked around the room, saw that nearly everyone was reluctant to tackle the topic. She quickly shifted gears.

Reese nodded. "What about Qatar? What's the latest word from them?"

McNally shook his head, "They're making noises about closing our bases, creating a no-fly zone above their airspace."

Several in the room laughed. The tiny nation of Qatar, one of the richest in the world, had long been a U.S. ally and a supplier of petroleum. For it to turn its back on the United States now seemed inconceivable.

"And they're going to defend that airspace with what? Learjets and bottles of Dom Pérignon fired out the windows?" Clarke waved the latest report in the air.

"Apparently they've grown a spine since the Mecca incident," Carter said.

"That's ridiculous. Those people worship at the altar of the American dollar. Tell them we'll put Allah on the hundred-dollar bill and they'll change their minds." The majority leader leaned forward with his elbows on his knees and laced his fingers together.

"They may be more afraid of what the Saudis, Palestinians, and Iraqis will do to them than what our failing dollar will do," Davis added. "Particularly in light of the mujahideen's success."

Everyone in the room stared at Davis.

An avowed dove, for him even to suggest what he seemed about to was as startling as an after-midnight phone call.

"The American people need stability restored at home, Madam President," Davis began before Reese waved her hands in his direction.

"This isn't the floor of the Senate, Mr. Davis, and I'm not here to debate any issues with you. Despite the fact that we're in a conservation mode and I know how you can energize a room, I'm going to have to ask you to refrain." Reese turned her own high-wattage smile at him. "At this point, we are the ones who are going to have to convince the American people of what they want. Now's not a time to listen but to act. Suggestions on what to do about Mr. Noir and his mujahideen? We'll reconvene tomorrow. Tonight the UN, tomorrow the rest of the world."

The Reverend Henderson Smith stood in the pulpit of his dreams, in the church of his dreams. The pulpit was made of beautiful hand-carved wood, and soared up in front of the congregation like the bow of a ship. He scanned the faces that peered up at him from the pews. The church was very big, open and airy, and almost every seat was taken. The faces he gazed upon were a colorful mix of all races, male and female, poor and affluent. A common desperation marked their countenance, fear, hunger for the Word. He knew that they were waiting for him to explain, to comfort, to give hope. He gripped the curved sides of the pulpit tightly, feeling his heart swell, finding his strength coming with his ingrained self-discipline. He knew that once he began his sermon, he would find the words.

But he lingered for a moment, watched the events of the previous days play out behind his eyes, blackening the edges of that swelling heart, singeing his mind. Miriam and the kids were gone. He had stumbled through his house like many, many others, calling out their names, looking in the closets, frantically trying to make sense out of the impossible. After finally coming to temporary terms with *knowing* they were gone, he had forced himself to get dressed and drive to his small church.

He arrived as a fire truck pulled away, and joined the small group of onlookers. His church was tumbled brick, melted glass, and burned cinders. Nothing was left but a charred skeleton of a house of worship, and a terrible stench. Two or three people standing across the street finally recognized him, ran to him, and almost knocked him down in their efforts to touch and embrace him.

"Lord — Lord — help us, Reverend Henderson, help us —"

"My babies are gone, Reverend. Are they with Jesus? Are they with Jesus?"

"Why am I still here, Reverend? Why are *you* still here?"

"Oh, no — not Miriam and the kids . . ."

"You taught us to pray, Henderson, and I've been prayin' like nothin' you ever seen. So where's my salvation? I pray every day. Now my kids are gone and I ain't heard nothin' from you at all —"

"Help us, Reverend."

"What happened?" asked Henderson Smith through dry lips. "What happened here . . . to our church?"

"Man done burned it down, Reverend, just burned it down, and himself with it."

"She's sayin' right, Henderson, your church is gone, man, burned on purpose."

"Who? Who burned it?" he asked.

"White man. A fat, crazy white man."

"That's right. I saw him too. Big heavy man, round face, white man in this neighborhood, you know, you look at 'im. Had him two big red cans. Gasoline, I guess."

"Sure it was gasoline, I know. He come strolling la-de-da down the sidewalk, big grin on his face, and walked right into the church. He put one can down, then began splashing the gas from the other one all around the building. Even back in your office."

"You . . . watched him?" said Smith. He tried to keep any note of peevishness from coloring his tone.

"If you mean why did we watch him and not do anything to stop him, sorry, Reverend, but this is one crazy day we got goin' on here, what with the riots and all. Police shootin' people that smashed into the grocery store, other people drivin' around just shootin' at each *other*. Then here comes this crazy fat white man with his gasoline. Man, we watched, but we didn't even get *near* him, you understand?"

"Yes, I do."

"Anyway, that man soaked your church, inside and out, then — he's laughing real loud so we could hear him from across the street there — he's laughin' and stands in the front doors and just pours the rest of that gas all over *himself*. Sick and crazy in the head. But man, you know today there been more than one poor soul took their own life."

"You see that one young girl? Cut herself all up 'cause her baby was gone —"

"What about the man in my church?" asked Smith, his stomach knotted with fear.

"Oh. That man soaked himself with the gas, like she said. Then he lit himself on fire. And man, that church of yours just *exploded* into this amazin' fireball, like a punchy blast. We could feel it, then all the fire. That man must have been standin' right up there by your pulpit, Reverend, and we could hear him laughing so loud, like laughing and screaming. We could hear him laughing."

"And then we couldn't."

"When that one fire department truck got here your little building was all gone anyway. We told the firefighters there was a man in there, but they went in and couldn't find a *thing*. Said somethin' like he had apparently been *consumed* by the fire. They didn't find a body, Reverend, and they couldn't stick around if they did."

"Reverend?"

"Reverend Smith?"

The Reverend Henderson Smith closed his eyes, bit his lower lip, and shook himself, still grasping the sides of his new pulpit. It was his new pulpit . . . it just came to be. When he turned away from the smoldering ruins of his small church, he got into his car and drove without thinking straight to this newly built, huge, gold, silver, polished wood, and glass cathedral. He parked in a space in the back with his name on it, walked the entire length of the imposing building to the street, and saw his name again. It was on the beautiful stone-and-copper sign that identified the place as the New Christian Cathedral. The Reverend Henderson Smith was listed as pastor, and the sermon for this day was "Don't Fight the Mysteries of Faith."

"Brothers and sisters," he began, "I see your tears. They look like the ones on my cheeks. I see the fear and confusion in your eyes. They're in mine, too. I can hear your hearts breaking all the way up here, and maybe you can hear mine. We have lost those closest to us, we have lost our loved ones. And don't you know it would have to be the children? After all, the children are more representative of what our sweet Lord tried to teach us than anything on this earth. Our children are gone, and gone too are those who were, well, our best. You know, how many times at funerals have you heard somebody say, 'Well, Jesus takes the good ones up to be with him in heaven'? I say to you, maybe he *has.* There has been a horrendous, worldwide *taking* of people. Hundreds of thousands — millions, perhaps — gone, gone in the blink of an eye."

He sipped cool water from a lovely crystal goblet, swallowed, and went on. "We can wonder about what happened to them, and we'll speak of it in a moment. First, what of *us?* Are we survivors of some unknown disease, plague, some virus? Did the aliens — I've already heard *that* theory — some powerful aliens take some and we'll be gobbled up later? What of *us?* Why are we still here? Why can't we go and be with those we lost? We've all seen on this day people who did just that. Simply killed themselves, too distraught to go on, or in the hope of being reunited with their babies. It could be argued that they did not make a bad decision. If this is some natural phenomenon, these millions of disappearances, then we could argue that those who are dead will go to heaven, or sleep until the judgment. All the things we base our faith on. So those who took their own lives might in fact be sleeping in peace, waiting to be judged and allowed to sit in heaven with their loved ones. Except of course most of us of almost any faith believe suicide is a mortal sin, right?"

He saw a few heads nod in agreement. Other than people sobbing quietly here and there in the pews, most were very still, listening. He continued, "*What if this is the end of the world?* What then? Okay . . . good. We would want nothing better than to know our sweet babies, our sweet husbands and wives and brothers and sisters, our loved ones have been *taken up* to be with their Lord and Savior. That's where we *want* them to be, yes? Yes. We don't want those we love to miss the lift, to miss the lifting up to where they can sit next to our all-powerful, knowing, sweet, merciful God." He paused, slowly looked across the sea of faces staring up at him, and said, "Did I say 'merciful'? Our *merciful* God? How can our God be merciful when he causes so much horror and sadness to come down on us in that blinking of an eye? What kind of merciful God is gonna do something like that to us? His children? He takes some, then he leaves some. . . . That's *us*. How can that be?"

He took another sip of water. The interior of the church was filled with a warm, sad silence. They waited, his congregation, waited for his words. He took a deep breath, confident now, knowing, ready to lead his flock out of the darkness.

"Brothers and sisters," he thundered, "I said we'd talk about what happened. Aliens?" He chuckled, "Well then, let's all put on our tinfoil hats and hurry on out to Area Fifty-one so we'll be ready!" He was rewarded with a few chuckles, and some heads shaking. "Megavirus? Maybe that one is more plausible, it *could* happen. But I believe a sudden disease of global impact would have to be otherworldly anyway. So what is it then? Oh, I almost forgot the secret death-ray thing. . . . One of our enemies has this laser-beam kind of weapon and they've been shooting us with it. Yeah, all right . . . but isn't it odd that they've been shooting *themselves* with it too? What about the Muslims of our world? They apparently have not been touched. Could it be them? I suggest they are so busy tearing at each other, they can't coordinate long enough to carry out such a sweeping plan. They seem to be at war with themselves. No . . . no way."

A beam of light shone through one of the high windows to his right. He could see tiny dust motes suspended in the golden air, and he felt his heart swell. "Children of God," he intoned, "let us look at the other, more probable scenario. Our Lord Jesus is calling us home. He has already taken our children, our most Christian-like. We can surmise that those of us who did not rise up are somehow not ready, perhaps not complete. No, someone else might say, you are simply *sinners,* and you are here because you are *not worthy.*"

He heard the uncomfortable silence, he heard his own heart crashing around in his chest. " 'But Reverend Smith,' " he said in a singsong voice, " 'you are a man of God, Reverend, you are not a sinner, you teach us about the Bible, about our Lord. It can't be right that you are still here.' " He let his gaze sweep the room again, then went on: "I say to you, perhaps I'm here, and you are here, because we still have work to do. Maybe our Lord wants more out of us, maybe we can still spread the Word, explain the Scripture, save a few more souls before it's our turn." Reverend Smith felt his own spirits lift at this point. Perhaps there was a reason why he'd been left on Earth.

"Am I prideful? Am I trying to rationalize? You be the judge. I say to you gathered here in this church, you are here for a *reason.* I don't think we can doubt that the end times have begun, my children. Like, yes, I'll say it, the end of the world as written in Revelation. It's all right there, been there for centuries, all laid out step by step. You know what, brothers and sisters? I believe it still. But let us not doubt this: We are here, and we will suffer."

He heard his own voice, amazed at the power, the richness of it. He carried on. "But" — he raised one finger in the air — "but even as it is written, we might still have a chance. There will come a savior, says the Book. A savior who will reign. I ask you: Does it have to be the Antichrist? Does it? No it doesn't.

"This is our God we're talking about here. Yes, our merciful God. Satan was defeated by our sweet Jesus ages ago, and Jesus and God will not let us fall. If we try now to understand, try to heed his lesson. We go now with the Scripture in hand, we testify, have I sinned, have I lusted for more? *Yes*.

"Am I lost. . . . Are *you* lost? No, I say, no. We must hold on to the mystery of faith, hold on to the faith that we will be shown the way, hold on to our hearts, and be ready for the one who will lead us. The one who will lead us home. Home, and back into the embrace of those angels we have so suddenly lost. Is it possible the God-knowing churches of the world — call them any name you wish — is it possible they already knew it was coming? You've heard it preached since you were a child. Yes, the churches knew, and the churches were preparing. There has been a not so secret entwining of faith and acceptance. A plan . . . it was given a name . . . a plan to start with, a plan that would be driven by one we would immediately *know*. I say to you now, don't lose faith. Be ready. We are not lost. There will be one who will bring us salvation, and we will be led home to where we belong."

He looked down at his hands. They were balled into fists in front of him. A ribbon of ice wrapped around his heart, then spiraled down into his groin. He shivered. God help me, he thought. God help me, God help me. He looked out at the hungry, frightened faces of his flock, and said, "Let us pray now, pray to our one and only loving and *merciful* God. Let us pray. . . ."

Chapter Eight

In the beginning, they conquered in a manner more like ancient Mongol hordes than a modern army. They waged war, it seemed, simply for the sake of waging war. Their goal appeared to be destabilization, in an already destabilized world. They were the Harakar ul-Mujahideen, Lashkar-e-Taiba, and Jaish-e-Muhammad, but the media simply called them the mujahideen Muslims. They had been warily ignored by most of the world as they ravaged what remained of Africa. Many governments, it seemed, overwhelmed with other, internal problems, pretended not to notice how the marauders ate the center out of the African continent, then chewed up the coasts, until only the northern countries remained. A few intrepid journalists sent reports out from the battle zones at great risk to themselves, only to be met with apathy by their editors.

During their first victories, the mujahideen had armed themselves with weaponry possessed by their defeated enemies. The arms trade worldwide had never really stopped flourishing, and everyone knew about the giant Russian armament flea market after the USSR disintegrated. Every time another country fell, the Muslims recovered more stores of explosives, ammunition, assault rifles, antitank missiles, heat-seeking Stinger-type shoulder-fired ground-to-air missiles, and armored vehicles. Soon they had tanks, trucks, support vehicles, and communications capabilities. It was rumored that they had also acquired limited-range ballistic missiles, some bio and chemical weapons, helicopters, ground-support aircraft, and electronic-warfare equipment like basic radar, false-signal, and Global Positioning System navigation instruments.

The mujahideen soldiers almost defiantly acknowledged that they had very little in the way of medevac, field hospitals, or long-term treatment centers. Again reverting to the philosophy of ancient plunderers, they warred with the acceptance of death or injury. If they were wounded but could carry on, they fought again. If they were wounded so badly that they needed help, needed medical specialists to care for them, they fully expected to be killed on the spot by their own.

Like the voracious hordes that decimated the combined armies of the European continent centuries ago, the mujahideen had no interest in rebuilding the governments or infrastructures of the defeated. They came to destroy, to kill, to loot, pillage, and burn. They took slaves, they took women for sport, and they either killed or ignored the very old and very young. Roads, bridges, airfields, homes, buildings, power plants, hotels — these were tangible evidence of what the "enemy" used to be. The radical Muslims destroyed all in their path, with no regard for what life would be like for those who remained after the battles moved on. They were vicious and animal-like, these soldiers of the mujahideen, led by men just that much more vicious, led by spawns of war. The mujahideen had for leaders men who attained rank by sheer brutality and cunning. They would kill their own as soon as the enemy if it suited their purpose. This caused the formation of warlords — tribal affiliations within the parent organization — and this "system" worked better than other, "professional" armies might have guessed. The key to success was having as an ultimate leader one who had proven himself to be the *most* cunning, vicious, rapacious, and cruel. Sure, it slowed the progress of the army down when units within turned on one another during a campaign, but the Muslims seemed to be in no hurry. They would forage and plunder while the infighting reached its apogee and then died down, perhaps jumping on their defeated sister battalions themselves if they thought they could come away with something of value.

Before becoming something more than just a small blip on the world's radar, they'd instigated uprisings in Indonesia, the Philippines, and other third world countries. The world began to take notice when the mujahideen attacked the North African countries — especially when the borders of Egypt were first tested. The Egyptian government immediately screamed for help from its Arab neighbors, and when their response was lukewarm, even petitioned the United States, and then Israel, arguing that if Egypt fell, the entire African continent would collapse. Diplomatic bluster and wrangling raged back and forth, but the mujahideen marched on. Ethiopia, the Sudan, Chad, Niger — these countries had already fallen. The Muslim fanatics did not linger on the parched lands of their victories, because those lands could barely sustain the native citizens in times of peace. A conqueror could not fill its belly on this.

They headed east, and north. Mauritania fell; then Morocco, Algeria, and Libya somehow sued for peace with Izbek Noir, and they were left intact, with the proviso that they become part of the mujahideen logistical base. The tatters of free world cooperation that existed offered no resistance, but the countries that had been the leaders before the fall began to pay attention as the mujahideen appeared ready to drive into Israel and the Arab countries of the Middle East.

That was all before the disappearance and the attack on Mecca. The mujahideen were galvanized by this attack on Islam's holiest of holy places, and the factionalism and in-fighting that had marked most of their efforts now paled in comparison to the sheer numbers eager to join their ranks. With them, these new recruits brought their own allegiances and enemies, but like a diffuse source of light brought into focus by a powerful lens, the Muslim world's distrust and hatred of the West could burn hot and intense and had the potential to consume everything in its path.

Izbek Noir's planned attack had worked better than even he had imagined. From paranoid outlaw to visionary leader, his transformation was complete. Initially, his recruits had been the displaced and the downtrodden; now even the most moderate Arab politicians and the most Western-leaning intellectuals and religious leaders saw his attacks on fellow Muslims as part of a ritual cleansing — leaving behind only those possessed of a defiant spirit ready to end Western repression.

Intelligence agencies and government advisers were caught off guard when branches of the mujahideen, Taiba, and Muhammad boiled up out of the chaos that was Argentina. It was known that the disappearance had taken its toll in South and Central America, as it had everywhere else on Earth, but the extent of the disintegration was not accurately gauged. Inexplicably, while the Muslims ravaged North Africa, their general, Izbek Noir, appeared at the head of the first violent mobs that ran amok through Argentina, then north into the guts of South America . . . much as it had in Africa. Bolivia, Paraguay, and Peru fell victim to the onslaught, and soon Brazil found it necessary to pull its troops farther away from its borders as the hordes flailed at them. More than one intelligence chief around the globe, keeping an eye on events in Africa and South America, noted the apparently impossible appearances of Izbek Noir. "This guy can't really be in two places at once . . . can he?" That the mujahideen and Izbek Noir were becoming a threat to whatever chance the world had at recovering from the disappearance was acknowledged. First stabilize the world, was the accepted plan, then make things whole again.

Cat Early was completely disoriented. She tried to open her eyes, but they were caked with dust and dirt. Her back hurt, and her neck felt strained. She realized she was upside down, plastered against a brick wall like a cartoon character. She moved one shoulder, and crumpled onto the rubble-strewn floor in a heap.

"What? What?" she said through gritty teeth. She heard a moan, and croaked, "Slim? Are you okay?"

"I seem to be breathing," Slim said from the other side of the enclosure, "and I've still got my cameras. Other than that I can't say right now."

They were with a group of international journalists invited by the Egyptian government to witness firsthand the destruction being done to the country by the invaders.

They had landed in Cairo the day before, and were now at a small airfield between Aswân and Luxor. They had seen several air strikes aimed at unseen targets to the south. Smoke from oil fires and dust from an army on the move filled the southern skies, and the booming of artillery was a constant thunder. They had seen and heard the impact of a few missiles, but who had fired them was not made clear. They were told of the Egyptian air force's valiant fight, and had seen many aircraft and vapor trails against the blue. They knew from their own research that military aircraft from other Arab countries had also been thrown into the fray, and there was a rumor that Israel might jump in to help. Strange times, it was agreed.

On the morning of the disappearance, Cat Early had awakened from a fitful sleep, thrown aside her camouflaged blanket, and looked around the misty battlefield outside of Islamabad. Along with many other Western journalists, a few tourists, and an odd assortment of diplomatic personnel and drifters, they were encamped in a compound a few miles from the fighting. She could hear the cries and wailing of the wounded, and sensed the fear. The sounds of artillery, often so rhythmic they induced sleep in her, had fallen silent.

She glanced a few feet away and saw Slim's empty bedroll. Beside it was a pile of clothes, a pair of boots, and what looked like his camera equipment. Nothing else. She sat up, pulled her hair away from her face, and saw and heard the panicked people screaming for their loved ones — even the soldiers. She had an odd and unsettling comprehension of what had occurred — not the how or why — that thousands, if not millions, of people had been "taken."

She had crawled over to Slim's gear and was pawing through it with a sinking feeling when he walked up behind her and said, "Listen, Cat . . . I want you to get into my bedroll when I'm *in it*, okay?" He wore his ragged campaign pants, no shirt, no shoes. She had been so relieved to see him she began sobbing, and he had turned away, embarrassed.

After a moment, he took her hand, pulled her to her feet, and said, "C'mon. There is a total weirdness to our world this morning, you gotta see it." Thus, they discovered the aftermath of the disappearance together. They had followed the reports of open warfare in Africa, the stories of the unnaturally brutal mujahideen, the death and destruction they caused even as the world was reeling. But nothing could prepare them for what they'd heard on CNN, read over the AP and Reuters wires. The world was waking to a brand-new day — one that was darker than any anyone had previously experienced. Until the attack on Mecca, when events seemed to crystallize. They wangled a couple of seats on a Jordanian military jet, and deplaned in Egypt, making their way to the defense position along the Nile. Other than some friends, Cat had no one close to her heart to lose. She knew Slim had a couple of sisters somewhere, and his mom. She had waited a few feet away while Slim made contact with a friend at home from a communications center in Cairo. He gave her a sad grin after hanging up, shook his head, and said, "They're gone. They were . . . good. Now they're gone and I'm still here and . . ."

They hadn't spoken of it since then.

They had been sitting in a small brick enclosure, pondering a message Cat had received from her home office on her cell phone. General Izbek Noir had agreed to be interviewed. He had asked for the journalist Cat Early. While they talked they could hear the sounds of battle in the near distance; then Slim lifted his head, held up one finger, and said, "Listen."

At that moment a crashing roar followed by a bone-rattling thud turned their world into a tumbling, choking cauldron of noise, burning powder, and dirt. Cat had been slammed against one wall of the structure. Two walls were blown away, and the wooden ceiling collapsed. Cat slid off the wall, tumbled to a sitting position, and carefully wiped the dirt away from her eyes. She saw Slim pushing a piece of ceiling off his hips and brushing the sand out of his hair, and looked to her left, where two Egyptian soldiers assigned to escort them had been waiting. She looked away from their twisted and ruptured bodies. "Let's get out of here," said Slim as he grabbed his things from the rubble and stood. She could see a trickle of blood coming from his left ear, and there was a red smear on his right elbow. "Must have been an unexploded shell, or maybe it was a bomb rigged a while ago," gasped Cat. "I'd hate to think it was a land mine."

Slim shrugged. "No telling." He looked around the wrecked building. "Aw, man. It killed our two guys."

They stepped outside, and found the bodies of three journalists who had traveled with them. They looked like mis-shapen piles of bloody rags. Cat turned away from two and went to the third. It was the French woman she had met in Pakistan. The woman stared at the hard blue sky that stretched above her, grasping a fatigue jacket over her chest and stomach. As Cat knelt beside her she saw the jacket turning dark red as it was soaked with her blood, and saw a thick puddle of it forming under the small of her back. She leaned close to the woman's face, and saw a half-smoked thin brown cigarette laying in the sand near her neck. She picked it up, carefully put it between the woman's thin lips, and said, "Hold on, Eva, we'll get help."

The woman grabbed Cat's right shoulder hard with one clutching hand, sucked on the cigarette, and said in a raspy voice, "No. I'm dead in a moment." She took a great gasping breath, and added, "Now I'll discover what is . . . really . . . going . . . on. . . ." Her face became still, the cigarette fell from her lips into the sand, and her hand dropped away from Cat's shoulder. Cat turned her face away, sat in the dust and rubble, and sobbed.

"Cat, look." Slim sat beside her and wrapped his arms around her. "This stuff is bad, but we've got to keep it together. I don't know how, I don't know why, but we're still here. Maybe we're supposed to somehow make sense of all this."

When Cat didn't respond, Slim closed his eyes and laughed. "You remember Ticonderoga pencils, Cat? The mystery behind the number two? Didn't you have kids in your class that always had to be different and use the two and a halfs, sometimes the threes?"

Cat stopped crying long enough to glare at him.

"I'm no good at comforting people, Cat. So all I can do is fill in the empty spaces so that you don't have time to think about the bad stuff. Had a dog once that could sing on cue. Fire siren would go off every day at noon and he'd howl." He could feel Cat relaxing into his embrace. "I feel like howling every noon, too, Cat. 'Dog Boy and Cat Found Safe Outside Islamabad.' Wouldn't that be a headline? Cat, I'm scared out of my mind half the time. Wouldn't be surprised that every one of my photos comes back out of focus or fuzzy from camera shake. My jaw aches so bad from grinding my teeth every night you'd think I could grind you a pound of coffee for the morning."

Cat sat up and wiped her eyes with the

back of her hands, leaving two swathes of mud as underliner. "What was his name?"

"Henry."

"That's not a good dog name."

"We called him Croquette after his favorite dog food."

"Croquette?"

"That's French for a small froggy thing, I guess."

Cat fought against it, but she had to smile at Slim's meager joke.

"Good to see you smile a little bit. Got to get you gussied up for your interview with the international man of misery."

"Slim, stop it, okay. For just a minute? We can feel bad, you know? We should feel bad. It's not like they took our hearts when they issued us a press credential or whatever." Cat could see that Slim was uncomfortable, but she pressed on. "You told me you were scared, and I appreciate that. Makes me feel less alone. I don't know that I can face this guy."

"I'll be right there with you, filming away."

"Why me, Slim? Why'd he pick me?"

Slim looked at the bodies of those killed by the explosion. "Seems like it could have been worse." He stood and held his hand out to her. "I've no answer to that one, though. That's better answered by minds greater than mine."

Two hours later, a few miles south of where they had been, they stood behind a large tank, face-to-face with General Izbek Noir. He was tall and dark, with piercing black eyes, a square jaw, and a permanent scowl. Cat shivered as she carefully examined him standing there; she knew he was either the soldier, Nacht, she had seen live through the grenade blast, or his twin. These guys are *both* the evil twin, she thought.

Noir wore battle dress, clean and tailored. He wore a large automatic pistol on his webbed belt, and had a folding-stock assault rifle slung across his back. The three mujahideen soldiers who had found them, taken them prisoner, and escorted them to their general stood a few feet away. All the others who had been around the tank as they walked up had been dismissed.

Cat glanced at Slim, examined his bruised right eye, split lower lip, and bloody nose, saw him shake his head covertly as if to shrug it off, then turned her gaze back to the general. "Thank you, General Noir, for granting us this interview. Before we begin, however, I must protest my treatment at the hands of your troops here." She pointed at the three, who stood relaxed, grinning at her. "This one" — she pointed at a heavyset soldier with a heavy beard — "tried to rape me. First he was to search me before bringing me to you, but then he began pulling at my clothes, and grabbing me. He threw me to the ground before my colleague" — she pointed with her chin at Slim — "stepped in to stop him. He is a fellow journalist, and was severely beaten by all three for his trouble. Doesn't the Koran instruct fighters for Islam to leave noncombatants alone?"

Izbek Noir shrugged. "I was to meet you, not you and your photographer friend, Catherine Early. My troops are without comfort for great lengths of time. I place no restraints on them. Captured women of defeated enemies are theirs to use as they wish. Perhaps you looked defeated. And a word of caution . . . don't try to throw the Koran in my face. Is it not written in your holy book that a man shall take an eye for an eye and a tooth for a tooth? I am not a mullah, but we all understand the key word in respect to any revelation is inter-pretation."

He waited for her response. She shook

her head but said nothing. "But," he said, "it would have been a pity if you had been damaged before you reported back on my message to the world. I wanted you to see and hear me. So this soldier jeopardized my little plan." With a glance he dismissed the other two, leaving only the heavyset man standing there. The man held his assault rifle loosely in his hands, stared blankly off into the distance.

"So, Catherine Early," said the general as he motioned for her and Slim to sit at a small field table surrounded by four folding chairs, "have you noticed anything different about the world lately?"

"You mean the disappearance?" replied Cat as she sat down warily. "All the people who have vanished?"

"Precisely," said Noir. "Interesting, no? Only Christians, isn't that something? Perhaps the beginning of the end. What do you think?"

"I don't know what to think," replied Cat honestly. "I hadn't heard that it was only Christians. Perhaps that's your interpretation."

The general waved his hand. "No matter. That is not why you are here today. You want to know about me, my plans."

"Yes."

"Listen, and then tell it, Catherine Early. This world was a mess before the disappearance, as your media like to call it. I was already taking my first steps toward fixing it, and now I am on a fast track. It is time for a world leader, one man with the vision, strength, and leadership . . . one man with the message for the people of the world. I have been called ruthless, cruel. It is said I only desire death and destruction. And what of the attack on Mecca? Thousands dead. Was this an act of mercy? And yet I am the one who is vilified. Yet I offer my enemies the chance to die honorably, to engage in battle, not come at them like a thief in the night." Noir took a drink from an earthenware jar that was placed before him.

"This world needs a new message and I'm the one who will deliver it. Life will be very livable once the various factions of the world come together under a firm guiding hand. My hand. At present, with all the different cultures, different mores, religions, the world is disjointed, an ineffective mess. Any tearing down of an existing system for the purpose of replacing it with a better system involves some pain, some . . . breakage. I can only tell you, and I want you to explain it to your readers, that to resist these winds of change will only make the pain last longer. This is a confused and frightened world right now, and the ones who have been downtrodden for centuries, those disenfranchised masses with no power, no voice, they should prepare to embrace me. It will be for the good of all. I am for the good . . . of all."

Cat checked to make sure that her digital recorder was still running. She saw out of the corner of her eye that Slim was quietly taking pictures while Noir spoke. She captured Noir's words, and shuddered. Sounds like another garden variety megalomaniac, another Hitler, another twisted child of Islam bent on world domination, she thought. But from what we've already seen . . . this maniac might be capable of pulling it off if he isn't stopped soon.

"My message," continued the general, "condensed, is this: Respect me, but do not resist. As a father must rule a household, so must I. I know what the future holds, what the world cannot yet see. Welcome the winds of change, help us, help me, make this world one where even the lowliest man or woman can live in comfort. Fear me, but do not resist. The world should understand by now that whatever deity you have prayed to through the centuries has clearly failed you, failed us. It is clear that the West has been punished for its sins of excess. So I offer my hand to any in need of assistance. This is not a world controlled by a divine force, it is a cesspool of greed, corruption, and manipulation. Follow me, lay down your arms as you see me approach, or simply turn them on your present leaders. They have failed you. I will not."

"I must say, with all due respect, General Noir," said Cat cautiously but firmly, "this message you want me to include in my story about you sounds like simple propaganda. I want to report who you are, where you came from, create a profile that will round you out as a human being and potential world leader. If you are successful —"

Izbek Noir smiled and nodded. "Rather than 'successful,' Catherine Early, I would use the word 'triumphant.' More direct and forceful, don't you think? As far as the propaganda, I agree. What politician ever interviewed hasn't spewed out his propaganda? This is what I want to say to the people of the world, that's all, and I'm counting on you. Your rise as a recognized journalist and the respect your words carry will help to warn and educate the masses.

If done correctly and accurately, your words could negate untold suffering."

"It has been reported that you 'miraculously' appeared in South America, seen there by many even while you directed your troops here against Egypt," said Cat. "Can you explain how that came to be?"

General Noir laughed, his head back. The heavyset, bearded soldier standing a few feet from the table, behind Slim, laughed too. "I like the word 'miraculous,' " said Noir. "Mysterious, unfathomable." He sighed. "I have cutting-edge transportation capabilities," he said, then laughed again. "I can be where I want, when I want, you understand? A general must lead his troops, must be where the action is. There's no mystery to it, really. Let others believe what they will."

"Were you in Pakistan or India, at the border battles throughout Kashmir?"

"Of course," replied Noir. "I just told you I go where I'm needed."

"But I thought I met —"

"Enough." The general stood. "You have enough now."

"But, General Noir." A plaintive plea rose in Cat's voice. She and Slim stood. "We still don't know who you are, where you came from, personal —"

"I am General Izbek Noir," said Noir quietly. "I was weaned in the stench of death and despair in Balkan Europe. I am a Muslim. Soldiers will die for me. The masses will follow me. I am very real, and intend to bring this sorry world under my guiding hand. Embrace me, do not resist me. That is all you need to know."

Cat clicked off her recorder and looked into Noir's eyes. They pulled at her, caressed her, penetrated her own eyes with a knowing stare. "Okay," she said. "Okay. Thank you, General." She glanced at Slim, then back at Noir, and asked, "Will you provide transportation for us to a safe location?"

The general looked at Slim and said, "You, Catherine Early, I will provide safe passage for. This one" — he pointed at the young, dusty photographer — "this one I am tired of seeing. He tags along where he is not welcome. You will no longer need to work with him."

"But, General Noir," protested Cat, "he is with me and —"

"No longer," said the general as he pulled his large black automatic pistol from its holster on his side. He pointed it at Slim's face, less than three feet from the barrel.

"*No!*" Cat shouted and she lunged for the weapon. Her right hand was within a few inches of his right forearm when it could go no farther. She watched as the pistol rocked back in recoil, then heard the punching blast as it was fired. She turned and saw Slim flinch, his eyes wide, his mouth open. He staggered backward, one hand coming up to the center of his chest. But he did not fall, and when his hand came away there was no blood.

Cat heard a gasp, then a throaty gag, and looked over Slim's shoulder at the heavyset, bearded Muslim soldier who stood behind the photographer. The man's head lay at an odd angle, and there was a huge bloody hole in the center of his throat. Without another sound, his shocked eyes locked on his general, the man slowly reached up with one hand, carefully fingered the gaping wound, and collapsed onto the ground, dead.

A lump in her throat, her mouth dry, Cat turned again to Izbek Noir. He smiled at her, and shrugged as he reholstered the pistol. He seemed pleased with himself. Slim, apparently afraid to move or attempt to speak, remained frozen in place, his eyes darting from Cat to Noir to Noir's gun.

"That soldier acted stupidly," Noir said

to Cat. He shrugged, his shoulders almost reaching his ears, and added, "His orders were to bring you unharmed. Simple. His orders also told him to bring you alone." He turned to Slim then and said, "Photographer, I've seen your work. You are good. I want you to stay with me, travel with me for a while. Take photos, record what I accomplish, what happens to those who resist."

"Thank you, sir," Slim managed, knowing he was being offered the chance of a lifetime. "But I travel with Cat, here. I mean, somebody has to watch out for her."

"Yes," said Cat anxiously. "Slim works with me, General. Though your offer is generous, I'm sure it would be better if we —"

"He stays with me," said the general coldly.

"Then I won't leave," said Cat through the lump in her throat. "He goes with me, period."

"Then I will kill him. Period," replied Noir.

The three of them stared at one another in silence. Cat glanced at the crumpled body of the heavyset soldier.

"Actually, General Noir," said Slim with an awkward grin, "your career options, as outlined, leave me very little wiggle room. I accept your kind offer, and we will both wish Cat Godspeed, bon chance, and good luck."

"No way," said Cat, her heart twisting under her ribs.

"Way," said Slim with a "Get out of here" look and a wink.

"I'm sure I'll see you again, Catherine Early," said Izbek Noir.

Within moments Cat was on her way out, hating him more than she'd ever hated anyone.

Chapter Nine

Ron Underwood, self-confessed news junkie, turned off his car radio. He had been listening to the news as he tried to make his way home from the campus, and he was overwhelmed. What he'd heard was just too much, the worldwide unrest, millions supposedly missing, scenes of destruction and despair. He didn't have to listen to it, he was living it, he decided. So far the drive home had been very bizarre, with scenes right out of a horror film taking place in front of his eyes. The power went out in the building where his cluttered office was on campus. No power, no phones, no computers, no elevators, no air-conditioning. He heard people cursing and calling to one another, and went into the hallway to see what was up. He heard someone crying, then people calling again, an edge to their voices. Some people seemed to be gone. They were there, then they weren't. Someone quipped that perhaps they thought it was a fire drill of some kind, and they were sitting at the coffee shop across the common from the building, having a latte and laughing their heads off.

Within a few moments a change in the overall feeling took place. Something was definitely wrong. Some professors had been in conversation with students, or a secretary, or fellow teacher, and observed with their own eyes that person simply disappear. More people were openly sobbing now, and one philosophy prof, a small man with bulging eyes, hot breath, and a habit of standing too close when he spoke to someone, approached a small group congregated in the hallway and said, "It's the Muslims. It's the Muslims. They're targeting us because we're the *intelligentsia!*"

Underwood tried to call his house. He wanted to speak with Ivy, and he wanted to know that Ronnie was okay. He had already heard about the children being "taken," and his heart burned with fear. He tried the office phone, then his cell, to no avail. Almost frantic, he ran down two flights of stairs, shouldered the fire door open, and ran across the lot to his car. Several cars were parked at odd angles, and two or three fender benders were scattered around. He made it to his car, heard a screech and looked out the side window, and saw a beautiful young woman walking in circles a few feet away. The girl was pulling at her long blond hair with her hands, yanking clumps of it out and throwing it to the wind. Her eyes were wild.

"It's the end of the world," she sang. "It is *the* end of the *world* . . . and I've been saving myself . . . saving myself for *the day.* But now it's the end of the world, and I've saved myself for nothing. . . ." She saw Underwood staring at her, screeched again, and began tearing at her clothing. Underwood put the car in gear and drove away.

He almost hit two people before he could even get off the college campus. People were running everywhere, often screaming or calling out names as they did. Here and there he saw young men or women crouched or kneeling, apparently examining piles of books or backpacks that had suddenly dropped to the ground. Cars driven by crazy drivers careened around him, tires squealing, and once he almost ran into a ditch to avoid an oncoming pickup truck. The scenes in the downtown campus area were equally unreal. He was fairly certain that several of the people he saw lying on the sidewalks, roadways, and parking lots were dead. A couple looked like they had been beaten or run over. The few police officers he saw appeared frustrated and angry, and he came across a huge fire truck, engine running, sitting at a large intersection with not one firefighter on board.

He redialed his house several times with his cell phone, and was rewarded with the busy signal. He passed the corner gas station near his house and saw a line of cars angled across the sidewalk, trying to get to the pumps. A small knot of men fought viciously with one another, and as Ron drove past he saw the owner of the station come out of his office and fire a shotgun into the air. While he did so someone threw a bottle, which hit the man in the back of the head. He dropped the shotgun as he fell, and it fired again . . . right into one of the gas pumps; a few blocks later Ron saw a flash in his rearview mirror as the station exploded into a geyser of yellow-orange flame.

A minute later Ron pulled into his own driveway. He saw the Belkers, his elderly next-door neighbors, sitting together on the front porch swing. He began reflexively to wave at them, then stopped and looked closer. They seemed to be hugging, but both had a splotch of bright red blood in the center of their chest, and what looked like an old black pistol lay in Mr. Belker's right hand. Ron fought back the urge to gag, called out, "Ivy! Ivy? Where are you? Are you okay? I'm home," and ran into his house.

Ivy waited for him at the top of the stairs, her face a mask of composure. He stopped just inside the front door when he saw her there, and said, "Oh, Ivy . . . thank goodness you're okay." She said nothing, her eyes bright. "Ronnie?" said Ron. "Is Ronnie up there with you, Ivy?"

"He said 'Mommy,' Ron," said Ivy quietly. "He said 'Mommy.' "

"He *did?* That's why . . . That's amazing, Ivy. How?"

"Then he was gone," added Ivy, her eyes locked on to her husband's. "I think it's my fault."

Confused and frightened, Ron rushed up the stairs, brushed past Ivy, and went into Ronnie's room. The wheelchair sat there, chrome, leather, sweat, urine, and tears. It was comforting to see it — the place Ronnie could usually be found. Ronnie was *not* there, though, and Ron turned to Ivy, who stood in the doorway, her arms crossed in front of her chest. He tried to speak, couldn't, swallowed, and managed, "How . . . gone? Not gone like all those others? What do you mean your fault?" Ron put his hand on the seat's back cushion, hoping to find some sign of Ronnie, heat from his body, the indentation from his head.

"He said Ronnie could be made whole," Ivy said as if to herself, "Ronnie could be made perfect. Like he should have been perfect when he was born. I wanted it to be, Ron, I wanted it to be."

"What?"

She stepped to him and put her hands on his shoulders. She turned her face up to his, her expression sad and gentle. "I know, Ron. I know it was my fault from the beginning. I pressured you, I wanted to be pregnant before you were ready to begin a family. I pressured you and had my way."

"What?" said Ron. "How . . . gone? Ronnie can't be . . . gone . . ."

"Listen to me, Ron," said Ivy. "It wasn't your fault. You have no 'crippled genes' in your family history like I accused. Ronnie had an unfair, crummy, stupid accident, and it severely damaged him. Okay. Ron? Are you hearing me?"

Ron Underwood pulled away from his wife's grasp and walked slowly to the empty wheelchair. He knelt beside it and placed his right palm flat on the seat. He turned and looked at Ivy, his eyes filled with tears and question.

"He's gone, Ron. Taken, like all the others."

"Taken . . . where?" Ron managed.

Ivy blew out a puff of air, shook her head, and said, "Heaven, I think. You believe in heaven, right, Ron? That would be a place where Ronnie could be 'made whole again,' right?" She turned her back on her husband and the wheelchair, and went on. "Here's the thing, Ron. I'm quite sure I met the devil in a restaurant the other day." Ivy couldn't believe that she was stating this all so matter-of-factly, as if she were telling Ron that she'd bumped into one of his colleagues in the grocery store.

Ron did not look up, but said, "You met the devil in a restaurant."

"I thought he wanted me to, you know, wanted to . . . fool around."

"You thought the devil wanted to fool around." Ron scratched his head and sighed. He looked around the room to see if Ivy had left any telltale signs anywhere — a glass, a bottle. She'd never been one to drink, but there's never been a day like this before either.

"I was into my 'tease' thing. You know, Ron. Being a bad girl, or playing at being a bad girl."

"And you thought the devil wanted you," said Ron quietly. He could feel Ronnie's absence expanding, filling the room and squeezing his chest.

"That's the thing, Ron," replied Ivy. "That's why this is my fault. It's like the perfect irony, don't you see?"

Ron remembered how reluctant he'd been to share with his family the news that Ivy was pregnant. He'd told everyone when asked that they were a long way from having a child. He had an idea for a book, and with it published, he'd likely be able to get a job teaching at the state university. From there, who knew?

"What is the perfect irony, Ivy?"

"I thought he wanted me, but he wanted to talk about Ronnie, and he told me he could make him whole. Make Ronnie a normal boy. Fix Ronnie. Fix his life, and ours."

"Nothing about our life needed fixing but you, Ivy," said Ron, his voice almost a whisper.

She stopped. She held each one of his words up to an inner light, and found them to be pure. They stung, and she let them. After a moment she said softly, "Yes. You're right, Ron. I needed fixing. I *need* fixing." She paused, and moved to the window. "Did you see the Belkers sitting on their porch when you pulled in, Ron?" she asked. "I watched them. It was an act of love, and for a few minutes I considered doing it to myself." She stared out the window, tears leaving silver tracks on her cheeks. "But I was afraid. I am afraid."

"What about Ronnie?" asked Ron.

"The guy . . . I think the guy was the devil, Ron," answered Ivy. "And he offered to make Ronnie whole and all I had to do was promise him my soul. I did. I promised him . . . I think. In my heart I said yes to him. Yes, make Ronnie whole, and I'll give over my soul to you. That's what I said in my heart."

"But," said Ron, "what . . . irony? And what happened to Ronnie?"

"What happened to Ronnie *is* the irony, Ron," she answered with renewed strength. "I gave up my soul as trade to make Ronnie whole again here on Earth, and not a day later Ronnie is lifted up."

"Lifted up?" repeated Ron. "Like lifted to heaven? The Second Coming and all that whistling in the dark? Are you crazy, Ivy?"

"I thought you were okay with my Christian beliefs, Ron," said Ivy, surprised by her husband's anger. "Isn't heaven a part of it? Do you think God lets kids like Ronnie stay . . . challenged . . . like that? No . . . God welcomes them, and they're whole, fixed, new, perfect."

"Oh, Ivy."

"Ron," said Ivy, facing him, "I sat at the window, I heard Ronnie behind me say as clear as a bell, 'Mommy,' I turned, and he was gone. He was in his chair, silent, his face peaceful like always, and then he *wasn't* there, okay? And it's my fault, and it's the perfect irony. I sold my soul for my son, and now he's in heaven and I guess the joke is on the devil this time." She hesitated, licked her lips, and added softly, "And me."

Ron sat for a moment, unsure if he should share with Ivy what he'd been thinking. He'd blamed himself too, certain that God had seen into his heart and known that he'd not really wanted this child, not at first, and that he was being punished for his selfishness. He'd loved Ronnie as much as he'd ever loved anyone or anything. The irony that Ron lived with was that most people saw his life, his son, as incomplete. The truth was that Ronnie had made him whole, brought him out of his insular self. Now his son was gone.

She watched as Ron stood slowly, then

turned and began searching all around the bedroom. He looked in the closets and under the bed. He went into the bathroom; she heard the shower-stall doors slide back. He came out, looked at her quizzically, and walked out of the room. She waited, following his search through the entire house in her mind. The electricity came back on twice while she waited, and went off again both times. She heard sirens in the distance, and someone sobbing loudly in the yard behind their house. After a while Ron came back to his son's bedroom. He looked at Ivy, looked at the empty wheelchair, and asked, "Ivy? Where's Ronnie? Where's my Ronnie-boy? I want to talk with him."

Ivy's eyes filled with tears as she reached out for him, and said, "Ron, oh . . . Ron . . ."

He pulled away from her grasp, walked slowly to the chair, turned, and eased himself into it. He placed his forearms on the armrests and laid his head against the neck brace. He pulled one foot, and then the other, onto the footrests. Huge fat glistening tears hung on the edges of his eyes as he stared straight ahead.

"Ron," said Ivy, very frightened, "don't do that. Ron. C'mon, don't sit there like that."

Ron remained silent, immobile.

"We have to leave here, get out of here, Ron. I . . . I've got a feeling in my heart, I can't explain it. I know we can't stay here. We must go east . . . east someplace. To a church to hear a lesson." Ivy moved around the room, straightening and dusting. "Do you hear me, Ron? We've got to go. I know it will be hard, and probably dangerous too. The radio has been saying the roads are a mess and it's impossible to get gasoline or food. But, Ron, I've got cash saved up, and we'll make it okay. Gas and food and stuff, we'll make it. There's a church, Ron, a preacher. I . . . I have to go hear him." She reached out and placed one hand on his shoulder. "Ron? Ron?"

Without turning his head, his voice weirdly strained, he said, "What if the preacher made the same deal you did?"

Ivy did not know what to say.

"Where is my Ronnie?" asked Ron Underwood. Ron spoke as though he were snapping each word off a tree and chewing it.

"Ron. Ronnie's gone," Ivy answered, her voice steady though her hands were shaking. "C'mon with me now."

"I'm not going to see any preacher, east, south, up, or down," replied Ron. "I'm sitting right here and waiting —"

"Waiting for what?" asked Ivy, already knowing the answer.

"For Ronnie, Ivy," said Ron through clenched teeth. "For my son, Ronnie."

The shadows in the room were long when she left him.

John Jameson stood in the doorway of his father's house. A complete emptiness, a void, stared back at him. The house had become a place freeze-framed, without purpose and without reason. He reflected on the last time he was home, how he felt it was the house his father had built, the place where he had grown from childhood, the home his father had told him he could always return to. Every reason for the structure that was wood frame, brick, and glass to be shaped into a 'home' was gone, he knew, and he looked at it now as sadly irrelevant like coming across a combination to a long-lost lock. He sighed, adrift and uncertain.

He had been given eight hours. His headquarters building, when he finally got there after jetting out of Morocco, was in disarray, as if a wide-ranging flu or a wild office Christmas party had decimated the staff. Security was tight but disjointed, and he had waited, frustrated, while hazmat and biochem teams in full regalia checked out him and others as they tried to enter the building. He was told that the secretarial staff, for some reason, had taken a good hit, and someone tried a bad joke about next time hiring younger secretaries. He was heartened to find most of his bosses in the building and struggling to rebuild the tatters of a worldwide intelligence network. Agents had disappeared, some as a result of the disappearance, some perhaps taken out by other agents under the cover of chaos, and some simply in the wrong place at the wrong time. Run over by a milk truck in Hamburg, or killed by a mob looting a bazaar on the outskirts of Calcutta.

He had been given a quick debriefing. The two years his organization had spent infiltrating various terrorist cells — the reason he had been in Algeria — were down the toilet. Forget them — different world situation, different game. Then he was shuffled upstairs, to the office of the agent in charge of operations. A few were missing from this area too, he noted, and word had already come in about a couple of agents who had called in to say sayonara before blowing their own brains out while sitting in empty places where their families used to be. A cold fist grew in Jameson's stomach as he listened to the reports.

The details in his new briefing were sketchy. He already knew about the mujahideen . . . the joining of forces within the radical Muslim sects, their intolerance for any other interpretations of their own book or protestations from other, more pacifist Islamic nations. He even remembered a short piece he had read by a female journalist, international type, concerning the ascension of Izbek Noir. He was told now that the scope of the Muslim threat had widened. Rather than facing an amorphous mass of cells, they faced a thing that had taken shape and was walking upright in a matter of what seemed days. Maybe the supporters of the virus theory weren't so wrong after all. Clearly the world was reeling, shaken and on the ropes as a result of the devastating losses of people, many of whom ran or worked in power plants, hospitals, transportation centers, water-purification sites, trash-hauling services, and the like. In Mexico City, for example, simple garbage disposal had collapsed completely. Tons of waste had begun to accumulate rapidly, leaving mountains of raw garbage in the streets, sewers, and waterways. Insects, disease, and pestilence were next on the agenda.

In the U.S., things were shaky, but already plans were being implemented to get the basic community needs covered. Great losses among police and emergency personnel required a call for volunteers. Retired officers and firefighters were being asked to report to the nearest headquarters. Old veterans of all the services were being hastily assigned to various National Guard outfits, to help gain control of the near-anarchy that existed in cities and towns across the country. The roads were being cleared by wreckers and bulldozers; vehicles sitting with their engine running, no driver, were either towed or simply shoved into the nearest ditch. Many places in the world, he knew from firsthand experience, were scenes of such despair already they could not get much worse. Perhaps they were the lucky ones in the new world.

First, he was told in the hurried briefing, we . . . the world . . . need stability. Most wealthy, democratic countries, like the U.S., were already working toward it. Many places around the globe were not. Now add rapidly growing, unbelievably savage Muslim armies into this sad and confused mix, and they could destroy any chance left. The mujahideen must be stopped, must be met by strong forces. A coalition was the only answer. One country alone could not do it, even America. The briefing became sidetracked momentarily as an acrimonious discussion erupted regarding the American Muslim community. Already suspect, already targeted — some said unconstitutionally — as potential terrorist havens, they were now openly looked at as the enemy, members of the numerically dominant religion in the world. This, of course, was counter to what America stood for, opined one staffer, while another stated firmly that desperate times required desperate measures. The agent in charge brought the briefing back to the matter at hand.

Jameson, he was told, was to stand by for a special assignment, TDY the White House. President Reese, through her chief of staff, had sent a broad-based ops warning order stating only that an agent or team would be made available for a high-priority limited-access mission.

"That means no one can tell you what you're gonna do, John," said the operations boss amicably. "And very few people will know about it"

Jameson said nothing.

"I can fill you in a bit, off the cuff here, John," said his boss. "President Reese, along with Britain, France, Germany, Japan, and of course Israel, wants to put together a coalition strong enough to shred the mujahideen. Set them back, maybe confine them to one area of the world. Neutralize Izbek Noir. The United Nations . . . still well-meaning, bumbling, and passive . . . couldn't find its way in the rain, as you know. You've probably heard of this rising star, this Azul Dante. Comes out of old Europe, had a hand in restructuring the Euro money, seems to be good at diplomacy, getting enemies to sit down and talk instead of shooting Scud missiles at each other. He's in New York to address the members of the United Nations. Oddly enough," he said with a twisted grin, "their ranks were largely untouched. So Dante is going to speak to the UN. After that, on the sly, he's going to meet with our president for a cozy chat. That is why I think she's asked for one of our teams to be on standby. It might be a hit scenario."

Jameson thought it over. The others in the room were quiet. "I guess since Congress has sanctioned those kind of ops, she could include it in her bag of tricks. You know, of course, getting close enough to Noir — always surrounded by his fanatics — might not be easy."

"We wouldn't be talking to you, John, if it was easy," said the operations boss. "And you will not be surprised to learn that this type of action is only one of several being considered." He shrugged. "They might be able to fix his position by satellite, then slip a smart bomb down his throat."

Jameson remembered part of a briefing only a couple of weeks ago during which Izbek Noir's apparent invulnerability was discussed in a laughing way. Guy couldn't be killed, said several reports; there were eyewitness accounts of Noir embracing a grenade, Noir taking artillery shrapnel through his body and shaking it off with a gleeful howl, Noir machine-gunned in his headquarters vehicle by a suicidal turncoat and being the only one in the vehicle to survive, still laughing. He remembered, but he kept it to himself.

"Anyway," continued the agent in charge, "Azul Dante might be able to give President Reese info that could create a doorway for you, or you and a team if you wish. Dante might be able to get you next to Noir, even while a coalition army stands against the mujahideen in what should be a pretty cataclysmic battle, whenever and wherever it takes place."

"I need to go home," said Jameson quietly. It was a statement, not a request. "My family."

"I've arranged military air transport, John," replied his boss. "Go. See if they're . . . Do what you have to do. Then stop off here again on your way to D.C."

"Thank you," said Jameson as he hurried out of the office.

He had returned home and found nothing. The aching pain in his chest was so bad as he walked slowly through his house, he thought he might simply collapse and lie there until hell froze over. As he opened the front door and took the first step inside he felt the total emptiness of the structure. Even if he had not already been told by his friend Conner Eagan that they were gone, he would have sensed it the moment he walked in.

Sylvia was gone. Sonia. Johnny. Intellectually he wrestled with possibilities, explanations, remedies. Emotionally he fought to maintain his will to carry on, fought to recognize the pure value of what he *had*, as opposed to what he had lost. Professionally he struggled with the concept of duty. There had always been a time to reap, a time to sow, a time for peace, and a time to kill. In his capacity as an agent for his country, an agent for *good* in this world, he accepted this as a time for extreme measures that might test the laws of man and the laws of God. Spiritually, he was adrift yet his feet were buried in shifting sands. All was contradiction and in some ways illusion. What did it mean? What did it all . . . *mean?*

He remembered the last time he had held hands with Sylvia. They had said a prayer together just before he left on his latest mission. She knew he thought kneeling in prayer was too demonstrative unless you were in church, but she had asked him to anyway. They had knelt, facing each other, her warm grip strong inside his. In her other hand she had held her Bible. While they prayed she had leaned forward until their foreheads touched, and he had felt her strength, felt her faith. That had been their last embrace. A small, angry voice deep inside his heart whispered, "So . . . were your prayers answered, John?" He shook it off. The last time he had held Sylvia's hand was during a prayer, right here in this very same living room. He ran upstairs, found Sylvia's Bible, and pressed it against his chest. He didn't have time to fully consider what she'd tried to tell him so many times. He knew that why Sylvia and his children had disappeared didn't matter to those he'd taken an oath to pursue. They would take advantage of the situation no matter what its cause.

A few minutes later he walked out, and firmly closed the door behind him. As he turned his back on his family's home for the last time, he heard that loving voice once more: *"The door to your father's house will always be open for you."* He headed back to the world, Sylvia's Bible close beside him.

The morning of his address to the UN, Azul Dante woke to a brilliant New York morning. High above Fifth Avenue, he was isolated from the street noise. Had this been a typical day, twenty-four floors would not have been enough to insulate him from the cacophony of taxi horns and the staccato chatter of jackhammers.

He was in the sitting room, leafing through a magazine; Sophia sat across the room from him with a cell phone pressed to one ear while she stabbed at an electronic organizer. Dante's staff was staggering under the weight of all the requests that they'd received for personal appearances. Even the Heritage Foundation had called seeking to have him speak at what had been scheduled to be a gala fund-raiser but was now reconfigured to be a more somber panel discussion. Sophia was scrambling to move meetings to accommodate the late, but certainly important, request.

She was amazed by how calm Azul Dante remained, how unperturbed he seemed at the prospect of making the most important address of his life in a matter of a few hours. She knew that most politicians hired a team of speechwriters, researchers, and assorted other handlers, but his personal coterie was small — just herself and Mr. Drazic. She rarely saw Dante sit at a computer or with a pad of paper, yet she'd heard him speak countless times and was amazed at his eloquence. She refused to believe that his remarks were off the cuff, that anyone could speak so passionately and so well about such a wide diversity of issues without spending hours in preparation or backed by a small army.

That ability was what had impressed her the most when she attended the seminar, his effortless command of the language and of content. She'd known an autodidact before, a boyfriend from her undergraduate years who was capable of reading and retaining nearly verbatim every bit of information that he'd come across. He was brilliant but troubled, almost as though every bit of information inside his head were jostling with every other bit for his attention. Dante was placid, but even in repose, as he sat with legs crossed, resting on his left hip, his chin in his hand, she sensed an energy emanating from him. She was reminded of a sprinter in the blocks, all coiled potential energy ready to be unleashed.

When the time came, Dante declined the use of a limousine. He preferred to walk the few blocks to the UN. Despite the NYPD's and the FBI's protests, Dante did as he wished. The motorcade wended its way across town to the East River and UN headquarters while Azul Dante walked among the sparse crowds that had gathered, hoping to discern the city's mood. The normally hectic streets were subdued, security gates pulled down over most of the storefronts, padlocks as big as frying pans hanging from chains. At Katharine Hepburn Park, a small plaza with a garden and a fountain, a meager band of protestors walked around in a tight circle surrounded by security police. Around the outer ring a crowd of still photographers and videographers from television news crews rotated for a better view.

Though the governor and the mayor had stopped only a few small steps short of martial law, Dante was still surprised to see this display. It was almost as if the powers that be wanted to let the media see that normalcy had returned. Sophia took out a small Instamatic camera and snapped a photo of the photographers. She smiled shyly at Dante, who extended his hand for the camera and snapped one of her. Later he did the same in the lobby.

Following his brief meeting with the UN Security Council, Dante addressed the General Assembly. Many of its members were not present, many still fearful that large public gatherings were easy targets, others recalled to their home countries. Still the house was full to overflowing, as many dignitaries from the U.S. including most of the House and Senate, were in attendance. The major networks as well as many cable outlets broadcast the speech live.

To those assembled and to those watching, Dante spoke his greeting in English, French, Spanish, Russian, and in a somewhat startling move, Farsi. In the first ten minutes of his address, he spoke of the recent events and the efforts being made on two fronts: to ensure that needed services were being provided to the people of all nations, and to protect them from lawlessness. He announced that along with the UN, and many leaders of the free world, multinational UN peacekeeping forces would be deployed, along with relief workers and medical personnel. He issued a call for more volunteers, and called upon governments to pool any available resources to begin humanitarian relief efforts.

"My fellow citizens," he continued after a politely enthusiastic round of applause, "the events of recent days should serve to remind us that while humanity has not always responded swiftly or effectively to crises in what we have perceived to be far-flung corners of our world — Rwanda, South Africa, East Timor, China — this unprecedented global occurrence calls for an unprecedented global response. While many of us are frightened, uncertain about the future — whether it be What shall I do today? or What shall I do the week next — we cannot afford to be shortsighted."

A fusillade of camera flashes seemed momentarily to blind Azul Dante, and he took a step back from the lectern and adjusted his lavalier microphone. He walked over to where Sophia was sitting and held his hand out. She pulled her camera from her coat pocket and handed it to him. Dante smiled sheepishly and shrugged, faced the battery of photographers again, and snapped a few shots. The audience seemed to breathe a collective sigh of relief. Dante ended his little performance by using his handkerchief as a white flag and waving it in surrender to another round of applause.

"Lest you think that I came here to surrender, I would like to use the words and issue a challenge that a great patriot used in this country many years ago. It was Thomas Paine who said, 'We have it in our power to begin the world over again.' " He paused and sipped a glass of water. "At another crisis in the world's history, another great leader, Mr. Winston Churchill, reminded us that, 'Success is not final, failure is not fatal: It is the courage to continue that counts.'

"I am reminded of the story of a man who was walking along the beach. He saw another man tossing something back into the ocean. As he approached, he saw that scattered along the water's edge were hundreds and hundreds of starfish. The first man stooped, picked up a starfish, and tossed it back into the sea. With each incoming wave, more starfish landed on the beach. But the man remained indefatigable. Finally, the observer walked up to him and said, 'Why are you bothering? You can't possibly save them all. It doesn't matter.' The other man paused, held the starfish in his hand for him to see, and said, 'It matters to this one.'

"While I know that many of you have heard a variation of this story before, I use it because it is comfortable and familiar. Something that we may share from our collective past. Besides, its message is clear: We must not merely stand by and watch as others begin the rebuilding process. Though the task ahead seems overwhelming, though many of us are bloodied and bowed, though we have suffered great losses as a people and as individuals, we must focus on the task at hand. Many of you may know that in recent months, a great initiative has grown from a grassroots effort on the part of people who believe in neighbors but not in borders. Their efforts have taken on a new urgency in the context of the many crises we now face. It is time for us to restore humanity. We have strayed far from the ideals and the values and the practices that each of us knows, deep in his or her heart, to be just and true. If nothing else, recent events should demonstrate to us that there is something essentially human that we all share. That something is more than the sadness and the grief that we feel for the loss of loved ones, though certainly we must grieve, we must honor those whom we have lost. But we must also acknowledge our responsibility to ourselves, to our individual nations, and to our humanity.

"The Prodigal Project is dedicated to the restoration of the one world family, to the restoration of the order we have lost, to welcoming back those who have strayed the farthest from the fold. You may ask why we should care about those who have wandered away from what is right and just and true and human. We must fight the urge to turn inward, to become insular, more guarded, more suspicious, more angry, more willing to strike out in defense of our own survival. What the past weeks have demonstrated is that there are forces at work in the universe that dwarf the individual. Collectively we can thrive; separately we will not survive.

"In a meeting earlier today with the UN

Security Council, we drafted a resolution forming the European Coalition. While I have urged the United States and many of its North and South American neighbors to join and form a unilateral front to battle the forces that seek to tear the world apart, they have not committed to this action. While I understand their desire to honor previously enacted treaties and agreements, I urge you as a people to join us in spirit if not in name.

"The Prodigal Project welcomes all those who have abandoned the world family. The promised restoration and eventual rejuvenation of the governments and peoples across borders, ideologies, belief systems, and political philosophies is possible only through the right individual action and response."

Dante spoke for another fifteen minutes, outlining the platform of the Prodigal Project. At the end, he unveiled a logo and a flag that would represent this organization. While the specifics of its aims remained a bit vague, in the vacuum that existed, Dante's words were enough. For many, the answer to the question What do I do next? was answered. For Clara Reese and the members of Congress, Dante's project presented them with more questions than answers. But they too were satisfied. If the Prodigal Project's aim was to restore order, then this looked as good a place as any to start.

Shannon Carpenter packed a small bag and collected all the cash she could find. She remembered the bank bag her boss had given her for "safekeeping" less than a week ago and carefully readied the house for her departure. She cleaned every room, folded fresh laundry, made all the beds, squared the kitchen away, neatly lined up all the shoes, and made sure all stuffed toys rested against their assigned pillows. She went about these tasks sobbing quietly, smiling now and then through the tears when she came across a particular T-shirt, old photo, or spot on the carpet or floor that reminded her of some tiny moment in the past . . . a moment of life through which she and her family had lived. The simple domestic tasks had a soothing effect on her heart, and she hugged each act and moment of it.

She felt immersed in the love the house held, surrounded by a warm and comforting mist of remembrance and appreciation. She made no attempt to watch the news, phone anyone, or learn anything new about the current situation. She was a wife and mother, a homemaker, and with loving hands she made the house right. Once when she picked up "Pookie-bear," a faded stuffed toy that had seen better times, she was rocked by an almost visceral replaying of Matt's birth. She relived the actual sweating, gasping, sweet, painracked moment of birth, the moment when Matt — his life surely confirmed in her womb months ago — physically came out from within her. Then the early weeks, the breast-feeding, the naps on the couch with his bundled warmth against her chest. Then the months and years as he came to be Matt. Including the day he got Pookie-bear, all the nights he fell asleep with the toy tucked under his arm, the days when he dragged "the Pookster," as Billy called him, across the yard and into the turtle-shaped sandbox. She kissed the bear on the nose, set him against Matt's pillow in his customary place of honor, and said quietly, "Thank you."

While she worked, Shannon thought of the conversation she had had with the old woman at Billy's church. She tried very hard to compartmentalize the various feelings of fear, loss, panic, sadness, and loneliness crashing around in her head, and to concentrate instead on what she could do now. She fixed a cup of tea, and sipped from it while she thumbed through Billy's Bible. It was comforting to know it as something he had held dear, had caressed with his hands, that he had found strength and solace there with his eyes as he read the words. She read passages, not looking for meaning or trying to dissect each line for exact comprehension. Rather, she read for the peace she found there. This Book, she reflected, was the written message given to us by God. It contained truths important enough for Him to want to share them. If you believed in God, and she did, then you believed in Him as an all-powerful, all-knowing entity — one who literally held all the universes in His hands. He was so vast, and incomprehensible to mere humans, and yet He worked a way to *speak* to us. He wanted us to get the Word, and through Him the Word was set down in black and white. All we had to do was read it, study it, open our hearts to it. Simple enough, she thought.

Why had she resisted for so long? she wondered. It would have been so easy to stand beside Billy and the kids, to embrace it as they did, to open her heart. That was the key . . . she had to willingly open her heart to the Word, then accept what she found as the truth from God. She shook her head as she sipped the hot tea and read different passages. There was no way, she was convinced, no way this taking of people all over the earth was some man-made thing. The alien stuff she dismissed out of hand; the Muslims were a threat and had been more active in demonstrating that through the recent years, but they were still human beings, capable of waging war, capable of perverting their own truths, but not capable of initiating something on a global scale. That left something spiritual, she concluded.

Billy had always counseled her to be patient and persistent. Instead, she'd grown frustrated that the peace that seemed to infuse Billy's very essence eluded her. When a person accepted Jesus Christ into his or her heart, he told her, there came welling up such an overwhelming feeling of joy and purpose it often taxed a believer's ability to describe it without getting all emotionally caught up in the message. Besides, he added, when you have discovered a truth that can literally save those you love, you have an obligation to give them the Word . . . even if you have to grab them by the shirtfront or spoon-feed them like a child.

She told him sometimes she felt as if she were being personally attacked by the person trying to give her the Word. She didn't like being told she was "unworthy" or a "sinner." He laughed — she still remembered it — and said that each of us is a sinner one way or another, and don't get all wrapped around an axle about it. He even conceded that there have always been great, learned discussions on what the word *sin* meant, anyway . . . less than, imperfect, missing the mark, falling short, purposely acting in a manner not consistent with the example set by our Lord. There are messengers and there are messengers, he told her; don't let a shrill or overzealous messenger turn you away from the truth embedded in his or her awkward enthusiasm.

She remembered these and other conversations she and Billy had had about it. He never seemed offended by her questions, even when it was obvious she was attacking him just for the reaction. "Hey," he would tell her eventually with his easy grin, "if I had all the answers for you, why . . . I'd have my own TV show, singing the praises, testifying, and rolling the words of Scripture around in my mouth like fine wine. All the while there'd be an eight-hundred number scrolling along the bottom of the screen, telling folks where to send their donations." She had laughed with him, loving him, knowing he spent many hours in front of the tube watching those very shows, and enjoying them greatly.

She thumbed through his Bible now, the teacup empty at her elbow. She saw where he had written notes here and there along the edge of the pages, and there were several Post-it notes inside the front and back covers. On one he'd written: "Prodigal Project!!" and "Keep contact with other churches, pastors." A few lines below this was: "Selma . . . Henderson Smith? What is *NCC . . . New Christian Cathedral?*" Near the bottom, in his neat handwriting, was one that caused a warm lump in her heart: "Try harder Shannon, don't give up, let your heart listen."

She closed her eyes. She had the feeling she stood on a precipice while gusty, tugging winds swirled around her soul, and she was pulled this way and that. She was close to something. She could sense it. She could discover something there, a reason, an explanation, and she was going to identify it and participate in it. She was poised on the edge of a journey, that much was clear. It would be a physical journey in search of answers, in search of a cause, and it would be a spiritual journey in search of peace. She smiled, her cheeks still wet from her tears, and knew that the seeds of truth had already been planted in her heart by Billy, and that the journey she would take would be an act of acceptance and confirmation.

A short while later she carefully locked the house, stood out on the sidewalk gazing at it for a moment, then got into Billy's pickup truck, made her way to the interstate, and headed south.

President Clara Reese knew from photos that Minister Azul Dante was an attractive man, tall, athletic, blue-eyed, with strong, craggy features, a prominent nose, and large, expressive hands. He wore tailored suits of good quality, had a full head of salt-and-pepper hair brushed back off his weathered forehead, and was well groomed and polished. What she wasn't aware of, but experienced as soon as he entered the Oval Office, was his powerful charisma and the patina of confidence that enveloped him.

She had already received the vetting reports done on him by the various intelligence agencies and had learned a very few facts beyond what the typical newspaper reader could know. For one, he had been married, but became a widower when his wife died along with their first baby during childbirth. He had never remarried.

The only hint of impropriety came in the form of a hand-written note on one of the security reports compiled on Dante a year or so ago. "This guy is too good to be true," wrote a chief analyst. "Perfect chronological records all the way, no gaps, no missing pieces. It's as if we had made up a legend for one of our agents." President Reese had seen the note, but any misgivings she had were swept away in the first moments of the meeting.

"President Reese," said Azul Dante as he strode across the office to shake her hand. "It is an honor to finally meet you."

"The honor is mine, Minister Dante," responded the president. "Welcome, and thank you for making time on your trip for this visit." Only the chief of staff and one secretary were in the office with the president, and Minister Dante traveled with one aide — an older man, Slavic perhaps, rail thin, with a dark suit that only accentuated his funereal countenance — and an attractive younger woman who could have passed as his daughter. "If it suits you, Minister," added Reese, "we'll talk for a while, then spend a few excruciating moments in the garden for the obligatory photo op. Yes?"

"Yes," replied Dante. "Sadly, I always appear very dignified in photographs, even though I'm really a very casual fellow."

Yeah, right, thought the president. She remembered how he'd handled the photographers in New York.

"I understand you were well received by the members of the UN in attendance," said Reese. Her new secretary of state had been there, and could not say enough about the minister from the Balkans. The secretary, a veteran politician who had seen his share of impressive people, was almost awestruck. The guy had bowled him over, and apparently had a similar effect on anyone who met him. Dante had the energy, her secretary of state told her, there was power in his speech, in his bearing, in his persona. The man made you want to listen, made you want to stand with him. In a world on its knees, Azul Dante was standing tall.

"Yes, I think my little speech went well," replied her guest. "I mean, who isn't receptive to reconciliation and healing? Forgive me if I sound like an ingracious guest, but in my opinion, the poor United Nations has lost its purpose. It flounders, blusters and makes demands, but is unable to back them up. Remember that description of a committee some long-ago spymaster supposedly uttered?"

"A committee is an animal with four hind legs?" ventured the president.

"That's the one," said Dante, nodding, "and that is how the UN is viewed by many in this world today."

"I agree it is a shame," responded the president.

"So," continued Dante, "If as you say my speech was well received, that is because I offered them strength, purpose, leadership. In all modesty, President Reese, it would appear it falls on me to somehow act as a catalyst to bring you into the fold of this European Coalition. If it comes together as envisioned, it will be a formidable state, capable of picking up the pieces of our skewed world civilizations, restoring order and democracy, and bringing peace to all the people." He paused, smiled at her, and added, "I don't have to tell you a partnership with the United States of America is the absolute best way to show the world we are for real."

The United States would never bargain from a position of weakness, never had a need to, but she didn't want to appear rude to her guest so she refrained from taking a more hard line stance. She nodded and said, "Of course we're always willing to listen."

They shared confident smiles.

"As you are probably aware," continued the president, "the media reports have greatly exaggerated conditions here. That's not to deny that America was hit hard by the disappearance. But if you were to believe everything you've read, you'd conclude that Wall Street has all but stopped working, our infrastructure has crumbled, the remaining members of Congress are fighting like hyenas over the bits of flesh and bone of our democracy with their bitter infighting, state governors are trying to declare independence. Let me assure you, America is in order. We as a nation can muster great strength when the need arises. Assuredly, the people who were not taken are clamoring for an answer. I have the best and brightest in our intelligence organizations researching the matter. A plausible answer is out there, and when we discover the *cause* of what happened, then we can attack it." She took a breath, and changed tack. "What do you think of this Izbek Noir, who leads the Muslim armies we call the mujahideen, Minister Dante? And how might a European Coalition stand against them?"

Dante first looked to his male adviser and then at Sophia Ghant. Her eyes widened in surprise — Dante seldom broke his focus when in a meeting. "Based on what I've read of him, Izbek Noir is a menace," responded Dante grimly. The president of the United States had just clearly told him America was wounded, but still powerful and capable of taking care of itself. She had issued a challenge, that much was clear. "I think he must have a powerful personality, so he is accepted by the children of Islam even though many of them must know he perverts their religion, bends it to his own purposes, and uses them as he wishes." He paused, and the color of his blue eyes deepened. "It is as I said in my speech at the UN earlier. A very strong coalition of nations, united for the purpose of peace and stability in this world, will always be able to overcome the forces of disorder. Whether we need to become a sword powerful enough to sever the ties the mujahideen have formed, or whether in the face of a unified opposition they will crumble, no one can yet say."

"What about Israel?" asked President Reese. "Will a coalition be in agreement regarding the Israelis? I don't have to remind you of the steady rise of anti-Semitism throughout Europe after the Palestinian affair."

With one hand, Dante rubbed his jaw. He pursed his lips, nodded, and replied, "If it is meant for me to form and lead a coalition, as long as I lead, Israel will be protected. Israel is historically important. I am very aware of America's relationship with Israel, of course, President Reese, and again, if the world needs stability — food, power, operational medical facilities, finances, scientific research — Israel is a country that can provide a firm foundation on which to build." He studied his manicured nails a moment, and added, "I may fly directly from here to Tel Aviv, President Reese. Prime Minister Pearlman and I have an ongoing dialogue. I don't want to tip my hand or in any way jeopardize something that is still so clearly in the formative stages, but we have hopes our talks may culminate in something conclusive and important."

"Yes," said Reese. She paused, looked away, then allowed herself to be brought back under his strong gaze. "I received your communiqué. I've studied your alternate suggestion and have taken it under advisement."

"I couldn't discuss *that* possibility at the UN." Dante's eyes once again sought out Sophia, measured her reaction. "You and I understand that certain expediencies are sometimes necessary in order to achieve a viable outcome. Sometimes a less direct salient while the front is engaged can prove effective."

"Spoken like a soldier and a diplomat, Minister Dante," responded Reese with a smile.

"I was the one before the other," said Dante easily.

"Yes, and I suspect that you learned the art of sleight of hand at an early age," said the president. "And if an extremely focused action can be taken against a single enemy — a leader — and successfully carried out with surgical precision, it would be *most* effective. As you know, our intelligence experts are fairly certain that the mujahideen can be fragmented, separated, and cut up piecemeal if their leader is neutralized. After reading your suggestion, and considering the help you have offered getting a team in place, I have already alerted the proper agency. They have had an initial briefing, and are on quick standby status."

"Excellent," replied Dante. "I feel much better having visited with you, President Reese. Since it seems meant to be, I will lead this coalition, and perhaps we can work together to get on with the business of peace."

"Yes," agreed President Reese. She admitted to herself that she was impressed with his aura of power and competence; he projected a larger-than-life energy, a clear understanding of the challenge. This just might be the guy who can make it work, she thought.

The chief of staff cleared his throat.

"Uh-oh," said the president. "Time for the never-sleeping cameras. Ready for the assault?"

"Only if you assure me a copy for my personal album," said Dante with a smile.

Chapter Ten

Ivy Sloan-Underwood liked her new car. Her old one had run out of gas someplace in Arizona, and although she had been able to find places where she could either beg for gas or pay crazy prices for it, this last time there was none to be had. There were plenty of cars up for grabs here and there, an old man with a dirty laugh had told her, if a person didn't mind sitting on a little pile of sand. The old bird was right, though. She got her things out of her car, checked out three or four along the side of the road, and picked the newest one. The gauge showed "Full." She knew it wouldn't be long before gangs began stripping them, or siphoning the gas, or just taking them, like she had. That's okay, she told herself, she was on a mission from God.

She continued eastbound, driving through a living *Mad Max, Road Warrior* sound stage. Once or twice she pulled into a roadside store only to find it eerily quiet. No one around, lights and everything turned on, drinks in the coolers, food on the racks. She helped herself, taking what she needed and extra. More often, however, anyplace that had food, water, gas, weapons, or supplies of any kind was torn apart, looted. More than once she had seen a frenzied individual wandering the streets, mindless, animal-like, terrible. She drove away from those places hoping not to be noticed.

Once she was pulled over by an Oklahoma Highway Patrol officer. She was flying down a ruler-straight stretch of highway, not even looking at the speedometer, when she heard the *whoop* of a siren, and glanced in the rearview mirror with her heart in her throat to see a big black-and-tan, blue lights flashing. It was so much a part of what used to be, she gave it no thought and pulled over onto the shoulder of the road. She watched in the mirror as the big officer climbed out of his car, straightened, and came toward her. She was actually digging in her purse for her driver's license when she saw the lace-up sneakers on his feet. Then he was close, and she saw how his uniform shirt was torn on one shoulder, how the buttons strained against his belly, showing a dark blue T-shirt underneath. The man's hands were dirty, with almost blue-black fingernails, he had a two-day stubble of beard on his jaw, and he had one gun in his holster and another tucked in front of his belt. The gun in his belt had blood on the grip. He reached for the door handle, leered, and said in a throaty voice, "Hey now, little gal . . . ain't you a purty one to be out here speedin' and all. I think it might be time for you to be nice to this here officer of the law, and —"

She heard no more, but threw the car into gear as she stared over her left shoulder at him. He lunged for her as she hit the gas, and she winced as his big grasping fingers dug into her arm. His other hand came up onto the window frame, and he hung there a moment spitting curses at her while the rear wheels of the car skidded in the loose sand and gravel along the side of the road. When the tires finally did get a purchase, they slung the car sideways, to the left, and the man screamed as the car bounced over his hips, the spinning tires shredding his pelvis before crushing his legs. She felt the bump as the car came down, then controlled the swerve back onto the blacktop. She slowed for a moment to watch him writhing and twisting in the dirt. Then she let out an angry sob and drove away.

She didn't know exactly why, and had stopped trying to figure it out, but she was headed for a place in Alabama, to a "New Christian Church," to a voice she had heard on the radio. The voice was melodious, strong, rich in timbre, comforting in tone. She had left her husband, Ron, sitting in their son's wheelchair, and followed the voice. She was partially motivated by the thought that there might be an answer, or some resolution to be found, but it was a hellish trip for her nonetheless. Her mind never stopped working, never stopped chewing on the events of the last few days, playing them over and over, digging, accusing, examining who and what she was with unrelenting cruelty.

She was Ivy Sloan-Underwood, elementary-school teacher, wife of Ron, mother of Ronnie. She was attractive, fit, and looking for love in all the wrong places. She had skirted on the edges of infidelity more than once, putting false "limits" on how far she might go with a man not her husband. She was a tease, and naive, and she had traded her soul for a chance to make her son whole. But her desire was not entirely altruistic. Oh no, a normal Ronnie would equal a normal life for *her*. Of this she was quite certain. She was not a churchgoer, had been angry for years at God, if there was a God. The whole thing — her life — was so unfair, so awful, that she could not accept the thought that an actual living, all-powerful God would let it go on. This was all old news, she reflected. Ron believed. She didn't know how, and he never seemed able to explain it to her, but the man believed. To him it was simple. He loved Ivy, and together they had a son, Ronnie. And the son equaled love to the father. This somehow validated God in Ron's heart.

Fine, she thought, but if I'm right, then the devil himself validated God in *my* heart.

She straightened in the driver's seat, unconsciously checked her hair in the mirror, blew out a puff of air, and thought about that validation. Religion was the "opiate of the masses," or it wasn't, she reasoned. It was fun to examine this complex argument like a college philosophy major while she drove a car she didn't own down dangerous and unpredictable roads. If an intelligent man hadn't made up the fantasy of religion to assuage his own fears about death, and a spiritual deity was real, then where was a sign? A sign! We need a sign!

C'mon, God . . . just one little miracle so we can really know you exist. Whaddya say, big guy? So, all right, we got the Bible, a divine revelation, we are told. It is the Word, we are told; you can find the Way within its pages. "And the Word is?" she yelled out the window at a huge billboard that showed a handsome man in a tuxedo holding his hand out to an elegantly dressed woman stepping out of a Mercedes. The Word is, Jesus Christ showed us the Way. That's the Word. Simple.

Too simple, she told herself. I need something tangible, something I can get my hands on and squeeze. So I'll know it's real. Faith, sayeth the spiritual ones. You gotta have faith, baby. All you see is the light from a long-dead star, you can't touch it, but you know it's real. You have faith in the reality of it. Same thing, sayeth the Bible troops. Even Jesus was reluctant to perform miracles for His hapless little band, lest it be too easy for their dim minds. Faith, have faith, He said. Man and woman, being the limited beings we are, she reflected, still want a sign.

And sure enough, she had a sign. She met a suave, smooth, confident, tasty-looking, bedroom-smelling male animal who called himself Thad Night. He knew how to rest his deep dark eyes on her, knew how to arouse her interest in more ways than one, and made her an offer she couldn't refuse. There he was, sitting with her in a little French restaurant . . . probably would never have happened if she had decided to go fast-food that day . . . the devil himself. Could have been one of his minions. Was her soul so in jeopardy that she could be approached that easily?

Her thoughts were interrupted by a problem in the roadway in front of her. A large gasoline tanker truck lay jackknifed on its side, blocking part of the traffic lanes. Several wrecked cars lay scattered around, along with three or four bodies in the grassy swale. She slowed, tightened her grip on the steering wheel, and tried to scan everything in front of her for trouble. There was no movement of any kind. As she eased her car around the tractor cab of the rig, she saw the door open, a burly man in a checked flannel shirt hanging out, his face bloody. Spaced around him were three young women, dressed in jeans and red long-sleeved shirts. Each of them was covered in blood too. The bodies were swollen and discolored, and Ivy turned her face away. She found open road on the other side of the truck, and accelerated out of there.

She went back to her thoughts. Minion. Does the devil have minions? Do beings such as lesser devils exist? Up-and-comers in corporate hell, trying to please the boss and climb up the ladder of success? Who knew? Didn't matter. Thad Night was the devil or *of* the devil, of that she was sure. And he was there for her soul, not just what was hidden beneath her Victoria's Secret. He spoke words, they discussed it, but he was actually communicating through his eyes, and her heart. He was there for her soul, and knew before the first word what her answer would be.

She stopped. What *was* your answer, Ivy? She left it, and finished her hypothesis. If religion is made up by man for man, so be it. Intelligent beings create a pretend world beyond their real world to comfort themselves. Fine. If God is real, how do we validate Him except by miracles, or faith? "Drumroll, please!" she shouted at a skinny cat sprawled on the vacant front porch of an abandoned house. If we meet the devil — the actual cloven-hoofed bad boy all dressed up and looking fine — and we learn right there and then that he is real, then it *all* has to be real. The Bible is real, the stories in the Bible are real, Jesus Christ really is God who came here to die for us and He's coming *back,* and *God is real.*

She felt light-headed, slightly sick to her stomach. She pulled the car into a large parking lot in front of some kind of industrial park. No one was around. Her thoughts had kicked her in the gut. She sipped from a water bottle, munched on some stale Cracker Jacks. She knew she was still on the edge of mild hysteria . . . knew she was tracking, but was a hairbreadth away from skidding right off the edge of sanity. Boy, it hurt so bad to lose Ronnie, to lose Ron. Boy, it hurt. She began to cry. Almost an hour passed before she pulled onto the road, headed east again.

She wondered what she was doing, really, what she hoped to accomplish. So you've determined God is real, she said to herself. He is real, but He is not a nice God, not a "merciful" God. Her life was a cruel joke, and what had happened to Ronnie, and to her, and Ron, was horrible, and not right, not fair. So there I am, hating life, missing life, but doing my duty, being a mother to him, putting my life and marriage behind my duties as a mother. She stuck her jaw out. Nobody could *ever* say I was anything but a good mother to Ronnie, a caregiver, twenty-four and seven, okay? So what do I get for my trouble? A nice little temptation from the Dark Prince himself. An offer that I had to take . . . and I took it.

But before it could come to fruition, the payoff, before Ronnie is made whole because I've forfeited my soul, he's taken up. Sure, I've heard Ron talk about the rapture, how the pure of heart will be lifted up. That has to be what happened to the world. So this should be the end times. Fine. I'm glad Ronnie's in heaven, I am. If God is real, heaven must be real, whatever it looks like, and it absolutely has to be a better place for Ronnie. Good. She began crying again, and said in a soft voice, "But all I got of a son made 'whole' was his sweet voice, saying just one word, 'Mommy.' That's all I got, that's all I got, 'Mommy.' "

She drove on, toward a place where the voice of a preacher might unwrap the toxic bindings that clutched her heart. Maybe the preacher could point her in the right direction . . . maybe even to the Son, if there really was to be a Second Coming. Believing in God was one thing, she knew. Giving yourself over to Him was another thing altogether. She drove on, through a tortured land seemingly abandoned by any guiding hand, through a land suffering in fear, helplessness, and pain. She drove toward the voice, toward the promise.

John Jameson sat with his broad back against a bulkhead in the officers' mess aboard the nuclear submarine USS *Finback*. He wore khakis with no insignia, but was treated with wary deference by the crew. They didn't know what rank he held, or even if he was in the navy . . . a SEAL team leader, maybe. He was in good shape, that they could see, his athletic body fit and trim, even though a flash of gray stained his dark hair at each temple. The guy was a spook, no doubt about that, pleasant enough, quiet, and totally wrapped up in the Bible he carried with him everywhere. One of the mess stewards had heard the captain say that the guy, Jameson, had lost his family in the disappearance, and that might explain why he seemed so distant. So what? Plenty of the *Finback*'s crew lost loved ones. Besides, even some of the crew themselves were taken. That doesn't mean we have to mope around with our noses buried in the Bible. They couldn't understand that Jameson wasn't moping. His quiet fascination and fixation on the Book he studied came from being totally *absorbed.*

John Jameson felt strangely at peace. "Strangely" because he was completely excited within the aura of peace that had formed around him. He had made a discovery, and it excited him. The world was probably coming to an end, he was several hundred feet beneath the Atlantic Ocean on a nuclear sub on his way to an extremely covert and impossibly dangerous assignment, he had lost everything important to him in this life, and he felt empowered, emboldened.

He had gone through the final briefing, been issued the communications codes, his gear, and his weapons, and been flown from Virginia to Panama to meet the submarine. His professionalism and many years' experience as a frontline operative kept him attuned and attentive during this process. Now was not the time to zone out under the pressure of personal grief. Rather than lose his edge, he found it was somehow honed sharp as ever, even though his mind and heart were divided as he prepared to go in harm's way.

He was told he'd be inserted into a relatively stable area some miles from the frontline mujahideen troops. He was given the names of two members of the mujahideen leadership cadre who secretly worked toward the destruction of Izbek Noir. These two secret informants did not work together, and probably did not know each other, but in case the first one had fallen or turned before he arrived, the second one stood ready. Either of these two might be able to escort Jameson into the command section of the mujahideen forces, to where Izbek himself would be directing things.

Jameson, with help or without it, was to kill Izbek Noir . . . plain and simple. If it could be done in conjunction with an air strike, artillery barrage, or any other distracting mayhem, Jameson might even be able to escape in the ensuing confusion. His clothing and equipment had been "sanitized" regarding personal ID or country of origin, and it was decided that he did not have to make an attempt to pass as an Arab Muslim, which he doubted he could. He knew rudimentary Farsi but was not a linguist, knew the basic protocols of the Islamic faith but would not withstand the scrutiny of a mullah. But he and his boss figured that the mujahideen were such a mixed bag of Muslims from all over the world, including the West, that no one would notice or care about him. The mujahideen at their core were Islamic fanatics, but the army's ranks were largely composed of mercenaries and brigands who would swear allegiance to any flag or deity if the price was right. He would enter their ranks, and appear to be just another soldier. . . . That part he could play perfectly.

He was told there was a westerner, an American news photographer with the headquarters group working as Izbek Noir's personal shutterbug. According to another journalist, the photographer was held against his will by Noir but was still allowed to send his photos, digital or film, to his parent agency for distribution. Apparently this was a form of rough public relations that kept Noir tapped into the news organizations of the world, able to spread his message and defend his actions when accused of war crimes or other indiscretions. His analysts did not know how the photographer, a young but experienced combat journalist, would react to Jameson's appearance or mission. Jameson's agency dismissed out of hand the thought of contacting the photographer's parent agency, too risky by far. Jameson could play that one by ear, he was told.

All of this had to do with his work, his job. It was another mission, dangerous, important, complicated by many potential problems, including a "recall" or "stand down" order from headquarters that would leave him in place, but in limbo. The huge twin inhibiting gasbags of bureaucracy and politics always loomed over any agent as he tried to do his job, ready at any moment to turn around in a fit of leaking certainty and stop the action cold. He'd been there, seen that. It came with the job, and he was a pro.

What was different about Special Agent John Jameson this time was what was happening to his inner self. Over the last couple of days — though certainly it had been in the formative stages through the years — he had not only developed, but accepted, a close personal relationship with God. After the initial shock and pain of realizing his Sylvia, Sonia, and Johnny really were gone, it did not take him long to understand what had taken place. The moment he picked up Sylvia's Bible, it was right there. He didn't even waste time saying to himself, "Gee . . . I've been a pretty good Christian during my life, member of the church, supportive of my wife and kids' involvement, always said grace at the dinner table, gladly allowed the tithing, which Sylvia had arranged. I attended church many times during the year, not just Easter, and I always gave money to the poor. Why wasn't *I* lifted up along with my family? What . . . wasn't I Christian *enough?*"

No, he knew he did not have the core of pure faith that Sylvia breathed in and out like the very oxygen in her lungs. She had always been gentle and patient with him about it, saying there was no way to force it . . . and to pretend was worse than not really getting it. He found himself reading passages in her Bible with an aching hunger; he couldn't get enough. He could hear her voice, as if she sat beside him as he read, explaining things, pointing out nuances, putting things into context. Even in his present state of emotional and spiritual openness and longing, it was difficult at first to understand the concept of "giving yourself over to God," or the admonition to "Place your life in the hands of Jesus . . . turn it all over to Him . . . and you'll be okay."

Sometimes in the quiet of night he could feel her hand on his as he turned the pages, and her neat handwritten notes in the margins always signposted something important for him to examine and comprehend. He was amazed. This was not the first time in his life he had read parts of the Scripture. He always read aloud in church when everybody did, and now and then would read a passage as part of a Thanksgiving dinner prayer or something. But this time the words seemed alive to him, the very pages vibrated with good news, and the passages wrapped around his heart with healing power.

He read John 5:24, "whoever hears my word and believes him who sent me has eternal life will not be condemned; he has crossed over from death to life." He read Romans 9:16, "It does not, therefore, depend on man's desire or effort, but on God's mercy." He liked Corinthians 13 about love, and he studied Colossians 1:27, "this mystery, which is Christ in you, the hope of glory," and 2:2, "My purpose is that they may be encouraged in heart and united in love, so that they may have the full riches of complete understanding, in order that they may know the mystery of

God, namely, Christ." He read, and reread, Hebrews 11, "By faith," and 1 John 5:11, "God has given us eternal life, and this life is in his Son."

Then, in the midst of his reading, his heart opened. It was not an outwardly dramatic event, and he knew that if he was asked to testify about it in front of a group, he would struggle to accurately describe it. He experienced an outpouring of emotion and spiritual infilling, and for several moments had the light-headed sensation of being swept up into a swirling cloud of faith and understanding. He was a pragmatic, no-nonsense man, not easily given to display, but now he found he could barely contain the urge to go *tell* someone, anyone, what he had discovered.

Christ was real, Christ lived, and he accepted Christ as his Savior. His desire was as simple and unbelievably complex as that. He gave himself over to God, turned his life over to God, and accepted God's will. He would not take another step in this world without Christ by his side, and there would not be a moment when he was not aware of his Savior. He studied His prayers, looked back at how He used to pray, what He used to pray for. There was only one passage in any prayer that mattered to him now: "Thy will be done." He would continue to study, he would try to learn and understand, he would keep fighting in this life, even as the world seemed to be collapsing around him, and he would not question his God. He savored the feelings as he was swept by warm emotion, and tears ran down his cheeks as he understood the love, the promise.

That his studies, and recent world events including the rapture, showed clearly the end times were at hand did not worry him. He knew the world would suffer many tribulations, there would be fear, and chaos, and he would be a part of it. He knew he had not been taken along with his loved ones, and he *accepted* it. God's will was what mattered, and if that meant he was to struggle through the wars, famine, and global destruction, so be it . . . it would change nothing in his heart. His heart held Jesus Christ, and he accepted God's will, and would do his best to work concurrently and parallel to that will.

He felt at peace. He missed Sylvia, Sonia, and Johnny, and he regretted having turned away from Christ for so many years — more apathetic than antagonistic — thus not sharing in the relationship with them. But he was at peace, settled, and after the initial rush of emotion, he still felt very strong.

The captain of the USS *Finback*, Campbell Sims ("You can call me Campy," but no one ever did), was a lean and whiplike man with iron gray hair, a creased and weathered face, flinty eyes protected by bushy gray brows, and thin lips. He looked like a man who experienced pain if forced to laugh. After the disappearance, he immediately began looking for enemies to attack. He liked the Muslim hypothesis, even if he had no respect for their weapons-making capabilities. They were out there, they had been fighting against America for years, and they could be shot at. The "alien baloney" he simply dismissed. The "rapture stuff," the "end-times stuff," he found intellectually amusing, and soft-headed. Any God he cared to know didn't have time for any of this nonsense, he was sure of that. Nope, this was another man-made problem, and it would have to be dealt with on man's level.

That his wife of over twenty years — secretly he adored her, and never understood why she was his — had been taken only angered him more. He was very grateful to be the commander of one of the most powerful weapons ever commissioned, and ached for the chance to put it to use against an enemy. Now he had this little diversion, however . . . this spook on some supersecret top-priority mission. Like most career men, he hated spooks. Dilettantes, most of 'em. This guy, this Jameson . . . he seemed okay. Old enough to carry himself with dignity. Didn't strut around like Rambo, didn't try to impress the crew, kept to himself, his nose buried in the Bible. Captain Campbell Sims had no problem with the Bible either. It told a wonderful story, even if it was sometimes an awkward read. Either way, he had to brief Jameson, and decided to do it in the exec's office.

"Have a cup of coffee, Jameson, it's good on this boat," said Sims as Jameson reported to him in the small cabin.

"Thank you, sir." Jameson sat where the captain motioned, pulled a full cup closer to him on the desk, picked it up, and sipped it.

"Supposed to fill you in, keep you updated," said Sims. "You know I got my brief on your deal, right?"

"Yes, sir."

"You're briefed on Azul Dante. He's designated friendly and useful by our, uh, new commander in chief. He's close to pulling together a coalition."

Jameson nodded. The coffee *was* good.

"The latest is this: Dante has an okay from almost all of the countries that will form his European Coalition. It is in place in principle, as the lawyers say, and he is taking up the reins without a hitch. He can put it together, and he gets it done. Got the major highways cleared, power plants working and sending electricity cross-border if needed. Food distribution is on track on the Continent, hospitals staffed again, employees being recruited to take up the empty spaces. The guy is good to go. I've never met him, have you?"

"No, sir," replied Jameson.

"I hear he's a man who holds your attention. No fluff, if you know what I mean. Comes into the room, and the room turns to meet him, and *pow* . . . they love him." Sims stopped, thought about it, and added, almost to himself, "So . . . maybe this toilet bowl of a world needs somebody like him to straighten this mess out. I'm not too keen on any coalition being a bigger superpower than the U.S., though. We're the best, and always will be." He stopped again, refilled both coffee cups, and charged on. "Anyway. I'm supposed to tell you Azul Dante is on track, all good. Looks like he's begun the process for a real showdown with that sand scum, Izbek Noir. Izbek Noir? What kind of name is that, do you suppose? Like sort of Russian with a little twist of French?" He shrugged, clearly not liking names that did not sound like they came from Nebraska, South Carolina, or Wyoming. "The mujahideen are a formidable force though, I don't have to tell you, and man . . . that will be one outrageous battle if the European Coalition gets it together and goes head-to-head with them." He frowned, then said, "Oh, the big news I'm supposed to tell you about Azul Dante is he and Prime Minister Pearlman have signed a pact. Dante called it a 'covenant,' where the European Coalition will let Israel live in peace and will protect it from attack. This, of course, puts him in good with Washington."

Of course, thought Jameson, but he said simply, "Yes, sir."

"In line with that, I've been given a sketchy outline of your mission. No details, just the premise. Personally, I got no problem with that type of limited, specific action if it can eliminate a problem. I believe the mujahideen will still be a dangerous crowd, though, even if their supposedly invulnerable leader develops a nine-millimeter head cold." He scratched his own head. It made a raspy sound. "We'll put you in on the north coast. Maybe west of Tunis, somewhere in there. The mujahideen are like fleas along that coast, so you'll be right in amongst 'em real quick. Hope you, uh, are prepared."

"Hey diddle diddle. . . ." Jameson answered with a small grin.

". . . Straight up the middle," Sims finished for him.

"I've been given a couple of contacts who might get me into the upper echelon, sir," added Jameson. "After that it's wait for an opportunity."

Captain Campbell Sims nodded but said nothing, still awed by acts of courage in the name of right.

There was a pause as both men sipped their coffee. Then the captain spoke again.

"I've seen you carrying that Bible everywhere you go, Jameson."

"Yes, sir. I've . . . I've gone back to it after too long." He thought about what he had just said, then added, "Actually, it's like I've gone to it for the first time . . . uh . . . if you know what I mean."

"Everything in this old world looks different now, Jameson," Sims said easily. "I'm not prying, I was just curious if you found it . . . helpful." He stopped, not comfortable talking about his personal life, and not wanting to appear weak or vulnerable.

Jameson looked at him a moment, then said quietly, "I lost everything. Everything real and important, sir. I mean, the job is important, *this* particular assignment is monstrously important, but it's still the job. They flew me home so I could see for myself they were gone, and then there was this emptiness."

He watched the captain's weathered face as the man nodded in understanding.

"It was my wife's Bible, sir," Jameson went on, "and I just picked it up, began reading, and . . . I don't know how to . . . It was there, in the pages. I found it —"

"Found what, Jameson?"

"Reason. Hope. Strength. I don't know, some sense to this whole thing." He paused, then said, "I am, right now, a totally different man after finding the Word, and accepting it."

"We had a chaplain on this boat, Jameson," said Sims after another long silence. "Some kind of preacher before he came into the navy. Big, friendly guy. Everybody liked him. Took his job seriously, held Bible studies, counseled the young sailors, handled all the, uh, religious events and what-not." He shook his head. "The day of the disappearance we were in Norfolk. Shipmates just *gone,* then the news from shoreside. So many people, crew members lost family, wives, kids. It was horrible. Well, while we're all speculating on the cause, here comes the chaplain. He was convinced within an hour, no doubt. Said it was the end of the world, called it the 'rapture.' Said Jesus was coming. He started babbling on about bowls, different bowls, of pain, or fire, or . . . I don't know. I mean, I know it's in Revelation, but I haven't studied it. So he's got it figured, and he's explaining it, and then his eyes sort of got real big, his face broke out in a hot sweat, and he started crying. 'Hey, what about me?' he said. 'Why wasn't I taken too? I should have been taken.' Then he's shouting to the overhead, like he's shouting to God himself, telling God He made a mistake and left him still here even though he most certainly is a Christian and always has been and how could God make such a stupid mistake and God better take him up right now or he is gonna really raise a stink." Captain Sims shook his head, remembering. "Truth was, I felt embarrassed for the man. Lots of people were suffering, and this guy was all about himself. And screaming at God because God left him here by mistake. Went into loud detail about why he was a good Christian. . . . It was awful. Finally he went berserk. Something just snapped, I guess. The boat was already at general quarters, so I had the security detail wrestle him to the deck and handcuff him. A little while later a shore party came for him, and away he went. Next day we got word he had hung himself in the psych ward." Troubled, the captain thought it over, then said, "He was assigned to this boat, so he was one of mine. Hated to see it, but what can you do? So many people looking for answers. Maybe the ones worst off are the ones who *thought* they had the answer before all this happened."

Jameson said nothing.

"Anyway," said Captain Campbell Sims, "I didn't mean to pry about your Bible. Guess I was just wondering if you thought it was worth a look." He looked away.

Jameson watched him a moment, then said, "Captain, all I can say is, it's in there, the Word. It was in there for me, and if I could find it, you probably could too." He hesitated, wondering if he should offer to pray with the captain, but he let it pass. It was too soon, it was too personal.

The meeting ended with a solemn hand-shake.

Chapter Eleven

Thomas Church was in an agitated state. After all the years of carefully constructing his perfect personal environment, his house with its built-in multimedia center, after all the hours sitting comfortably inside while the world careened on its crazy axis around him and he observed it from his sanctuary, now he was literally bouncing off the walls. He couldn't figure out why it was affecting him so irrationally; it simply *was*. The disappearance was too crazy. For some reason, the very real possibility that it had to do with the Bible, with God, infuriated him even more. He wasn't even frightened — he was angry. Angry that such a stupid thing could be perpetrated on the human race by the spiritual being, the all-powerful entity, we call "Father."

Maybe he had been a cynic even as a young man, when he first saw for himself the hypocrisy of the church. With the condescending benevolence of youth, he had viewed the discrepancies, the inaccuracies, through benign and forgiving eyes. "No big deal," he would always say, "whatever makes them feel good." The church was part of the neighborhood, part of the society, like other familiar structures — schools, for instance, bowling alleys, movie theaters, skating rinks. The church edifice, and the people who filled it, were all simply part of the script. Harmless, not a bad thing. The church actually lent an air of dignity to human events like birth, marriage, and death. It was created and fine-tuned to help us go along to get along, he figured.

But this, this monstrosity. It was totally unacceptable. God? He was okay with the notion of God, it seemed more reasonable than the entire human race being a biological accident. God was supposed to watch over us. He created us, and He had the certain obligation to care for us. So He had created this incomparable planet Earth, had formed us into these incredible electrochemical flesh-and-blood mechanisms, given us intelligence, the power of speech, free will. All great gifts. Well, why not? If we were to be created as *life*, to exist in this world, why wouldn't He make us more than capable of surviving?

He did, and we had, until the day He decided only some of us had made the grade, or stood in His favor, or passed some kind of spirituality test. Let us not forget, he argued, this same God who gave us all these gifts so we could survive in this world also gave us built-in shortcomings. We were *human* beings, imperfect beasts a couple notches up from primal, grunting and grasping through our uneven lives, making mistakes, impregnating each other to insure there would always be more incapable fools to stumble along in our footsteps. We were human, not perfect, not godlike.

"I'm not perfect . . . I'm forgiven," says the bumper sticker, he mused. Yeah, you're forgiven until the day He decides to end it. Then *maybe* you're forgiven, and then maybe not. It just rankled him, the injustice of it. God, who could do such wondrous things, and had — that same God then snapped His fingers, brought a select number of "good Christians" to sit with him, and turned His back on the rest of us, leaving us to make our way through a world turned to shambles, more dangerous and unforgiving than ever.

This really stinks, he thought. The worry about his son pounded the walls of his heart like a drumbeat. He was very close to deciding whether to leave immediately to try and locate Tommy — last heard of in Texas, for crying out loud — or to hang tight in the comfort zone of his multimedia center, where he could keep his finger on the pulse of the world and had many forms of communication available. He was unsure, on the fence, until a visit from his neighbor settled it with a searing intensity.

She was young, tall, lithe, and lovely. Missy, she told him. Missy and Mark, a great couple. He played golf, she did yoga. He was a sales rep for a huge sporting goods company, she was a part-time assistant at a neighborhood veterinarian's office. She had great eyes, great skin; and Thomas Church, good neighbor, tried not to stare when Missy washed her little Honda while wearing a two-piece. Then the neighborhood buzzed about Missy's first pregnancy. Lovely news, and everybody smiled when they passed Missy and Mark's house. She was more than a couple months along before she even started to show, remembered Church as he thought about it.

Missy was the last thing on Church's mind when he cautiously answered the incessantly ringing phone. When he heard who it was, he relaxed, until she began yammering, obviously on the edge of hysteria. Church hadn't seen her or her husband since the disappearance.

"Missy," he said. "What? Did something happen? Oh, no . . . not Mark . . ."

"No, Thomas, not Mark," she hissed. "Of *course* not Mark. He's still here. My family, his family, some gone. Some still here —"

"Well, what is it, Missy? What?"

"Who *is* missing, Thomas?" sobbed the young woman. "Who do you think is gone?"

Thomas shook his head. He let the pause lengthen.

"It's the baby, Thomas, you fool," she cried. "My *baby*, the baby that was inside me. She was in me, the first sonogram showed her to us. We saw her heart beating. She was there, Thomas. Now . . . she's gone . . . gone like she was never even . . ."

"Oh, Missy," said Thomas, genuinely saddened by what was a horrific loss, "I'm so sorry. You poor thing. What a terrible thing. . . ."

"Sorry. Sorry. That's what my mom said, my sister too. That's what the neighbors, the ones still here, say. Sorry." He heard her set the phone down for a moment, followed by a rustling and what sounded like a door being opened. "They're all sorry. They can't *fix* it, but they're sorry. Even

Mark . . . my husband, the father of my child . . . even he was sorry . . . so . . . sorry."

"Missy, what can I —"

"Know what our priest said?" she interjected. " 'All the children, Missy,' he said. 'Even the unborn.' Then he said . . . 'sorry' . . . and instructed me to go home, be with my husband, and pray on it. He said we should pray on it! I went home, Thomas, and I got with my husband, and I pushed him into bed — I didn't pray about it — and told him to . . . to . . . Well, you know what I mean, don't you? I wanted him to do what he did, Thomas, to do what he did to make me pregnant with my most beautiful little girl who was curled up inside me so sweetly." She was sobbing now. "And then she *wasn't*. I lost my child, and I wanted Mark to give me another. He looked at me like I was crazy . . . kept saying, 'No way, Missy . . . It can't work like that. . . .' "

He did not know how to answer that. He couldn't make himself speak anyway. He was frightened for her, terribly saddened, and angered by her suffering.

"Don't worry," Missy rambled on. "That's what I told myself after I hit Mark with the lamp. There was blood everywhere, and he just slid off the edge of the bed and lay there so . . . still. He wouldn't listen, he wouldn't listen. But don't worry, I said. Mark isn't the only man around here. There are others. Men are everywhere, and almost all of them can give me . . . I mean, men always want it anyway . . . so I thought . . . I thought about you, Thomas . . . right next door. You've got snow on the roof," she said with a twisted grin, "but there's still some fire inside, right? Right."

He could hear Missy sobbing on the other end of the line, heard her stuttering inhalations and her nearly feral moans. All Thomas could do was chant the mantra of the ill-prepared and the reluctant: "It's okay. It's all right. You're going to be okay." In a few minutes, he heard her breathing grow steadier. In a small voice, she said to him, "Well, thank you anyway, Thomas. Sorry to disturb you. I'll . . . I'll . . . find someone who has . . . what . . . I need." He heard the phone rocking in its cradle before its final click.

It had taken him a long time to get through to the local police department. When a dispatcher finally answered, all he could report was that a woman in his neighborhood, possibly insane, might have hurt or killed her husband. "We'll get over there when we can get over there," he was told, and the line was disconnected.

That did it for Thomas Church. He loaded up his SUV with his guns, extra cash, clothing, camping gear, first-aid gear — everything he would need for his adventure. This included two laptops, a Palm Pilot, a Blackberry, a cell phone, chargers, and several other techno-treats for good measure. He opened a floor safe he had installed a couple of years ago and pulled out a bag of gold Krugerrand coins from long-ago South Africa. Gold was a good thing when the world was a wild place and the Federal Reserve was on its ear. He, much like Shannon Carpenter in Ohio, very carefully prepared and secured his house before leaving it. He would go to his daughter's place in Virginia first, get all the info he could, then move on in search of his son. God had proven Himself to be a capricious and arbitrary father, and Thomas Church figured if nothing else, he could show Him how it was supposed to be done. At that point, he didn't care about anything he had read about Izbek Noir, Azul Dante, the Prodigal Project, or anything else. The script of life was a lie, plain and simple.

Ron Underwood sat in his son's wheelchair in an upstairs bedroom in his house in California. His mental processes had fragmented into different facets, and one part told him quite clearly that he was experiencing a classic breakdown. He had not the will to fight it, and that was comforting in its own nonproductive way. He did not know how long he had been sitting there, or how long it had been since Ivy left the house. Where did she say she was going? No matter. It just didn't matter. The daylight had gone, then there was night, then day. He did not know how many. He knew he had soiled himself sitting there, but that was okay too. . . . The chair had already suffered through the various indignities a non-functioning human body could visit upon it.

Another part of his mind examined the fact that Ronnie was no longer there. Ronnie had disappeared, and even though Ron had demanded an answer from Ivy, deep inside he knew Ronnie had been taken. He had, at some point, felt under his bottom for the traces of sand and bits of gravel that lay on the orthopedic cushion. His fingers felt gritty when he brought them to his face to look at them.

"Ronnie . . . Ronnie-boy?" he had said to the empty room. Something very bad had happened to the world, he remembered. The children had been taken, and perhaps some others. The most important thing was Ronnie, and he was gone.

I really should have gone with Ivy, he thought, gone with her to try and find the answer to this . . . problem. It was her fault, she said, but I don't think so. Not her fault, she would never do anything to hurt Ronnie, even if she never understood the gift he was to us. A large, fat, silvery tear welled up in the corner of his left eye, hung there a moment, then began a winding descent across his cheek. I should have gone with her.

He was not a simple man. He was learned, well-read, and educated. He was a college professor, and a news junkie, respected for the depth and complexity of his knowledge. He was conversant with Scripture. He had tried, gently, cautiously, timidly, to bring faith and his wife, Ivy, together. He had believed in his heart she would deal better with their son's situation if she had some kind of relationship with God. She might even be like other moms of special-needs kids — joyful, grateful, accepting — and just possibly happy. At the end, she thought she had caused Ronnie's disappearance because she had made a pact with the devil. What a shame. She had caused nothing, and the devil doesn't go around meeting people in French restaurants anyway.

Then his mind jumped, blanked out, sped forward to questions, then reversed at high speed, reversed back to scenes of his son, Ronnie. He remembered the night of Ronnie's birth, how quickly the joy turned to concern, how everything became a jumble, and he had to be strong. Everyone's eyes were filled with apologies, and he could not understand it. Ivy was cold, distant, wouldn't even look at him, cried when she held the baby when they finally let him out of ICU. He overheard somebody talking about the birth, heard the word "damaged." He thought of his son, damaged. What an awful word. Like he was a piece of merchandise that needed to be returned. But when he finally got to hold him close, to look down on Ronnie's angelic face as he held him in his arms, he was swept away by the feeling of pure love and joy. Ronnie was a sweet baby boy, with beautiful eyes. His expression always told his dad, "No worries, Dad, no worries." Ron simply could not understand how anyone could dismiss the child as "damaged." The child was simply love.

He was the father of the son, and the son was love.

Ron Underwood sat in his quiet house while his neighborhood went through throes of agony, fear, and survival around him. Ivy was gone, there was nothing to do, no *reason* to do anything. He had no intention of moving. One of the fragments in his mind, thinking of Ivy's quest, wanted to remind her of the information he had gathered weeks ago about the church . . . about that "project," about some expectations the church had. Then it was not there, and he didn't want to worry about it anyway. He wanted to let his mind go back to Ronnie's birth, to begin there, and then painstakingly resurrect every single moment of life, every day Ronnie was alive and with him in this world. That was the essence, the substance of Ron Underwood's reality: the life of his son. He would not move from Ronnie's wheelchair. He would stay right there, basking in memories, sustaining himself on morsels of love gleaned from the parade of images of Ronnie. He would never leave.

He looked up suddenly, a frown on his face. He wished he could have heard Ronnie say, "Mommy."

He was the father of the son, and the son was love.

The touching was not something the Reverend Henderson Smith had counted on. People wanted to touch him. If he stood at the massive front doors of the magnificent cathedral to greet the flock as they gathered to hear him — he could not stop himself from likening it to descending from the mount to mingle with the great unwashed multitudes — they would touch him as they passed. Of course, he shook hands all the time, but he became aware of people reaching out and touching his arm, or passing their fingers over the hem of his robe, of gently squeezing his shoulder. More than once people had collapsed at his feet, crying and sobbing, twisting the folds of his robe in their grasping fingers, rubbing their wet faces against it until one of the church staffers politely but firmly pulled them away. He sighed, and guessed it came with the territory.

On this day he had finished his sermon with a talk about Ephesians 4:20. He had read to the silent, attentive congregation: " 'You, however, did not come to know Christ that way. Surely you heard of him and were taught of him in accordance with the truth that is Jesus. You were taught, with regard to your former way of life, to put off your old self, which is being corrupted by its deceitful desires; to be made new in the attitude of your minds; and to put on the new self, created to be like God in true righteousness and holiness.' "

He closed his Bible and spoke to them, his voice quiet but intense. "To put on the new self . . . the *new* self. All of us in this wonderful cathedral today better be puttin' on our new self . . . because this is surely a *new world*. 'But Reverend Smith,' you'll say to me. 'Reverend, this is the end of the world, not a new world. It's the end, not the beginning, not something new.' And I'll say to you, *Listen*. . . . Go back and read Revelation, frightening and unforgiving as it may be. Can you not see it as a *warning?* Just one step in God's plan for our eventual redemption and salvation?"

He moved to Ephesians 5: " 'Be imitators of God, therefore, as dearly loved children and live a life of love, just as Christ loved us as a fragment offering and sacrifice to God.' " Then Ephesians 5:8, 5:10, and 5:13 and 14: " 'For you were once darkness, but now you are light in the Lord. Live as children of light and find out what pleases the Lord. . . . But everything exposed by the light becomes visible, for it is the light that makes everything visible. That is why it is said:

> . . . *Wake up, O sleeper,*
> *rise from the dead,*
> *and Christ will shine on you.*'

"Be imitators, brothers and sisters," called the Reverend Henderson Smith to his flock, "as 'dearly loved children.' 'Live as children of light.' Did you hear that? The children have been taken, but we are enjoined to 'Live as children of light,' and we are to 'find out what pleases the Lord.' Then we are told to 'wake up' . . . *'rise'* . . . and Christ will shine on us." He let his gaze scan the upturned faces, each listening, waiting. In the crowd of faces two stood out on this day, both women's. Both seemed to hold his gaze as his eyes met theirs. He was startled by the first. She was attractive, with honey-colored hair, a strong face, bright eyes; her face held the stamp of *survivor*, the stamp of someone who had lost loved ones. But in her eyes was a certain strength, a . . . light, the light of conviction. She held him with her eyes, and in them he saw hope.

Several pews back from the first was the other. She was a beauty, her hair brushed

395

out and shiny, her face angular and challenging; her female body, even sitting in the crowded pew, was carried with a sensual ease. Her eyes burned too. Again strength, again conviction, but with a seasoning of anger embedded deep. Anger, and a secret. He pulled his eyes away from them, took a deep breath, and finished his thought.

"Stay with me now, brothers and sisters, for I am here to sing a message of hope. *Hope*." He held his Bible high above his head. "Sure, we are taught from a young age not to try to get too creative with the simple gospel in this Book, right? Read it, hear it. Don't try to make it fit something so you can justify your actions later. I say this because it may appear I'm trying to do just that today. Take words from this Bible, bring them out into the light of this dark day, this day when we've all lost so much, when it quite literally looks like we might be seeing the world come to an end, this day when the children have all been taken up. The children and those who were among us and had a light in their hearts we didn't quite have. I'm saying to you, there are words in here, these are the words of *God*, words that can help us. Words that can give us hope. The children were taken. It is a scary possibility that *we might not be able to make any more!*" He paused, and allowed a teasing smile to play across his face as he wagged one finger at them and admonished, "Now I don't want you-all leavin' here trying to prove or disprove that as soon as you get home." He was rewarded with a smattering of laughter and some head shaking throughout the pews.

"But what I'm saying to you, fellow Christian wanderers," he continued, "is this: If we are enjoined to live as children of light, then we will be looked at as 'children,' we will still be Christ's children. And he will *not* forget us. We must remain strong, remain faithful, study hard, try hard to hear his message, and perhaps we won't be lost." He paused, then went off on the tack he had been angling for: "We Christians in this world that's been torn asunder . . . must we be lost? Must we give up, and sit out there on the street just cryin' and fussing like you can see out there every day? No, I say to you. N-O. This church isn't called the New Christian Cathedral for nothing. We *are* the new Christians. We are surviving Christians, and we must be united. Strength, unity, cohesiveness. These things are necessary for survival in this sad world today. Let this church become a worldwide church. Let us join in a worldwide one church with no more time for varying nuances and subtle differences. Let us speak with one voice, let us hear one voice as a teacher and guide when he is shown to us. Let us prepare for the possible end of time as *new* Christians." He stopped, waited to make sure the words fell upon them, then said, "Now let us end this sermon today with a prayer."

Shannon Carpenter liked Ivy Sloan from the first moment she saw how the woman spoke to the thin black reverend who had such strength, such power. Shannon had waited — it had been almost a half hour — before the crowd of people clustered around Smith began reluctantly to leave him. She heard Ivy introduce herself, heard her say she had traveled from California to Alabama on the strength of the reverend's voice and message.

Apparently the end of the world would not stop the woman from keeping herself attractive and appealing, observed Shannon as she looked over how Ivy was dressed, the carefully applied makeup, the hair, the way she held and moved her body. If men-women games still had any effect in this world — and Shannon, though not a participant, had no doubt they would — this Ivy Sloan would be a high scorer if she wanted to be. But it wasn't that. Ms. Sloan — she had first introduced herself as "Ivy Sloan-Underwood" — had an undeniable depth of feeling, emotion, and experience in her soul. Her eyes and voice were challenging; she had anger in her, sadness and loss — well, who didn't — and some kind of determination.

"Yes, Ivy," said the Reverend Henderson Smith as he held both of the young woman's hands in his, "I do have time for a chat, especially for someone as nice as you who has managed to drive through the craziness that our roads have become. All the way from California to Selma."

Ivy smiled, and said, "Thank you, Reverend Smith." Then she pointed at the woman who stood on the other side of the preacher, obviously waiting, and added, "Reverend, I think she wants to —"

Ivy Sloan watched as Shannon Carpenter introduced herself and shook the reverend's hand. She thought Carpenter was pretty, in a carefully controlled way, coiffed, smoothed, and made-up with muted freshness — as if she had snuck off with her teenage daughter's cosmetic kit. The woman's clothes were casual chic, slacks and a top with three-quarter sleeves, both in a crème color that brought a little life to her boring hair. Sensible low-heeled shoes, matching bag. The old Ivy would immediately have characterized Shannon Carpenter as nonthreatening, but the new Ivy was immediately uncomfortable with the woman's quick use of the name of Jesus in the first sentence in her conversation with Smith. Something about "having Jesus by my side the whole way down here from Ohio." Ivy Sloan was ready to dismiss Shannon Carpenter as irrelevant, somehow cut the reverend away from her and sit down with him for a talk, when she heard Carpenter tell Smith, "something about a 'Prodigal Project,' Reverend Smith. My husband, Billy, was a Christian, taken along with our kids. He had mentioned it, and actually wrote it into the margin of his Bible, along with the name of this church. And your name."

Ivy Sloan cleared her throat, touched Smith lightly on the arm, and said, "Reverend Smith, would you mind if we both visited with you, talked with you. I mean" — she looked at Carpenter and Smith, and grinned — "looks like we're all heading for the same thing, here."

"Yes," said Smith, aware that these two women being here, now, was extraordinary somehow, perhaps preordained. "Let's go into the back . . . the cathedral has a lovely kitchen and dining area. After I visit with some of the ladies who volunteer there, we'll settle in my private dining room and talk."

Shannon Carpenter was tired but excited. Her road trip had been harrowing, but devoid of any really bad moments. She had stayed on the main highways, managed to find gas and food without too much trouble, followed behind a National Guard convoy a long way for safety, and found the New Christian Cathedral with the minimum of fuss. She knew that the Shannon Carpenter whom Reverend Smith and Ivy Sloan met was not the same woman who had left Ohio in her husband's pickup truck. Like everyone else, there had been a Shannon before the disappearance, then quite another Shannon after. The Shannon who lost her family was a sad and frightened woman, aching inside, confused, lost, bitter. The world had become a horror, and when she had first begun to clean her house after realizing her husband and children were in fact forever gone, she thought she might just stay inside until she died. Billy's Bible had driven out the immobilizing uncertainty, and she had headed south with a purpose.

But it was during the journey that the totally new Shannon had appeared. She smiled to herself as she remembered how she used to dislike that old, trite phrase *born again*. Well, she was. . . . She was born again in Christ, and she didn't mind it at *all*, and she had been busting at the seams waiting to tell someone. It had happened while she aimed the dusty pickup truck down the highway, mile after mile, trying to steer and read passages from Billy's Bible at the same time. The images of Matt, little Billy, and Laura floated in her heart as always, but her husband, Billy, he was right there, riding shotgun in the truck.

Like John Jameson, Shannon had the feeling that her partner, her husband, turned the pages with her as she studied different passages. He was there for her, explaining things, delving into meanings he had gleaned from the words years before. She was comforted by the book itself, the physical paper, ink, and binding that were the Bible. It was Billy's Bible. His hands — the same hands that had held hers, that had touched her, had let the book lay open in his palm while he thumbed through the pages, his eyes caressing the words even as they caressed her when they lay close in the soft shadows of evening. She could feel his strength, his love, when she held the book, and it comforted her. Many times she simply pulled over to what looked like a safe spot, made sure the truck doors were locked, and read over a passage that had impacted her as she drove. She would sit quietly, studying, thinking, then sip some water, have a snack, and pull back out onto the roadway.

She knew that if she had been on one of those televangelist shows that Billy liked to watch, and the host had asked her to pinpoint for the listeners exactly when it had happened, she would have had difficulty putting it into words. Just as her children had been there, then they were *not*, Jesus was not in her heart, and then He *was*.

It had been early morning, of that she was fairly certain; she had been feeling bone tired and edgy. She had promised herself she would pull over the next time she saw a group of highway patrol cars or National Guard trucks parked somewhere, close Billy's Bible for a while, and get some sleep. She had closed the Bible, and held it close against her chest as she drove, her mind full of what she had experienced and what she had read. Then, in a rush, it happened. Her heart felt a warm swirl of energy, a full flow of joy welled up out of her chest and into her throat, and she *accepted Him*. Jesus Christ was suddenly in her heart, standing with her, holding her hand, smiling at her with an unbelievably soothing and comforting look. She simply gave herself over to him, hearing Billy's words about putting your life in his hands, and she did. Her tilting feeling of empowerment came with her acceptance. He had been there the whole time, she understood. He had been there, but she had to open her heart to Him, to turn *to* Him, instead of away. And she did.

After the initial welling up of energy, joy, completeness, grateful surprise, she learned more. She learned the aching loss of her children, her husband, would not be diminished. They were still gone, she missed them, she wanted to be with them, and it *hurt.* But with her acceptance of Jesus into her life came *reason,* the knowing that even if she didn't understand why, they were gone but they were okay. They were with *Him,* and though she wanted them with her for selfish reasons, she knew they could not be anyplace better, and if she loved them as she knew she did, then she would *want* them to be with their Savior, period. Simple, exciting, a little scary, but simple. She had a mother's pain in her heart, but with it sang a child's joy. The child who has found her Father, and with Him . . . hope.

With equal certainty, Shannon realized as she accepted Christ, she accepted the Scripture as real. Revelation described what this was all about, and Shannon no longer intellectually fought it. These were the end times. She had not been taken up, understandably and deservedly, and it was all right. She had a purpose here, that much she understood. If she had found Christ too late to be saved, had found Him now because there was something more for her to do before it all went black, it was *all right.* She was late, she knew, but she was now reporting for duty as a servant of her Lord. For now she would follow the lead Billy had given her in his Bible. Head south, find this Reverend Henderson Smith at his New Christian Cathedral, testify to him about Christ, and see where it took her.

Henderson Smith felt unnerved. He had received visitors after a sermon before, often, and often the conversation turned to where the New Christian faith was heading, if there was a world leader on the horizon who might make the movement global in scope. He had slipped into his skin as pastor of the cathedral, and in that role had realized all of his dreams. True, he had lost Miriam and the kids, but that fact actually helped him in his new post. His loss of family validated him; his being left on Earth and not lifted like the others confirmed for his congregation his simple humanness. His sincere hurting over their loss made him a sympathetic figure, and he had already seen that the congregation included many attractive women, from all the neighborhoods of Selma, who would consider it their duty, and pleasure, to stand at his side.

But he had it now, had all he had longed for as a young preacher. The biggest church, a congregation lost and hungry for guidance, a facility and organization, even in these tumultuous times, that had everything at his disposal to make him a multimedia star. His recorded radio voice carried far and wide, and the church television station, though local, made videos of his sermons, which were being distributed all over the world. He had respect, and a large, hardworking staff . . . that again included young women who wanted to be with him in the worst way. He was the Reverend Henderson Smith, and he stood tall in that beautiful high pulpit, anointing his flock with the Word.

Of course, there was an undeniable dark

side to it too. He could not stop himself, as he scanned the faces of his congregants, from looking for the smug, porcine, sweating face of Andrew Nuit, the man who had made him the offer he could not refuse. Sure, witnesses had told him it was probably Andrew Nuit who had burned his old church, and himself with it. But Henderson Smith suspected that Andrew Nuit — or whoever he was this week — probably bathed in those flames, pleasured by their caress. He shuddered.

More darkness came from his internal struggle — maybe there was hope for him yet — over his deliberate and covertly guided selection and interpretation of the Scripture to get his message across. He had a theme buried in all of his grand speeches, a theme that pushed his listeners toward the world church, and one specific world leader. Way, way down deep in his heart, a bone fragment of the original Henderson Smith still existed. And that fragment of Preacher Smith hated what he was doing. It was unsettling to blithely pervert the pure Word. It was actually harder for him to do than he had thought it would be when he sat across his old desk from the seducer.

Now he sat at a nice table covered by a

thick white tablecloth with place settings for four. One of the ladies who worked in the kitchen brought coffee and pastries, then left with a smile. Smith's two visitors sat on his right, and across from him. They were both attractive, strong, professional females, he already knew both had lost loved ones, and both had been "called" here, to him. Shannon Carpenter, the lady from Ohio, had that old effervescent, barely contained luminosity he had seen many times in the past and secretly longed for. She wore the purple J for Jesus emblazoned on her heart and in the expression on her face. She had recently been born again, and the Spirit welled up in her, and she was bursting at the seams with His presence.

Henderson Smith's personal commitment to God was real, but his biggest secret until recently was that his "salvation experience" had actually been fake. He had studied it, had been around it, understood what it was supposed to be, went through the motions of acceptance, then manufactured the excitement and zeal that often came with it for his audience. In his work he had come across the genuine thing enough times to recognize it, and to understand that his was counterfeit. This

Shannon Carpenter had it for real, and he was glad for her in his heart.

The other one, Ivy Sloan, whoa boy. There were some energies crashing around inside that lady, uh-huh. She also had a glow. He recognized those fires too. The raging fires fueled by the wooden frame of a person's own soul. That the woman was genuine he had no doubt; that she had driven all that way on the strength of his voice he could accept too. She had suffered during the disappearance, and had come from that to him. She was searching, and wore her anger and bitterness like a spiritual bandolier of ammunition draped across her torso. He turned to Shannon Carpenter.

"You made mention of Christ being with you on your trip, Mrs. Carpenter," said Smith. "Do you want to tell me about it?"

"Do you mean testify about it, Reverend?" asked Shannon shyly. Then she shrugged. "Nothing new to you, I know, but I . . . I was born again on the trip down here. I found Jesus, accepted Him into my life, and there it is. We all" — she nodded at Ivy — "know my timing stinks, seeing as how it looks like the end times are here, and I missed the lift." She shrugged again. "Now I understand what my husband,

Billy, tried to tell me all those years. I have his Bible, and now I'm with Jesus. Oh, and please call me Shannon, Reverend Smith."

"Why are you here?" asked Smith.

"My husband wrote your name in the margin of his Bible," replied Shannon. "Your name, your cathedral here in Selma, and 'Prodigal Project.' "

Smith nodded, then turned to his other guest. "Mrs. Sloan? Did you find Jesus too?"

"Not like Shannon did," Sloan answered evasively. "You can call me Ivy. I lost a son, left my husband, who could not accept the reality of what happened. I heard your voice, your message, and I felt compelled to come to you. I'm not sure what I expect to learn, or what I'm supposed to do, but I'm sure I'm with the right person at the right place. Even your sermon today helped me. A worldwide understanding, someone who would put it all together. I can't go back home, I've got energy and questions, and I want to *participate* in something that will make things better."

"I'm sure there is a reason for the three of us to meet like this," said Smith sincerely. "These are extraordinary times, exciting times." He sipped from his cup of coffee, wondering where, in fact, this would lead.

Ivy Sloan looked at Shannon Carpenter and said, "So you found Jesus, Shannon, and through Him, God?"

"Well, yes," replied Shannon carefully, not sure if she heard accusation or mockery in Ivy's tone. "I have always believed in God, but it wasn't defined or focused. My new relationship with Christ has solidified things for me."

"Well, I may as well tell both of you right now," said Ivy as she looked first at Shannon, then at Henderson Smith, "I never really was sure about God, and certainly not at all about Jesus Christ. There was just never anything to really grab hold of, you know? I had . . . a child, a son, and he suffered severe neurological damage at birth. He was massively 'challenged.' Carried or in a wheelchair his whole life, could not speak, react to anything, couldn't feed himself or . . . care for himself." She raised both hands, palms facing out, as if to ward off any attempt at sympathy or understanding. "I handled it, okay. I'm not the first or only mom to raise a special-needs child. But recently I had an experience, right before the disappearance, and it made me believe in God."

"But that's wonderful, Ivy," said Rev-

411

erend Smith as Shannon nodded in agreement. "I thought you said you had not accepted Jesus."

"I sat face-to-face with the devil himself."

"What?" Smith blanched. "You . . . what?"

"Yes," confirmed Ivy, "it was the devil, or one of his lackeys. Standing up, walking around, talking smooth, and looking fine."

Henderson Smith felt a trickle of sweat run down his spine. He was very frightened.

"I don't understand," said Shannon. "Why would the devil talk to you? What did he want?"

Ivy looked at Shannon, grinned, and said, "I *thought* he wanted what men always want. My husband was home with Ronnie, I was out playing hooky, and this hunk makes a pass at me in the restaurant, and I thought it was like, you know . . . some tawdry hot little romance, or something." She seemed to stare inside for a moment, gulped her coffee, then went on. "So I'm twitching and winking and throwing out my chest, and all he wants to talk about is my son. He didn't want to, you know, with me. He wanted to see how I'd react to an offer to make my son whole." Her cheeks turned crimson, and tears formed in her eyes.

Shannon Carpenter, seeing it, hearing it, imagining it from a mother's point of view, began to cry softly also.

Henderson Smith sat there, terrified. He did not want to hear any more, because it would make *his* little meeting all that much more real.

Ivy took a deep breath and continued. "I don't know about my answer, I don't know. Maybe you can help me figure it out. It doesn't matter now. That's the joke anyway. It doesn't matter because the next thing I knew all the disappearances happened, and my Ronnie was gone. Gone to heaven, gone to hell, whole again. I don't know." She stopped, turned her face square to Smith's, and said, "What I *do* know is this. The devil is real, I sat with him, he exists. Thus, if the devil is real, then *God* has to be real. Because it was God who cast Satan out and all that stuff, right? Yes? I saw the devil, and he convinced me God is real."

Shannon reached across the table and took one of Ivy's hands in hers. She gave it a squeeze, and said tentatively, "Ivy. If you sat with the devil, and he proved God is real to you, then it only follows that God's *Son* is real too. Right?" She turned to

Smith. "Isn't that right, Reverend Smith? Sure, it's a strange way to come to our Lord. Serves the devil right, I'd say. But why not? Ivy's reasoning is sound, right, Reverend?"

But the Reverend Henderson Smith did not know what to say.

Ivy looked at Shannon, liking her more, gave a squeeze back, and said, "God I'm okay with. Jesus I'm still not sure."

Both women fell silent, holding hands. After a moment, they turned to Reverend Smith, waiting. He stared at them, licked his lips, and came within a hairbreadth of admitting that he, too, had met the devil. Problem was, he knew what his answer had been to the offer made to him . . . see huge cathedral and pulpit as exhibit A. He played with his coffee cup a moment, collecting himself. Then he looked at them both, smiled, and said, "Where are you ladies staying, have you thought of that?"

Both women shook their heads, and Ivy said, "Nope."

"Okay, let me ask you to stay here as my guests. The cathedral has its own dorms." Smith turned and pointed through the window to a row of handsome redbrick buildings on the far side of the parking lot. "We get people in from all over for retreats, seminars, different events, and the dorms are really like small apartments. You'll be comfortable there. When you are our guests you can take your meals right across the hall in the dining room. Coffee is always good; the meals are hit-and-miss, but always served with enthusiasm."

"You are too kind, Reverend Smith," said Shannon Carpenter. "I admit I never even gave it a thought."

"Yes," agreed Ivy Sloan, "I was wondering where I'd find a place to stay. Can we make an offering or something? I mean, I know it takes funding to run an organization like this, especially with the things you have. Can we contribute somehow?"

Reverend Smith waved his hand, dismissing their offer to help or their worries about it. He enjoyed being the gracious host. "Funding," he said, "is never a problem with this church."

Puzzled, Shannon looked at him and asked, "Reverend Smith, what will we do now? I mean, we'll stay as your guests, but what is our next move? What action do we take?"

"Yes," chimed in Ivy, "there has to be a reason why I was called here. What will we do?"

Smith hesitated. His face went slack, and he seemed to be far away for a moment;

then he came back. "I've asked myself that same question. Prayed on it. Asked for guidance from God. If it were possible, I would have sought the counsel of church elders, but as much as it pains me to say this, most of them have been taken. That's why I feel it is so important that my ministry be active." He paused, made eye contact with them both, and added, "There is a reason why you've both come to me. It has to do with continuing this ministry to the people. Perhaps you are to help me. It has fallen to me to stay here on Earth and be a voice, a voice of truth and explanation that can assist the people of the world in the preparation for what lies ahead. There will be a battle between good and evil, a cataclysmic fight, and the Christian souls who still have a chance at salvation will live or die depending on with whom they align themselves. I've no doubt of the outcome, but that doesn't guarantee that there won't be suffering."

Smith's eyes searched the scene outside. He marveled that his cathedral had remained untouched by any of the violence that had racked so many other places across the world. His was an island of peace in the storm-tossed seas. When he spoke again, it was as though he were trying to convince himself as much as the two women seated across from him. "You may have heard of Azul Dante, and the European Coalition he has worked so hard to form. There is another, the leader of the Muslim mujahideen, the dark forces. Azul Dante stands alone among the remaining leaders of the world, stands against Izbek Noir and the mujahideen. I believe that he can't do it in the secular role only, he must also be aligned with a Christian church, in partnership. Perhaps he will be at the head with people like you, like us, who have given themselves over to God for the good of this Earth and all the souls who still inhabit it."

He paused, and studied their faces carefully. Two sets of wide eyes were riveted on him. "I believe that his Prodigal Project will ultimately bring the churches together," continued Smith, more sure of himself now. "It will help the world prepare for the Second Coming, for the return of the Son."

"Azul Dante might be the one . . . ," said Shannon Carpenter quietly.

". . . to pull it all together?" asked Ivy Sloan.

"He may not even realize it himself," replied Henderson Smith. "The Lord, well, the Lord has a plan for all of us. I'm sure that it will all be revealed in good time. So in the meantime, we work with the church. When called, we'll try to help Dante and his coalition any way we can, and stay strong."

"But what can we, what should we do now?" asked Shannon in a quiet voice. She and Ivy held hands and waited for the reverend to speak.

He pursed his lips, reached across the table, took their hands in his, and said, "Stay with me for now. Listen, study, learn. Pray. Pray for answers, pray for guidance, pray for strength. Examine your hearts. Don't lose hold of faith, don't lose sight of truth." He heard himself say those words, and looked hard into his own heart with unforgiving eyes. "Last, keep the promise in your heart, and hold on tight. Tight like a newborn holds tight to its mother's fingers. Hold on tight to hope."

Chapter Twelve

Cat Early was aware that she knelt in a moment of perfect stillness, held in a kind of suspended animation that stopped movement and sound. It was as if life, the world and all that existed in it, held its breath for a length of time elastic and finite. She was alive in this cocoon, insulated, on hiatus from the abrasive reality that normally surrounded her. She was sure that her whole life had been designed to prepare her for this one specific moment. To understand, evaluate, and appreciate the pristine cessation, it would be necessary for her to be completely comfortable being alone. Loneliness had to be the air she breathed, and aloneness the oxygen. And so she was prepared, ready, capable. Let the moment drift there, captured by an unseen hand, float above the careening moments of time-space like the breath of an angel . . . pure, silent, silver-gold.

It passed.

She dug her fingers into the warm dirt by her right knee. It was granular but fine. It was Mother Earth, her world, the physical place where she as a human animal had come to be. She listened to the beating of the strong, steady heart that lay beneath her breast, and wondered at the sadness that pumped through her like blood with each pulse. She wanted this, she reminded herself again, she wanted the chance to get out into the world and observe real events, earth-shattering conflicts, soul-searing triumphs, mind-numbing loss. Her cup ran full now, and what spilled out looked like tears leaving silver tracks on her cheeks.

She had just said a prayer.

Prayer was not something she turned to very often. It had been her belief, since she was a young girl, that simply being born with a working mind and body, waking to see the sunrise, having the chance to experience life as a human traveler on Earth, was gift enough. To petition God for more, or something specific, seemed disrespectful. But this morning she had prayed, asking God to give her strength, to keep her moving forward with conviction and purpose, to make her work be of some value to her fellow travelers. Shyly, awkwardly, she asked God to watch over her friend, Slim, the photographer. She knew how ridiculous it sounded even as she asked for it. The very world might be coming to an end, millions had been taken in the disappearance. For many, war, up-heaval, famine, and despair were their daily lot; but she asked anyway. She even prayed that God the Father would not forget the rest of His children, for surely they *were* His children, even now. She ended the prayer in the name of Jesus Christ, which she normally would not do, and was pleased with how natural it seemed.

She saw the helicopter curving over the near ridgeline, stood, and grabbed her bag. She had missed Azul Dante when he visited Tel Aviv, but had word that he would stop on the Spanish isle of Ibiza for a meeting with several finance ministers from various governments. She intended to be there. She wanted to see him, watch him work, learn for herself if the rumors were true that this one man might be the one who could turn this self-destructing world around. The dark forces, she knew, had their champion. She had met him more than once, felt his power, been seared by the blinding intensity of his eyes. Izbek Noir was a man — Cat kept thoughts of his being somehow other-worldly at bay — bent on destroying the world in the act of saving it from itself. He was a stone killer, on an international level, and a personal one.

That her destiny was somehow entwined with his, she had no doubt. Her sister, Carolyn, had sensed it first, had brought him out from the shadows with an early report of him in soldier guise on a long-dead and horrific field of battle and massacre, and had died not long afterward. Cat was known to him too, and twice he had let her go away from him after displaying fragments of the beast he was. The last time he had taken her friend, Slim. She knew Slim was still alive because she had seen some of his published photos, and somehow she just knew. Izbek Noir was darkness, and hate, and she would follow, observe, and report on his actions in the hope of being there the day he was destroyed.

Battle loomed, possibly the biggest, or most important, battle in the history of man.

The forces of the mujahideen, led by Izbek Noir, had a strong toehold in Morocco, and their limited-range missiles were pointed at Spain. Egypt was in ruins; only a small area around Cairo, and Alexandria, were still secure. Israel was already threatened, and the mujahideen were pouring across the Red Sea from Eritrea, into the southern regions of Yemen, and from the northeast corner of Egypt into the vastness of Saudi Arabia. Both of these

Arab countries cried to the United Nations and the United States, begging for help against the onslaught, but stood by and watched as the mujahideen simply moved through them toward another destination. Israel was bypassed, which led some observers to guess that Izbek Noir simply was not ready to face the totally committed forces of America if Israel was attacked. Once into Iraq, then Iran — the first welcomed them with open arms, the second with cold acceptance — the mujahideen appeared to be consolidating their forces, bringing in their armored divisions, moving attack aircraft and antiaircraft missile units closer.

To the east lay Afghanistan, Pakistan, and India. These countries were battered, war-torn, helpless. They would be no threat to the mujahideen. Farther east lay China, and so far it was anyone's guess as to what the Chinese would do, whom they would side with. Many observers thought it was in China's best interest for now to simply sit back and watch. They were strong, they were militarily prepared and equipped, and if they bided their time the whole world — what was left of it — might be handed to them on a bloody silver platter.

North and west of Iraq lay Turkey. Historically a place of religious conflict, a pathway for crusades and conquerors, Turkey might be in the wrong place at the right time. Analysts agreed that the European Coalition of Nations, with or without Russia, but almost certainly with Britain and America, must draw a line in the sand somewhere, and Turkey looked like the obvious choice.

On the Continent, before the disappearance, Germany, France, Britain, Italy, and Poland had had the strongest military forces on readiness status, but like everything else in the world, these forces had been wounded by the sudden disappearances of so many souls. The mujahideen did not have that problem. With the exception of China, the Muslims could field more soldiers than any group on Earth. Some analysts attributed Izbek Noir's apparently callous sacrifice of ground troops to this abundance; others figured that Noir's "pile-on" strategy ate up his own troops but that he as a leader simply didn't care, as long as it was effective. To date it had been brutally so. A radical Islamic cleric in Iraq, when asked about the brutality and cruelty of Izbek Noir's mujahideen, twisted an old American Special Forces saying, and sneered, "God has already sorted them out, now he is killing them all."

The hard blue skies over the Mediterranean Sea, surrounded by the historic battlefields and playgrounds of the world, became a three-dimensional arena of supersonic high-trigger danger. Free world, Arab nation, and Israeli air controllers saw their radar screens painted with converging targets at all hours of the day. The skies were filled with MiGs, Sukhois, British Tornados, French Mirages, F-15s, F-16s, and F-22s, the occasional Saab Viggen, a few Chinese-built Chengdu J-7s, and here and there even the venerable F-4 Phantom. They wore varied livery, and were flown by pilots with skill levels from clumsy-but-game to top gun. All were armed to the teeth and spoiling for a fight.

Scattered through the deserts and cold mountain ranges were the hidden missile emplacements. These varied in range and payload, and everyone tried to figure out who had nukes, where they hid them, where they would be aimed, and whether an enemy would actually use them. On the ground, masses of infantry and armor waited, resting, equipping, planning. The world's oil crisis made obtaining and distributing fuel a priority. The armored-division commanders screamed the loudest, complaining that the flyboys always got the good stuff, while the infantrymen of any nation's army wanted only good boots and clean socks.

The world, already in anarchistic chaos following the disappearance, was poised on the brink of total war. It was not a good time to be an innocent, if there were any innocents left, and refugees from African and Middle Eastern horrors only moved from one bad place to another. Most of the world's international news organizations rarely bothered to show footage of dead bodies strewn alongside the roadways leading out from some hell on Earth . . . civilian bodies . . . people who had simply been trying to get out of the way of the fighting. Some of the mujahideen soldiers who shot, cooked, and ate the huge rats that infested the battlefields chided one another about "cannibalism, once removed" because of what the rats feasted on before ending up on the spit. Wild, lawless bands of thieves, grave robbers, and "comfort girls" shadowed the battalions of troops, and hung on the periphery of every battlefield.

In one short piece Cat had sent to her

editor, she described how the term "grave robber" was not really accurate. They were actually roving gangs of carrion eaters, she said, picking their way among the dead, who are *rarely* buried, taking anything of value they can find. The military commanders, concerned about disease and the terrible stench if the corpses remained on any battlefield too long, called in the combat engineers to deal with the problem in the time-honored way. They brought in huge bulldozers, dug long trenches in the soiled ground, used the front blade to push hundreds of bodies into the trench, then covered it with dirt before moving a few feet away for another dig. Very rarely did anyone observing this process take a moment to "say a few words" or offer a prayer. One photograph seen on many news Web sites — Cat believed it had been taken by Slim — depicted row upon row of small, dark Buddhas sitting along a stretch of desert highway. A closer look showed them to be people, wrapped in tattered blankets and robes, who had simply died while sitting in the sand, no longer having the will or strength to take another step.

Now, as Cat waited in the shadow of the chopper for the leased pool aircraft that would carry her and several other journalists to Ibiza, she pondered the state of the world. The disappearance had ravaged the Christian populations of the planet, and the Muslims were attacking without respite in an attempt to take over completely. The dark forces were led by the unstoppable Izbek Noir, with his cagey strategies and merciless brutalities. It appeared that nothing and no one stood in his way. The only hope, it was widely viewed, lay in Azul Dante — a positive, bright spot on the dim landscape of leaders — and an army composed of troops from his European Coalition. Dante's forces would meet Noir on the field of battle, it was said, and destroy him. If he could not, the darkness would only deepen.

Cat had no way of knowing that a dusty, quietly efficient, apparently non-Arab Muslim soldier who had been accepted into a ragtag battalion of mujahideen troops in North Africa was Special Agent John Jameson, a man she did not know but was destined to meet. She thought about Slim, worried about him, and prayed for him. She did not know of Ron Underwood, who sat hunched in his son's wheelchair, silent and brooding in the gloom. She could not know about the edgy anger crashing around in the mind and heart of

Thomas Church, or of his hunt for his son, or about the similar anger mixed with shame that had driven Ivy Sloan to the New Christian Cathedral. She might like Shannon Carpenter, if they had a chance to meet, but she could not know of Shannon's teaming up with Ivy Sloan and the forceful Reverend Henderson Smith, he with his own inner turmoil. She had heard of the prodigal son, and of the Prodigal Project; she had seen the aftermath of the disappearance, the taking up of so many, and the apparent abandoning of the rest. She wondered, and hoped that the Prodigal Project could in some way save them.

Among the notebooks, pens, tape recorder, camera, cell phone, and cosmetic case in her dead sister's backpack, given to her on a distant battlefield, had been a small, well-thumbed Bible, its pages smudged, a tear in the cover repaired with tape.

The Bible was hers now, and she carried it close to her heart.